Waterfall

Also by Mary Casanova
Published by the University of Minnesota Press

Frozen
Ice-Out

Waterfall

A Novel

MARY CASANOVA

University of Minnesota Press -»※«- Minneapolis

The right of Mary Casanova to be identified as the Proprietor of this work has been asserted by her.

Photograph on page 256 courtesy of the Ernest Oberholtzer Foundation.

Photograph on page 258 courtesy of Atsokan Island Archives; reprinted by permission of Jim Hanson.

Photographs on pages 259–60 courtesy of the Minnesota Historical Society.

Photograph on page 261 courtesy of Koochiching County Historical Society.

Published by the University of Minnesota Press
111 Third Avenue South, Suite 290
Minneapolis, MN 55401-2520
http://www.upress.umn.edu

ISBN 978-1-5179-0174-5 (hc)
ISBN 978-1-5179-0175-2 (pb)
Library of Congress record available at https://lccn.loc.gov/2020053654.

Printed in the United States of America on acid-free paper

The University of Minnesota is an equal-opportunity educator and employer.

26 25 24 23 22 21   10 9 8 7 6 5 4 3 2 1

FOR JIM HANSON,
KEEPER OF ATSOKAN ISLAND
AND ITS STORIES

1

Northern Minnesota
Early June 1922

ON THE DOCK AT HER EASEL, Trinity Baird worked to capture the morning light—orange scallops across slate-blue water—then stopped mid-brushstroke, her senses on alert.

From the island's highest point, the windmill turned—*thwup, thwup, thwup.*

A muskrat swam past, leaving a faint *V* of ripples.

A seagull cried and circled above, then flew off toward giant cotton balls gathering in the east. Lake clouds.

And there it was.

The low, familiar thrumming.

After two days of sleeping, sunning, and swimming, she had started to feel hints of her old self again. Now everything inside her tensed.

Breathe, she told herself. *Remember, they can send you back on a whim.*

She cleaned her paintbrush in the folds of a cotton rag, smoothed her painter's smock over her overalls, and willed herself to gaze out across the bay as the yacht came into view. The fifty-foot Elco rounded the island's pine-studded peninsula, its bow slicing through water, as it sent reverberations through the sun-warmed boards beneath Trinity's bare feet. She knew the vessel well. Her first name, after all, was painted boldly across its transom.

The horn sounded, a deep resonant bellow.

The engine slowed to a rumble.

A whiff of fuel oil drifted in.

Mallard ducklings scuttled away as waves sloshed against the dock's rock-filled log cribs.

The boat loomed closer and glided toward the length of dock. In its wheelhouse George waved from behind glass, his rumpled hair newly salted white.

She waved back, feeling a surge of gratitude that he'd been willing to tell her parents about her early arrival two full days ahead of schedule. She braced herself, hoping to smooth things over with them.

As George reversed the engine, slowing the boat's forward motion and skillfully sliding *Trinity* into place, Mother emerged along the boat rail, with Father at her shoulder.

"Without telling us?" Mother called. "You arrived ahead of us?"

Trinity looked past Mother, refusing to meet her eyes. She wanted to shout back, *Do you have the faintest idea of what you've put me through?*

She forced her hand up in greeting.

George jumped onto the dock and secured lines, bow and stern. Then he extended his arm. "Ma'am."

With a nod, Mother took it and stepped down. Standing as tall as her five-foot frame allowed, posture flagpole straight as ever, she looked around, as if assessing her realm. But when she walked, something had changed. She walked more slowly, hesitantly, as if she couldn't trust her own footing.

"There you are, lovely girl!" Father lifted his fedora skyward. "I want to see what you're painting!" In his dark suitcoat and trousers, he strode down the dock and kissed the top of her head, engulfing her in the familiar scents of cigars and shaving cream. "You're here," he said with finality, "and that's what matters."

She tried to smile.

He acted as if days—not months—had passed since her visit home to Davenport last Christmas. A whole year had passed since she had last stepped on the island, and then only for seven days. This time she had needed to arrive ahead of them. Her survival had depended on a few days alone before their barrage of questions and judgment.

"I'm sorry for any worry," Trinity said, "but I . . . I thought I'd surprise you."

Mother drew closer and whispered, "You'd do well with fewer surprises and more predictable behavior."

Trinity bristled, but nodded, as if she wholeheartedly agreed. She chose her words carefully. "You smell wonderful," she said—and meant it.

"Chanel No. 5," Mother replied. "The latest fragrance from Paris. And, oh, we had the loveliest trip there last month."

Trinity couldn't miss the irony. When she should have been studying again in Paris, they had been there instead: strolling along Île Saint-Louis; dining at Café de Flore, and rubbing shoulders with renowned artists and writers; delighting in the Luxembourg Gardens; admiring the freshly rendered sketches and paintings by street artists along the Seine. All this had been theirs to enjoy, while she was confined for one year and nine months behind the walls of Oak Hills Asylum in St. Peter, Minnesota.

She swallowed back her rage and forced herself to act politely.

"I'm glad to be here this summer . . . with family." She was the daughter they could count on to know how to socialize, be witty, and make pleasant conversation. For two and a half months, she would play whatever role they needed her to play. She had already sent her letter of intention to resume studies at Sorbonne University and expected a letter of re-admittance any day.

"I'm sure time will fly," she said, keeping her voice melodic and hopeful. "Before we know it, August will be here and I'll return to my studies."

Mother took a step back and threaded her arm through Father's. "Well, that depends," she said.

Trinity's heart stalled. "But . . . Dr. Stratton agreed it's essential to my well-being."

"Your future depends on how things go this summer," Mother said, her smile thin as fishing line.

"Father," Trinity said, imploring him to counter Mother's conditional words.

But he winked, as if telling her not to worry, that everything would turn out fine, and he looked away toward the yacht.

"Ah, Trinity, here's one of our newest," he said, waving as an unexpected passenger climbed off the boat. "We've been bringing in young architects to B&B." Baird and Beecroft, under Father's ownership, now shipped predesigned houses, precut and ready to build. "Now that we're offering financing and advertising through the mail, we're trying to keep up. Growing by leaps and bounds."

Sporting a cream-colored fedora with a charcoal band, round-rimmed black glasses, a striped tie topping a crisp white shirt, and cuffed trousers, a young man hopped off the yacht looking more prepared, Trinity thought, to be a window mannequin for Marshall Field's than for the rigors of wilderness. He carried a suitcase and gripped something football-sized under his arm.

Something small and furry and wiggling.

Ah, a dog! She welcomed any dog to visit on the island, but especially now when she needed a distraction from her parents.

Mother rested her hand on Trinity's shoulder, leaning in as if to share an important secret. "Mr. Bern rode the train with us clear from Davenport. He's the nicest young fellow. And he comes from a good family."

In other words, wealthy.

Another of Mother's marriage prospects? *Well, whoop-dee-doo.* Sometime soon she'd tell her straight out: she had no plans to marry. Ever. Once in Paris, she would date whomever she wished. But first she had to get there.

"Trinity, this is Mr. Maxwell Bern," Father said. "And Max, this is our youngest daughter, Trinity."

"Nice to meet you," she said, glancing up as the architect set down his suitcase and extended his hand. With a high forehead and intelligent, close-set brown eyes, the architect was oddly good looking. Then she extended her hand in hello to the dog. "What's its name?"

The dog's marble-black eyes were nearly hidden under its wiry black hair and shaggy, pointed ears. It licked Trinity's fingers with its little pink tongue.

Mr. Bern lifted an eyebrow, but he didn't answer.

The dog struggled to be free.

"You can set it down," Trinity said. "It can't get lost on the island. But if you hear an eagle cry, I advise picking it up right away."

"First, she needs a name," Mother said, her voice tart.

Trinity wasn't sure what Mother was talking about. She tilted her head, trying to understand. Why would the dog not have a name? Unless . . . She had always wanted a dog, but she'd long ago given up on the idea. Surely not, after all these years . . .

But Father's grin turned into an ear-to-ear smile. "A welcome home present—for you, my dear."

At that, Max set the dog down and it scrambled along the dock, dashed up the granite slope, and disappeared into a patch of underbrush.

"It was your father's idea," Mother said. "But I still wonder if you're truly up to the responsibility."

The dog must be their way of dealing with guilt, or perhaps controlling her behavior. Part of her wanted to resist their gift, but the little dog was adorable. And it needed a name.

Father laughed. "She's a cairn terrier. They come from Scotland, just like our family. They're bred to go to ground and keep rodents on the move."

"And good thing, too," George added, waiting with a luggage-filled wheelbarrow. "Red squirrels are a nuisance. We don't want 'em taking up residence in our cabins."

Father asked Trinity, "So, what will you name her?"

She felt pushed, rushed, hurried.

They wanted a name.

But, she told herself, she didn't have to come up with a name on the spot. But then she knew. The little dog made her think of the one person who could light up the dreariest day, the one person who had managed to bring a smile to even the most iron-faced nurses.

"Louise," she said. "Lou, for short."

Mother crossed her arms and tilted her head. "Well, if you must, but that's a rather strange name for a dog." Mother was skilled at using a firehose to put out the smallest flicker of happiness.

"Yes, that's good," Father declared, the edges of his eyes crinkling. "Now you have a dog. Thought we'd get the summer off on the right foot."

A dog of her own, Trinity thought, trying on the idea. "Thank you."

Mother sniffed.

Father nodded, clearly pleased with their gift. "You're welcome." Then, arm in arm, her parents walked to shore and George followed.

The architect remained, looking confused.

"Say," he said to Trinity, picking up his suitcase. "Do you know where I'm to stay?"

Pointing to two small cabins a short distance from the main lodge, she said, "First one, over there."

Max Bern nodded, then added under his breath, "Mr. Baird said he wanted to get this summer off on the right foot." Then he shuffled a few light dance steps in his polished boots and just as quickly stopped, his left foot extended. "But I say, why not start off on the *left* foot?"

She grinned, heartened by his humor.

Then he tipped his cream fedora and strode off.

Beyond the guest cabin, the little dog sat on the top step to the lodge kitchen's door.

Poor pup. She must be hungry, tired, and confused. She needed something to eat and eventually a place to sleep.

They shared something in common.

Neither knew quite where they belonged.

2

Two Days Earlier

AS SADIE WORTHINGTON paid the taxi driver, Trinity climbed from the back seat out to the sidewalks of St. Paul. She closed her eyes and breathed in her new freedom. Before finishing their three-hundred-mile train ride to the Canadian border from southern Minnesota, she and Sadie had stopped at Union Depot and caught a cab. Now light danced across her eyelids. She inhaled the city—the mixed scents of blooming lilacs, horse manure, automobile exhaust, cigarette smoke, grilled meat, perfume—and winding through it all, the ever-flowing Mississippi River.

"Are you all right?" Sadie whispered, her hand at Trinity's elbow.

Trinity nodded and slowly opened her eyes. Everywhere colors and images: a halo of pink blossoms against gray brick, a young woman pushing a pram with a wailing baby, men in bowler hats, a horse and carriage, followed by a backfiring Model T. It was as if she had lost her ability to see, hear, and smell, and those gifts had suddenly returned, overwhelming her.

"Going to a barber is the latest trend," Sadie said, her mahogany waves cut fashionably short. "Better than to risk dreadful results at home. Besides," she added, with apology in her gray eyes, "Mrs. Baird, I mean your mother, insisted."

When they stepped inside, heads turned. *A shift in the order of things,* Trinity thought as she stepped on the footrest of an empty barber's chair and took a seat. She crossed her legs beneath her navy sailor dress and gazed out the window at the barber's pole of swirling red and white.

Dizzying.

Everything was happening so fast.

One moment she was a patient with no rights, and the next she'd been set free to do as she pleased. For months on end, she'd wandered ghostlike behind locked doors. Except for her one week at the island the previous summer, and a week home in Davenport the past two Christmases, she had been shut away. Other than an occasional letter from Mother, her parents had passed all responsibility for their daughter onto Sadie's shoulders.

It had been a peculiar arrangement. Mother and Father had offered to pay half of Sadie's tuition to nearby Gustavus Adolphus College. Father had said that they would have gladly paid full cost, but they didn't want to embarrass the Worthingtons by doing so. It was all quite awkward at first, because Sadie wasn't the kind of person who demanded payment for friendship. But Trinity was glad the arrangement helped Sadie go to college. In exchange, Sadie acted as chaperone on trips. She was Trinity's only regular visitor. When Trinity had first met Sadie, their three-year difference had seemed much greater. Now she felt the younger of the two.

She was twenty-one, for crying out loud. She should have answers for her questions, should know the next steps to take toward independence. But she didn't. She felt wobbly, as if she were recovering from a long bout of influenza.

"May I help you, Miss?"

Reeking of cologne, a parrot-nosed barber stepped close.

She blinked wide. "Oh, yes. Thanks. I hope so," she managed. "The style straight from Paris—bobbed short, please. Mine has grown out."

He chuckled. "Get a request at least once a day for the past year. Now let's see what we can do." He ran his fingertips through Trinity's hair, from scalp to scraggly ends, and she tensed. At his touch, her heart dashed ahead, picking up speed. Racing. She willed it back into her chest. She'd felt this frantic anxiety before and closed her eyes, imagining her favorite white pine, beginning at its trunk and its upward sweep from the ground into an arc. It must have once bent to a storm and was more beautiful for its imperfection. Her pulse slowed. With a deep exhale, she willed her shoulders downward.

Her stay at Oak Hills Asylum was behind her now.

As she willed the knots in her shoulders, neck, and jaw to loosen, her hair fell to the floor like feathers from a molting chicken.

She closed her eyes, then drew an uneasy breath.

SHE HAD NEVER KNOWN much about chickens before Oak Hills, which was a giant farm and village unto itself. No matter your background, everyone worked to keep things operating. She'd worked at the poultry barn, gathering eggs and cleaning nesting boxes; in the kitchen she had diced onions until her tears flowed; in the sewing room she learned to stitch patient gowns; and in the admissions office she wrote out the doctor's diagnoses in shorthand. She flashed back to her first day, almost two years ago, when she was admitted.

"Undress, please," the nurse had said, not unkindly, in the room covered in white ceramic tiles.

"Undress? Right here?"

"It's standard admitting procedure," the nurse replied.

Piece by piece, Trinity undressed down to her chemise, then stopped. Surely, they didn't expect her to drop every stitch to the tiled floor. She asked with her eyes.

And the nurse nodded.

Never had she felt so powerless.

With goose bumps rising, she was told to leave her clothes in the pile and step into the next room where a hot bath waited. The room smelled of disinfectant and the claw-foot tub steamed. She climbed in, uncomfortably aware that her bum was exposed to the world before she sank into the warm water as two nurses began to scrub her from scalp to toes.

"Honestly, I can scrub myself!" Trinity pushed their hands away.

"You might be the Queen of Sheba, but it doesn't change our policy. Some patients come in crawling with lice, and we can't let that start spreading."

"Well, I'm not one of them," Trinity insisted. "This must all be a mistake."

"That's for us to determine," the second nurse said, resuming her scrubbing, but harder this time. And so Trinity had entered the asylum squeaky clean, wearing a squarish blue patient gown, coarse as burlap, with her sense of self swirled down the drain.

After that first thorough scrubbing, showers and bathing became infrequent. Her dirty hair often clung to her head.

NOW, AS THEY WALKED out of the barbershop, Trinity loved how her hair bounced with each step.

"Trinity, you look wonderful!" Sadie proclaimed.

"Thanks," she said. "To some, we're sporting the look of independence. To others, our bobs mean we're just brash and brazen hussies."

She looked to a high point beyond, where wisps of lavender clouds floated above the Cathedral of St. Paul, its dome pressed into a deep azure sky. She stopped. A moment worth capturing on canvas.

But Sadie drew her back to their purpose. "Next, we must bring your wardrobe up to date."

"Oh, is that truly necessary?" Trinity sighed. She felt a wave of overwhelm and stopped. The city and its bustle were enough, let alone trying to reenter the world of fashion. "I just want to return to the depot," she said, imagining the farms, fields, and forests drift by as they clattered north toward Rainy Lake, with its granite islands, bare and creviced cliffs, and sublime sand beaches. She longed to return to those waters that stretched nearly one hundred miles, even though in her entire lifetime she would never see the whole of it.

With seeming uncertainty of how to handle the situation, Sadie brought her fingertips together as if in prayer and touched the base of her chin. "Your mother said you'd know the way to a good dress shop. Irene's or something like that? And she encouraged me to suggest two words."

"Oh?"

"*Thrifty* was one. *Sensible* was the other."

Trinity bristled at the words. "Sadie, honestly. Whose side are you on?"

"Yours," she said, "but you know how your mother can be."

"I'll shop, but truly, she can be so penurious at times," Trinity replied.

"And that means—?" Sadie asked with a tilt of her head.

"Penny-pinching. She gets some odd pleasure in acting as if she's one step up from poverty. I honestly don't get it. She wasn't that way until we started summering up north. Those first few years of camping, she dressed almost identical to Father: canvas jackets, tall leather boots, and jodhpurs."

Sadie laughed. "Jodhpurs? Those balloon pants people wear riding horses or on archaeological digs?"

"I know," Trinity replied with a grin and a shrug. "After we built cabins, Mother dressed like someone on safari, or worse. Shabbier. Like a poor new immigrant. If that's her idea of sensible, I could skip shopping altogether and just stitch up some rags for a dress."

"Oh, no," Sadie replied, threading her arm through Trinity's. "Lead on."

She steered them to the block with Irene's Dress Shop. "Here we are."

The high tinkle of chimes sounded as they stepped inside. The stork-like clerk wore a cloth measuring tape as if it were a long string of beads. "Miss Baird, welcome back! How may I help you, young ladies?"

"I'm nearly two years out of date," Trinity said.

The clerk pushed open the curtain to the dressing room. "Wait here and I'll bring you dresses guaranteed to make you swoon—just as if Valentino himself stepped off the big screen."

When she was out of earshot, Trinity whispered to Sadie, "We had film nights at Oak Hills, but never one with Rudolph Valentino. The staff probably feared he would increase levels of hysteria." She half-smiled.

Sadie nodded soberly.

They'd talked before about *hysteria,* the diagnosis given to countless women, young and old. After giving birth to her first baby, one young woman could not shake her blue feelings and get out of bed. Her baby was put up for adoption and she was committed for life. Another patient, a fifteen-year-old girl, was found in bed with a traveling salesman. The verdict? Promiscuity—a symptom of hysteria.

She thought of Marta, whose bed had been next to her own. Wide-set blue eyes and hair so blonde it was almost white, a rounded shape, and well-endowed. She was admitted because she'd "falsely accused" her uncle of unwanted advances. "My family claimed I was delusional," she had said. Delusional—another form of hysteria—and now her family was willing to let Marta return home only if she would agree to quit talking nonsense. Trinity ached for her, wondering how Marta was managing now in her small town in such a predicament. Freedom for silence.

Not until her time at Oak Hills, Trinity recognized,

had she fully understood how privileged she was. Not just because she came from wealth—though granted, that was part of it. But she learned her life had been far easier than that of the other patients. At home she hadn't been beaten. Or sexually molested. She wasn't confined because starvation had driven her to madness. She wasn't locked up for excessive drunkenness. She wasn't born with a damaged brain that kept her a child. To cope with being locked away, she had imagined herself back on the island. It helped, especially at first, but eventually she had needed a way to engage—rather than only escape—and she offered to teach drawing and painting to other patients. Now, at last released, she was going to have to learn once again a new way of being in the world.

WHEN SHE STEPPED OUT of the dressing room in a daring, sleeveless short dress with matching blue fringe, the image in the mirror made her frown: average height, well proportioned, blue eyes, and bobbed hair. The eyes looked faded, as if someone had reached into her depths and stolen her soul.

"Trinity, it's stunning, but are you sure?" Sadie asked.

"I'm not sure about anything right now!" she snapped, instantly regretting her shortness of temper.

But Sadie didn't back away or crease her brow in worry. Her gray eyes brimmed with compassion and a seeming willingness to understand before making snap judgments.

"I'm sorry," Trinity began. "But if I try to be exactly what my parents want, I'll shatter. I showed exemplary behavior as a patient, but was that enough to release me after the first year? No, I'm released now only because my parents have decided it's time. So am I sure? No. I'm not sure about anything anymore." Her voice wavered, jumping like a child from one step up to the next, higher and precariously higher. "My parents will insist on their cocktail and lake parties, and I'll play my part. Father will want to show me off, but this time I'll be a conversational curiosity, fresh from the asylum!"

Sadie stopped her with a wave of her hand. "Oh, Trinity. I doubt anyone knows. I'm sure your parents kept it all quiet. And besides, you're done with all that now." Trinity hoped she was right, but her chest tightened, almost as if a python from a Burroughs novel was squeezing the last bit of air from her lungs. A sickening mix of weakness and anger flooded through her, and her legs threatened to buckle.

Sadie pulled her close, holding her upright.

"Is something wrong?" asked the clerk.

"I'm not sure," Sadie replied, leading Trinity to a pink upholstered chair beside the full-length mirror. Lightheaded, Trinity put her head between her knees.

The clerk looked on. "A glass of water?"

"Yes, that would be kind," Sadie said.

Trinity gulped deep breaths. It was as if she had set off in a motorboat, but a morning fog had settled in and all she could do was wait for it to lift before she could see where she was headed.

Take care of your needs.

What's really going on?

In the past, she might have told herself she felt fine.

Now she could almost hear Dr. Stratton, the youngest physician on staff who had shown abstract prints to Trinity. "There's no right answer," he'd assured her. "But what you see might help us understand what you're thinking and feeling."

If she had to look at any Rorschach image now, she'd see only dark and frightening shapes. She was feeling something in her body. Something raging, pushing out against her ribs.

She felt a swirl of dark feelings.

She ran through a list of possibilities.

Fear, perhaps.

A storm of indignation.

Anger. That was it. She was angry.

Damned angry.

Because she hadn't proved to be a danger to herself or others at Oak Hills, and because Dr. Stratton deemed her "highly intelligent with an artistic temperament," she had been granted access to the latest books and research articles at the asylum's library. She read journals and the latest theories by Sigmund Freud about the ego, id, and libido. She read the latest articles on eugenics, the growing field focused on family pedigrees and limiting "undesirable traits" such as pauperism, mental disability, dwarfism, promiscuity, and criminality.

But who decides? For God's sake, who in a family or in society has the right to decide what's "normal"?

Good or bad, she and both of her sisters had inherited certain genetic traits. She shouldn't have been institutionalized any more than her sisters. So why? A burning anger coursed through her belly and throat, and she wanted to flee. She was a jackrabbit pursued, desperate to run away, race down a hole, and disappear.

She waited out the overpowering feeling. After several breaths, she felt it lessening. Her heart slid from her throat and returned where it belonged.

When her breathing settled back to normal, finding a more regular rhythm, Trinity opened her eyes and sat up straight.

"Oh, Miss Baird. There now!" the clerk said. "You're looking so much better. Have you decided on any particular items?"

"I'll take everything," she said.

The clerk's head cocked like a robin's at an unexpected earthworm.

"Put it on my mother's account."

The clerk beamed and started wrapping up the items. "Yes, ma'am!"

3

THREE SUNDRESSES, three pairs of shoes, two bathing suits made of the finest wool, one traveling hat, one evening gown, and one adorable flapper dress later, they flagged a taxi and climbed into the back seat.

Sadie said, "You know, I feel as if I've held my breath, waiting for you to be released. In my opinion . . . it's not my place to be so straightforward, and I don't want you to think me out of hand, but—"

"You're my friend," Trinity said, reaching for Sadie's hand. "Say it."

"I'm so glad you're out, and it pains me to say it, but I honestly don't know why you were sent away in the first place." Her chin puckered and her eyes filled with tears. "Last summer I told your mother I truly believed you were ready to return home."

"You did?"

With a nod, Sadie continued, "Her words? 'Absolutely not.' She believed you were being helped by staying there." She glanced away, then met Trinity's eyes. "And now I'm worried. I mean, aren't you . . . worried about going home?"

When Trinity thought of returning to the island, she felt like an acrobat tottering high above the ground, a mixture of elation and dread.

"If I had my way, I'd leave today for France."

"Why don't you?" Sadie asked. "I'm serious. You could take a train from here to New York, then a ship . . ."

But as Union Depot appeared, Trinity shook her head. "Money. I'm completely dependent on my family's wealth. And I'm not allowed to manage my own affairs."

"Not yet," Sadie said. "But eventually, don't you think? I mean, you're the apple of your father's eye."

Trinity shrugged. She had never asked to have a yacht named after her. It had only caused hard feelings and resentment. Why not name it after one of her sisters, or Mother? But Father didn't seem concerned about his favoritism. And yet it was baffling, because if he favored her, then why send her away? Or more exactly, why hadn't he stood up to Mother's insistence that she be sent away to St. Peter?

The taxi pulled to the curb. "Allow me," the young driver said, jumping out. He stacked shopping bags and her cherry-red hatbox on a cart. Then he pushed the cart at a brisk pace through the depot, and Trinity couldn't help but notice his slim waist, sturdy shoulders, and fine backside as he moved. At their train, he unloaded their items and tipped his derby.

Trinity reached into her handbag and removed her coin purse.

He waved the money away. "The pleasure has been mine," he said and then strode away, his body silhouetted against a shaft of daylight.

A warmth filled her, surprising her. A flush of feeling, yearning, wanting. The tantalizing sense of being wanted and allowing herself to want in return. At the asylum, she'd learned to lock such feelings away in a cupboard.

At that moment, she felt herself tottering—somewhere between her new need to be in control of her actions and her old urges to dive into someone else's arms and give herself away. For days, weeks, months she'd tried not to think about Victor Guttenberg, his body fit from miles of paddling a canoe. Now she was returning for the summer and that cupboard door creaked open on rusty hinges, ever so slightly.

Sadie touched her elbow. "Trinity, are you okay?"

She answered with a nod.

"We should board."

Another nod. *Breathe in.*

She'd have to be careful . . .

Breathe out.

She trembled at returning to the island she loved and the family who had sent her away. How could she ever forgive them for thinking they knew what was best for her? She would watch her every step until August, when she would leave for Paris.

But three months with Mother, a hovering presence watching her every word and gesture with the scrutiny of a raptor . . . the very thought made her want to dash for cover.

She filled her lungs, straightened up, and boarded the train after Sadie.

They found the first class car, stuffed their purchases in an overhead compartment, then settled in velvet armchairs at a table, facing each other. "Heading north," Sadie said.

Trinity gave a nod, grateful for her company. Sadie possessed a depth that belied her eighteen years—born perhaps from tragedy. Sadie had shared that she was only five when she had been found in a snowbank beside her frozen mother and narrowly rescued from a similar fate. That night, Sadie's exposure to brutal temperatures took its toll with a resulting fever and severe ear infections. After Sadie recovered, she didn't speak for eleven years. When Trinity met her a few years back, Sadie was still communicating with a piece of white chalk and a small, black slate before she eventually found her voice. If Sadie could overcome such an ordeal, Trinity reasoned, then she could as well.

After the porter gathered their tickets, Sadie asked, "Our luggage, sir. Was it transferred to this train as requested?"

"Oh, most certainly," the porter answered. "Ladies, when you ride first class, you haven't a care in the world."

Trinity closed her eyes.

Nothing could be further from the truth.

4

AS THE ARCHITECT hefted his suitcase up the stone path to the guest cabin, Trinity left her easel and walked toward the lodge. Pine boughs murmured overhead and along the path, lanky red columbine bloomed amid beds of radiant green ferns, newly unfurled.

Ahead, the little dog sat on the top step, its eyes fixed on Trinity as she approached.

"They tell me you're mine," Trinity said as she drew closer. "But we don't even know each other, do we?"

The dog's tail started swishing back and forth across the step, and Trinity took it as an invitation to sit down. Not too close, which might scare her off, but a respectful foot away. She had learned a few things with wary patients. Maintain physical space. Watch for signs of unexpected aggression. Avoid sustained eye contact, which could be interpreted as predatory behavior.

She looked out, facing the bay. "I can tell you're smart," she said. "You've picked the right place if you're hungry."

Every day, amazing scents wafted through the kitchen's screen door, from fresh baked bread to cinnamon rolls, skillet-fried walleye to roast turkey. Agatha worked magic every breakfast, lunch, and supper of the summer. And since Trinity could remember, Agatha and George, the island's caretakers, had always made her feel welcome and comfortable hanging out with them, whether in the kitchen or the boathouse.

Trinity called in a singsong voice through the screen. "A-ga-tha!"

Agatha appeared, a welcoming smile set in her melon-round face, her arms soft and dimpled as bread dough. "Yes, dear?"

Trinity motioned to the dog, its nose lifted toward the door. "Meet Lou. I guess she's mine. My parents brought her."

On the other side of the screen door Agatha tsked. "Strange. Mrs. Baird has never much liked dogs."

"I think she's hungry."

Agatha turned away. "I'll see what I can gather."

In moments she returned with a ceramic bowl filled with meat and bread scraps.

"Thank you!" Trinity said, taking the bowl and intending to lure the dog across the island. "If you want some, Lou, you have to follow."

Nose high, the little dog trotted alongside.

They passed the boathouse flanked by two long docks and walked across the sand beach that joined the two sides of the island like a top-heavy hourglass. Then Trinity led the way up the slope and down to the south side of the island.

Her side of the island.

Eventually more guest cabins would be built, but for now she shared this half of the island with George and Agatha, though they rarely crossed paths. Where they would follow the path to the left, she headed to the right and up the slope under the shadowy pines. Talking to Lou, she reached the top, then followed the curving path down to her studio.

The square log structure sat on a rock outcropping, the bare ends of its logs painted red, matching the geraniums in its flower boxes. George and Agatha somehow succeeded in transplanting them each spring after storing them in a basement during the winter months.

But when Trinity stepped inside, Lou stayed back, planting herself at a distance. "C'mon, girl. It's okay. We're going to be friends." She held the door open, but the dog wouldn't budge, as if afraid of the consequences of crossing over the threshold.

"You've been locked up before," Trinity guessed.

The dog gazed back, its round, black eyes soft and unflinching.

"That makes two of us," Trinity said. For the moment, mosquitoes were absent, or seemed to be. Despite the price she might pay that night, she propped the screen door wide with a stone—at least for a time, until Lou came in on her own. Trinity turned away and walked to one of the narrow windows on either side of the hearth and gazed out at the channel. A northwest breeze drove the water into choppy waves.

"Do as you like," Trinity called over her shoulder.

Eventually, Trinity turned from the window and stretched back on the chaise lounge, crossed her ankles, and picked up a book. She set the bowl of scraps on the floor beside her, waiting for Lou to make herself at home. When she came closer, she'd give her a treat. After a page, she glanced out. The pup still hadn't budged.

Other than her dear friend Sadie and her adoptive parents the Worthingtons, Trinity had no idea who knew the truth about where she had actually been. Two days earlier, she'd lied to Owen Jensen when he had met her at the train depot and gave her a boat ride to the island. She hadn't planned to lie, but she'd felt overcome by a sense of shame. She'd told him she'd been in St. Peter in her own apartment and had taken classes at Gustavus. It had spilled out before she could admit to the truth of being locked away.

She returned to reading *Main Street,* enjoying getting lost in the characters of a small Minnesota town. Though the author, Sinclair Lewis, had painted a picture of something similar to International Falls, she had never really known small-town life. She knew life in their nine-bedroom home in Davenport, where staff waited on their every whim. During summer stays on Rainy Lake, she'd rarely ventured into International Falls, the paper-mill town on the main-land. That's why she often joined George by boat to the port village of Ranier for supplies and mail.

She glanced around at her work from past summers.

An oil painting of spring tulips in Central Park.

The unfinished waterscape she was working on now.

Sketchbooks filled with faces rendered in charcoal and pencil from the island . . . from Chicago, Paris, Davenport, and St. Peter.

Her mind flooded with images.

Faces of patients.

Nights at the asylum.

As memories rose, her chest filled with an overwhelming sense of dread, and she pushed the feelings down, put the memories away.

Stop, she told herself and turned back to reading.

Breathe.

Read.

But she couldn't concentrate. Her eyes glazed over the printed words on the page as she remembered that first night at the Oak Hills dining hall.

***

TRINITY SCANNED the rows of wooden tables and bench-es filled with women and teens all wearing the same cotton blue gowns. When she spotted an open table, she pushed back her shoulders, aimed for it, and took a seat.

Next thing she knew, a pale-skinned teenager with hair the color of molasses appeared, standing at her shoulder. "Hi," she'd said, like they were old friends. Then she plunked down beside her.

"My name is Louise . . . ." She added her last name, which started with "Petra-" and turned long and difficult to pro-nounce. A Slavic name, Trinity guessed.

Trinity wondered how this young woman ended up at

Oak Hills. Newspapers reported concerns about closing America's borders to waves of immigrants, largely Catholic, from Eastern European countries.

"So why are *you* here?" the young woman asked. Her eyes were alert and steady, unlike some of the patients whose eyes darted, fluttered, stared, or seemed utterly absent. Before Trinity could answer, she continued, "Me? Since you asked? Epilepsy. Scares the shit out of people."

The edges of Trinity's mouth crept upward. Not that this was funny. "I've heard of it. Something about seizures?"

Louise nodded. "I've been getting them since I was ten. I'm sixteen now."

"Is it scary?" Trinity had never seen someone have a seizure. She felt apologetic for asking. "Oh, I'm sorry. I don't know much about epilepsy."

With an easy shrug, Louise answered matter-of-factly. "I don't remember much of what happens. But stick around if you care to find out. I give regular shows." Her eyebrows arched above laughing eyes.

Trinity grinned. She appreciated this girl's grit and hoped never to witness a seizure firsthand.

A few months had passed when Trinity and Louise were playing checkers in the parlor, which was as nice as the photographs used for the Oak Hills postcards: fringed lampshades, rocking chairs, tables, shelves of books, and windows looking out on the grassy lawn all the way toward the town of St. Peter below. Louise was a shark at checkers and always seemed to know how to place her first checker to ensure she'd win the game. Halfway through the game, something changed. It started with a change in her face, a blank stare, then a twitching of her face and hands. Louise wobbled in her chair and Trinity rushed to keep her from crashing to the floor. As the seizure set in, Louise's body became rigid. She began shaking violently. Trinity was there as Louise fell sideways off her chair.

Trinity broke her friend's fall but lost her balance and

flopped backwards, creating a human mattress. At least Louise didn't hit her head, but she was now on top of Trinity, twitching and making gurgling sounds.

"Help! Somebody help!" Trinity yelled, trying to ease out without making things worse.

She kneeled beside her, calling for help as Louise's eyes rolled back in their sockets.

As other patients pressed closer, Louise started choking.

"Oh no!" someone wailed.

Another woman drew her fingernails to her mouth. "Poor girl! In the name of Jesus we call upon Heaven . . ." and then she started shouting. "I'll pray the blood of Jesus and command these dark powers of Satan to leave. Be gone! Be gone!"

"I hate these fits!" a teenager shrieked. "Can't she have them somewhere else?"

White-uniformed attendants rushed in, strapped Lou's rigid and contorted body on a wooden stretcher, and carried her off toward the asylum hospital.

⁎

THAT NIGHT AT BEDTIME Louise returned. Shortly after "Lights Out," Trinity hurried across the women's dorm to sit on the edge of her friend's bed. Louise's face was a shade darker than her white pillowcase, circles of gray pooled under her eyes, but she grinned. "I've started a scandal!"

"You had a seizure. That's not a scandal, Louise," Trinity said soothingly.

"No," Louise said, drawing her dark eyebrows together. "But they say I was on top of you. Rumors are flying I was trying to 'make whoopee' with you."

"What? That's ridic—" Then she understood it was another of her friend's crazy jokes.

She cracked up.

Before long, others in earshot started laughing. That's

how it went around Louise. She'd set off a spark of laughter until others at the edges of the room, who had not heard the joke or had the ability to understand one anyway, would start laughing too. In that way Louise was an artist. She set something in motion, something beautiful.

On the morning of the first light snow, Trinity and Louise bundled up after chores and strolled through an inch of fresh snow, leaving footprints.

"How do you keep your sense of humor?" Trinity had asked.

"I always feel better after a good laugh," Louise replied. "Sometimes for a full half-hour. Besides, better to make the best of things since I'm never getting out of here."

"How can you say that?" Trinity said. "Maybe you'll get better."

"Even if I were to get better, epileptics are put away for life."

"Life?"

Louise nodded. "And now there's talk about sterilizing us so we won't pass on our bad genetics." She closed her eyes for a moment, then added with a grin, "Doctors should save their money. Most of us don't make it to old age anyway!"

Almost a year later to the day, Lou was on kitchen duty sweeping the dining hall floor when a grand mal seizure struck. She lost control and cracked her head on the square edge of a solid oak table as she fell. She didn't recover.

⋇

WHEN TRINITY GLANCED UP the next time from her book, the little dog was gulping down the last of the food scraps. Then she sat back on her haunches beside the empty bowl, staring at Trinity.

"Good girl," she said. "Come here, sweetie."

The dog jumped up next to Trinity's feet and Trinity reached out and scratched behind the dog's ears and under her chin. Then Lou exhaled—as if she had been waiting for the moment when she could relax—and she rolled on her back, her pink underbelly exposed.

"Lou," Trinity whispered, "I don't know why they gave you to me." She swallowed back emotion. "But I'm awfully glad you're here."

5

AS TRINITY SAT AT THE STERN sipping an ice-filled gin rickey, she studied the sunset. Others sat on the long bench behind George, who steered for the edge of the world—a lava-red sunset spewing layers of magenta, rusty-orange, and pink.

Cigarette and cigar smoke drifted from the wheelhouse to the stern.

Soon Max Bern drifted back as well. "May I join you?"

"Of course," she said, motioning to the three other red wicker chairs around the table.

"You do this every evening?" he asked, taking a seat and offering her a cigarette from a silver case.

"As long as the weather holds," she replied with a shake of her head.

When George cut the engine, they drifted, enveloped by warm, humid air.

"Say," he said, "are you a fan of Frank Lloyd Wright?"

"Yes. Why?"

"Such an innovative architect!" he replied. "All straight and simple lines, but I prefer a style that, well . . ." He paused. "A style that both harkens to past traditions and creates something new."

"I bet you're not a fan of Cubism," Trinity said.

"I guess you could say that. I'm a good fit at B&B with its penchant for cozy bungalows. I find ways to be creative within the traditional lines."

Trinity tilted her head, aware that Max Bern was studying her. She had kicked off her shoes and wiggled her toes.
Bare legs crossed at the ankles: she refused to wear stockings
in warm weather. In her sleeveless sheath dress, she loved
the feeling of sun and air on her skin.

In a worried tone he asked, "So I can sleep tonight,
should I worry about cougars or wolves or bears?"

She smiled, not sure how to answer. She didn't want him
to panic. A bull moose could swim to the island and, if it were
later in the summer, might charge. Bears could find their way
and had done so, drawn by fish guts or ripe garbage. Though
there was a bounty on wolves, they still roamed the north; if
he was lucky, he might hear them howl from the mainland,
but they didn't have reason to swim to the island. Winter was
another story, when the lake froze solid enough for cars and
trucks—and wolves. But she'd only ever been on the island
in the summer.

"I wouldn't worry. You're safe here."

He shuddered. "Makes me a little nervous, actually.
I know I'm hundreds of miles from real civilization . . . in
genuine wilderness . . . and I suppose I should expect such
things, but I'm worried every time I step out of my cabin that
I'll run into a bear."

"Not likely, but it's possible." Trinity waved away his concern. "Really, just make yourself look tall and make noise.
You'll be fine."

She thought of Victor, in contrast. If he had been afraid
of bears, she mused, he would have stayed home and never
dreamed of canoeing with his Ojibwe guide to Hudson Bay
and back. In the past she might have teased Max, but after
her experiences away she knew better. Sometimes fear was a
thing born of the imagination, and other times it was ground-
ed in reality. So instead she said, "Chances are you won't see
one during your time with us, which is how long, Mr. Bern?"

"Please. Call me Max," he said. "I'm sure I'm only a few
years older than you. Until July, according to your Father."

"Then I advise you don't keep any food in your cabin, and when you head outside after dark, bring a flashlight so you don't end up dancing with a bear."

He looked only half-relieved. "Not many bears where I grew up."

"And where was that?"

"In Chicago."

"I believe that," she said, having been to the Windy City. "But Max, our fears can take many forms, wouldn't you agree? If not bears, then something else."

"What keeps you awake at night?" he asked, leaning back.

She laughed away his question, not sure if he was being forward with her or asking sincerely. "We're on a glorious sunset cruise. What could possibly cause me to worry?" She met his eyes.

But Max only smiled in return.

She followed his gaze to the deepening horizon. In silhouette, a flock of pelicans soared against shades of magenta. The boat drifted. Waves lapped against the wooden hull. As if on cue, a loon broke the surface, nearly standing on the water as it stretched its wings wide, then floated, white stars strewn over its black feathered back.

Max reached inside his sport jacket and pulled out a metal flask. "Canadian whiskey," he said, offering it. "Compliments of Mr. Baird."

"No doubt," Trinity said. "I have a drink. As you can see, Mr. Bern . . . Max," she said, "Prohibition doesn't really apply here on this boat or on the island. Father wouldn't think to risk his guests' expectations. He acquires only the best whiskey from Canada, none of the moonshine being brewed on our side these days."

"There's a reason they call it *rotgut*," Max said.

"Yes." Trinity nodded in agreement. She'd heard dreadful local stories. That's why Father had connections with a factory that still produced distilled whiskey. "Every summer

Father takes the yacht across to the city dock in Fort Frances, Ontario, to buy cases of gin, whiskey, fine wines, and rum. The big cache is stashed at an outlying island on the Canadian side. They head home and George takes out the Garwood—a twenty-eight-foot speedboat and by far the fastest boat on the lake at forty-five miles an hour—to bring back the booze, one case at a time, and masterfully hide it on the island."

"Inventive," Max said.

"There's a reason he's good in business," Trinity said. "Probably didn't know that you're part of a bootlegging scheme, did you?"

Max looked worried and glanced beyond the boat, as if expecting federal agents to converge and arrest them at any moment. "What do you mean?"

She smiled. "The cabin you're staying in. There's a discreet little wire outside. When you pull it, the trap door lifts inside the closet."

"I didn't notice."

"No, you wouldn't. It blends in perfectly with the wood floor."

Max took a swig and then said conspiratorially, "We're both artists, granted, of different sorts," he said. "But I can't wait to share my sketches and perhaps . . . you'll share what you're working on with me."

Before waiting for an answer, he reached into his jacket and set a small notepad and pencil on the table. "Minute sketches, I call them." In a flourish, he set down straight lines and in short order presented her a cozy cabin with a tapered stone fireplace and wide screen porch. Then he turned to the next blank page. "Your turn?"

She studied his face, committed it to memory, and started sketching, entering that place of knowing—a certainty that flowed from her mind through her fingers. When she showed him her quick portraiture, a flush of pink spread from his neck to his cheeks.

"Oh—it's me. You captured me, didn't you?"

"That was my goal." She enjoyed the moment—a small measure of flirtation and an outlawed sip of whiskey—but she had no intention of becoming romantic with him or anyone. With each hour, each day away from Oak Hills, she became increasingly aware of her need to focus on caring for one person—and only one person. Herself.

As Mother stepped from the wheelhouse and began making her way toward them along the gangway, Trinity grinned at Max and whispered, "Keep the flask handy."

He put a hand to his chest and winked. "My solemn duty."

Before sitting down to join them, Mother made a noisy point of closing the hatchway to the stateroom below, where two beds fit into the curved sides of the boat with a dresser and mirror dividing them. Did Mother think that peering into the space was enough to give her daughter scandalous ideas?

"There," Mother said, latching the wooden hatchway door securely.

"Mother," Trinity said, "join us, please."

"I was planning to," she replied, taking a seat as the chair cushion wheezed in protest. She removed a newspaper from under her arm. "First we have a woman doctor, and now she's sharing her offices with an eye doctor. An optometrist who comes up one week a month."

"Seems like a good thing," Trinity said, assuming there was a reason Mother was holding court and choosing this issue.

Mother drew a breath and sighed. "I'm all for the Nineteenth Amendment and the right to vote. But surely that doesn't mean women need to fill men's jobs?"

"Another female doctor?" Trinity asked. "I can't imagine why that should be a problem. I mean, maybe I'll continue on at university and become a professor. I could teach art to college students someday."

Mother humphed. "Really, Trinity. Who would marry a woman who is already married to a profession? No one."

"Ha!" Max cocked his head. "I'd gladly marry such a woman. Let *her* wear the pants in the family! Then I could read and sketch away my days, just for the sheer pleasure of it."

Trinity flashed him a grateful smile.

"And let me ask, Mr. Bern," Mother pressed, "under such an unconventional scenario, who would raise the children?"

He glanced at Lou, sleeping on Trinity's lap, then winked. "The dog, of course!"

Mother wagged her head in mock disgust, as a faint smile played at her mouth. "I can see I'm outnumbered here," she said. She rose from her chair with her newspaper and returned along the gunwale to the wheelhouse.

Trinity lifted her glass in a toast and whispered. "Thank you!"

6

THE FIRST WEEK OF JUNE, nights were chilly. Trinity slept under two Hudson's Bay wool blankets with Lou snuggled in the crook of her legs. When the sun climbed early and sent brilliant shafts of light across the studio's wood floor, Trinity lingered in bed and studied the light and changing shadows. The light was golden, stunning in its perfection.

Outside her windows the lake was ever changing. Some mornings it lapped gently. Other times it hurled itself in rage against the rocky shore. This morning it whispered.

Trinity willed herself from under the blankets, wrapped herself in a cotton robe, and built a small birch fire in the hearth. As it crackled and warmed the air, she began sketching whatever came to mind.

Another friend came to mind.

Marta.

Large blue eyes under a strong brow.

Petite nose and chin.

Generous dimples.

Marta's bed had been directly across from her own, yet Trinity now found memories of her were slipping away. Determined to remember, Trinity rummaged through papers and photographs and found the image Sadie had taken of the two of them. It was Visitors' Day at Oak Hills, and Trinity and Marta were serving tea at the end of a long table. In the photograph Marta poured and Trinity offered sugar and cream. They smiled. But when Trinity studied the image now, she noticed the pain behind her own eyes and Marta's, plagued with the constant question, *Why?*

Why am I here?

Working off the photograph, Trinity sketched quickly, her fingers re-creating Marta's commanding eyes, full lips, petite nose. Marta shouldered the burden of being pretty—something that seemed to fade a little with each day of her confinement. Ever since Marta had been released two months ago, Trinity had worried about how she was faring after returning to her mining family in Hibbing. Patients' families paid for their stays, until a doctor determined if they were candidates for lifelong commitment, in which case the state took over all costs. Marta had fretted her family couldn't afford her care and would turn her over to the state instead of allowing her to return home. She couldn't stop chewing her nails. And she had reason to fret. A stroll through the asylum's cemetery was a visceral reminder that countless patients never left. Many families, Trinity learned, upon committing a son or daughter or wife or mother, sent an obituary to the local newspaper. By declaring a death in the family, they must have found solace in its finality—and believed that commitment ended their responsibility. They could wash their hands and family name of mental imperfection, whatever its form, and start anew.

Trinity stood back from the image taking shape on her easel. She missed whispering with Marta after "Lights Out." She missed afternoons outside in the gardens, whether spring, summer, or fall, with Marta reading nearby as she sketched. She missed the brutally honest times when they shared their most painful secrets.

Trinity had never told anyone else about that first year in Paris. One day when they were on kitchen duty and shucking corn, she finally told Marta the whole story: how she'd lost her virginity to a thirty-two-year-old artist named Jean

Marc and how she'd first seen him on Île Saint-Louis, painting portraits of wealthy tourists. That first day when she'd stopped with a group of university friends to watch, he had glanced up. "You," he said, pointing his paintbrush directly at her until she felt heat searing her cheeks. "Someday, I will paint you."

Later the other students, at their easels in Mademoiselle Turrant's class painting the nude subject of the week, would jest, brush poised, "Someday, *ma chérie*, I will paint you." Trinity always laughed. His comment was flattering, but she never expected anything to come of the street artist's declaration.

She shed much of her traditional sense of modesty that year. At her first drawing class she was told to expect to paint from live models, but she didn't really expect a fully nude model. The woman was roughly fifty years old, with ample padding that more resembled models preferred by Renoir than the lean, straight lines of modern fashion. This model was all breasts, buttocks, and belly. It took the entire first day just to get comfortable looking at her. Reminding herself that this woman, who wrapped in a robe on her breaks and smoked by the open window, was paid to pose, Trinity saw that the woman seemed completely at ease; she was the one who had to get beyond her discomfort. By week's end, her painting had become its own creation, inspired by the woman's form and being, yet wholly its own entity. After that, they had a new subject each week: an elderly man, a young man, a young woman. A study. She started to see them in lines and shadows, their eyes something to be studied, ascertained, a life apprehended in that singular moment in time.

So it took little pressure on Jean Marc's part to get her to agree to sit for him. He was exotic. Beneath untamed brown hair, his intense gaze nearly hypnotized her.

"But I don't need a portrait of myself," she protested as the river flowed past.

"No, no," he said, his white linen shirt rolled to his elbows, his body lean. "I am the one who should pay. Just sit, *s'il vous plaît*, for a short time." When he finished, he handed her the small canvas. He had painted her in miniature. "Perhaps not for you, but for your parents. America, yes? Send it to them. I'm sure they must miss seeing your lovely face."

After that, whenever she strolled outside the university, she managed to pass by him at his usual post along the Seine. One day, he confessed. "Trinity, I do my best work in my studio," he said. "Here, my portraits are mainly for tourists, to help pay my bills. But someday I would give anything to have you come and pose for me in Montmartre."

Montmartre. She nearly swooned at the name of his neighborhood, famous for the history of its resident artists. She hadn't yet seen his *arrondissement.* How could she say no? "I'll come and pose, but I intend to keep my clothes on."

"I would have it no other way," he said, bowing his head.

On her first session, she ignored the cracked window, the restroom he shared down the hall, and the many portraits surrounding her of women, mostly in stages of undress. At her second session, he asked so politely if she might lower her dress straps, just enough to capture her shoulders and collarbone. When she did so, he stepped away from his easel and with gentle hands adjusted her dress. "*Oui, oui,*" he whispered, before stepping back to his paints. On her third visit, she felt so comfortable with him that she dropped every stitch of clothing and let him paint her. Before many more sessions, beneath the gaze of Sacré-Coeur Basilica, she gave herself to him and in return he showed her pleasures she'd never before imagined. She was smitten by him in every way: his accent, his touch on her skin, his deep-set eyes that expressed more than words could convey. And when she left his atelier, the streetlamps glowed more vividly, the city felt more alive.

She admitted it.

It was almost a cliché.

She was in Paris and she had taken a painter for a lover.

Only after a few breathless weeks did she worry about getting pregnant. She was nineteen, for God's sake. How could she not have thought about that? At her sleeping quarters on Île Saint-Louis, she died myriad deaths at night, worrying. If she was pregnant, would they get married? And if not, then what? The day her menses returned in the middle of an art history lecture, she was so relieved that she determined then and there to break off her sudden affair. Besides, she had lost her focus and was falling behind with her studies. She would do the honorable and modern thing. She would tell him face to face that what had started between them must end. She took a taxi to his atelier, only to round the corner and spot him on the sidewalk holding hands with another woman with two young girls at her skirt.

"Maman! Papa!" the oldest child, no more than five, sang as she skipped a circle around them. They stood beneath the second-story studio with the cracked and dusty-paned window.

Sick to her stomach, Trinity redirected the taxi driver and left, feeling stupid. Ashamed at her ignorance of things. She had never thought to ask if Jean Marc had anyone else. A family, for instance. She'd made it as easy for him as a knife through soft butter. When she returned to her own painting, which she'd felt was inferior to his work when she'd been with him, she poured her pain and humiliation into her art— lost herself in hues of light and shades of dark. The more she painted over the weeks ahead, the more her instructor commented on her confident hand, her bolder lines, her willingness to try for blinding brightness and shades of pitch darkness, saying, "Like hope . . . and despair."

7

NOW SHE GATHERED A BREATH in her lungs and exhaled. She and Marta had been there for each other—with a bridge of hope between them. You don't make a friendship like that and toss it to the wind, as if it had no significance. Damn the policy of not making contact with other patients once released; she'd find a way to contact Marta.

She pulled out a page of cream-colored stationery and a matching envelope from her writing desk and penned her thoughts, telling Marta about life on the island. What she really wanted to ask she couldn't put into words. But she paused, holding her fountain pen in midair, challenging her assumption. This was an exchange between friends. If she couldn't be honest here, then where? She wrote:

> . . . *And, Marta, are you still waking with nightmares? More to the point, is your uncle leaving you alone? If he is bothering you, then you must—must!—take the train to Ranier and come stay with me on the island this summer where you will be safe.*
>
> *The island is a world apart, and I sometimes feel I could stay here forever, letting the days pass by reading, sketching, painting, and swimming. But then I remind myself that fall will return and soon after, winter with temperatures dropping at times to forty or fifty below zero. You understand this kind of*

cold better than I can, as I always leave here by late
August for Davenport. But this year—God willing
and my parents allowing—I will be in Paris again,
with temperatures similar to Iowa's.

I miss you and wish you the very best, dear
Marta.

Your loving friend,
Trinity

It was a small action.

But important.

She folded the piece of stationery, placed it in the envelope, and addressed it:

Marta Sentzke
Street unknown
Hibbing, Minnesota

She'd join George on his next boat run to Ranier and mail it herself.

8

THOSE FIRST CHILLY MORNINGS breakfast was set in the warmth of the kitchen. But when the morning sun burned intensely, promising a day of heat ahead, Agatha served breakfast on the east-facing screen porch.

Trinity sat across the table from Max, divided by a silver platter of scrambled eggs and bacon garnished with parsley; orange slices dusted with powdered sugar; and cinnamon-sprinkled coffee cake warm from the oven. He smiled as she placed the linen napkin across her lap. She glanced down. After being away so long, the simplest things—a scrumptious breakfast in the company of a guest she enjoyed—took on new pleasure.

Mother lifted her glass and announced, "We'll have the Guttenbergs here for dinner soon." She smiled, seemingly pleased to be maintaining a social agenda.

Father looked up from the newspaper. "Splendid. Whenever you can pin Victor down," he replied, then tapped at the page. "Say, I see here First National Bank got it right in its ad this morning. It says, 'Unless You Start, You Won't Arrive.' That's absolutely true, not just in saving money but in life in general!"

"Makes sense, Major Baird," Max said.

Trinity made a mental note to herself: *Unless you start, you won't arrive.* She took pride in her efforts while at Oak

Hills to send her letter of application to study again in Paris. Now she waited for a reply.

Agatha appeared through the swinging doors with coffee service. "Miss Trinity? Coffee or tea?"

"Coffee, please," she said, and after it was set before her she added cream and a teaspoon of sugar. It was one vice that helped her face her mornings the past two years.

"By the way, the name *International Falls . . . ?*" Max asked. "There must be a magnificent waterfall here somewhere. Might I see it?"

Father laughed. "Not much to see!"

Max looked confused.

Trinity explained. "It powers the paper mill in International Falls."

"Just as we started coming up here," Father said, "they built a dam across it. All that water flowing through the lakes up here and down through Rainy River is now harnessed for hydropower."

"It was beautiful once," Trinity added, then left to retrieve the small framed photograph from the living room. It showed visitors picnicking along the shore in top hats and suitcoats, parasols and full-length corseted dresses. Upstream, the river appeared calm, then dropped sharply over a wide edge in torrents of white that plummeted into a swirling tumult below. She felt a certain resonance with that sudden, dangerous force of nature, though not sure why.

She handed the photograph to Max.

"Oh, thanks. Beautiful. Looks like people went there just to see it."

"More likely to be talked into investing in Ennis's dam," Father said. "Alas, the price of progress. Everything changes. I guess that's why I love our island." He stretched his arms wide, crossed them behind his head, and relaxed back in his chair. "Still untouched wilderness."

"Unless Ennis gets his way," Trinity added. "It would change this area into a water reservoir for as far as the eye can see." Then she brought Max up to date on the local David-and-Goliath battle between Victor Guttenberg and E. W. Ennis, who aimed to turn the intricate weave of inlets, bays, and lakes into a dozen or more hydropower dams. She didn't need to add how much she admired Victor for leading the fight. Ennis was one of the wealthiest men in the country, and he wasn't going to back down easily. As Victor described it, he was in for the long haul and willing to see the battle through in the courts, if necessary.

"Agatha!" Mother's tone was overly loud, overly harsh. She stopped the conversation sure as a moose stepping in front of an automobile. "You know we always take marmalade and butter with toast."

"Mother, we have plenty here," Trinity said, motioning to the remaining coffee cake and eggs on platters.

Agatha finished refilling Father's cup of coffee, then hurried in and out again through the swinging kitchen door. "My brain is a sieve," she said apologetically, shrugging with a little laugh. "More holes than metal."

"And you've quite forgotten," Mother continued. "I see not as much as a single bowl on the table, and you know Trinity loves corn flakes." She looked to Trinity, as if this somehow proved her affection. "Do you care for a bowl this morning, honey?"

That Mother remembered one of her preferences was a surprise. Trinity answered, "Uh . . . no. Not this morning. I'm quite content."

"Bring it," Mother said. "She might yet want it."

"Right away," Agatha said, disappearing again.

"Just once," Father said under his breath, "could you please not find fault with Agatha? Are you trying your best to drive her away?"

"Once again," Mother returned, "may I remind you that she and George are both paid fairly for their services? It's *our* job to set the standards, and I aim to keep our standards high."

Trinity winced. It was hardly the first time her parents argued, but she didn't want them to ruin Max's breakfast, too.

When Agatha returned, she set down a dish of marmalade, a butter tray, a bowl filled with cereal, and a small pitcher of milk.

"Thank you, Agatha," Trinity said, meeting her eyes. But what she really wanted to do was to apologize for her mother's rudeness. More than once, Trinity had suggested that Agatha and George take their meals with the Bairds, but Mother would never hear of it. She was, after all, a Druthmore from Prince Edward Island—and more concerned than the Queen of England about appearances. Though, ironically, while she stayed on the island, she dressed more like a frumpy washerwoman than the heiress of a major shipping company. She was a conundrum. There was no other word for her.

Mother sat forward on the edge of her chair. "Mr. Bern," she said, "just so you know, our oldest daughter, RuthAnne, and her husband will be coming in a week."

"Early this year," Trinity said. She couldn't say she was thrilled that her oldest sister was coming early, for her sister's presence always had a way of making the island shrink in size. RuthAnne and her husband, Emmett Pennyford, always visited the first week of July. "Why?"

Mother whispered, "That's the big mystery! RuthAnne said she couldn't tell us and it would have to wait until she arrives."

Father grinned. "Bet ten to one there's a bun in the oven," he said. "Somewhere between their bickering those two figured things out."

"To have a grandchild," Mother said with a sigh of longing. "Wouldn't that be something!"

Trinity lifted a spoonful of cereal and milk and asked, "What about Liz and Anthony?"

"Unfortunately," Mother said, "they're too busy to get

away from New York, what with Wall Street and her hat designs."

"Oh, too bad," Trinity said. Perhaps because Liz was second born, she never acted as entitled as RuthAnne. She had a different way of looking at the world, and not because her eyes were slightly off center—her left a tiny bit lower than her right—but she had an artist's eye. She didn't sketch or paint: she dabbled. On the island she made little creations of feathers, birchbark, and stone, and after she married and moved away, she'd somehow stumbled into hats—using feathers, ribbon, embroidery, jewels, and tassels to embellish styles ranging from toque to turban, from tam-o'-shanter to cloche hats. Two years back, on Trinity's return from her first year at the Sorbonne, she had enjoyed stopping in New York to visit Liz in her flat on the Upper East Side. It seemed so long ago.

Scritch! Lou raked her claws down the screen door.

"For God's sake, Trinity!" Mother yelled. Trinity choked down her cereal. "Stop that dog or we'll get it off the island!"

Max's eyes widened as he met Trinity's. She lifted her eyebrows, acknowledging the sudden craziness as she pushed away from the table.

"I'll give her some scraps," Agatha added quickly. "I've put away a few bread crusts and meat scraps. I don't mind, really. She's a sweet little girl!"

"Sit back down, Trinity," Mother commanded. "Agatha can handle this."

What was wrong with Mother? She'd never been a warm or snuggly person, and she always gave orders rather brusquely, but since Trinity had returned, everything set Mother on edge.

Something had changed.

In truth, Mother was the same as ever, only more pronounced in her shortcomings.

Trinity saw it for what it was: she was the one who had changed.

9

AS THE SUN ROSE HIGHER and warmed the beach, it beckoned Trinity to sun and swim. She brought a book along to read, and one afternoon as she was turning to her novel's next page, a canoe appeared in the distance, heading her way. The only white person she knew who preferred a canoe over a boat and motor was Victor Guttenberg.

She closed her book as he paddled into the bay and glided softly onto the sand beach. Shirtless—how could she not notice—he climbed out. The summer was young, but already the sun had browned his skin and lightened his sandy hair.

As he pulled up his canoe, Lou scrabbled out from under the lounge chair, barking shrilly, her guard hairs bristled.

"Lou! It's okay. It's a friend."

She jumped up, met him halfway across the beach, and grabbed Lou's collar. Then she planted a kiss on Victor's cheek. "I'm happy to see you!"

"Good to see you, as well, Trinity," he said, then stretched out his hand toward Lou. "And who's this?"

"She's mine," Trinity said with a grin. "Her name is Lou."

"Good for you." Victor untied the rumpled shirt from around his waist. "Need to maintain some level of decorum," he said jokingly, then pulled the shirt over his torso and buttoned it.

Lou quieted as she sniffed and then licked Victor's hand.

"Just like that?" Trinity said. "As if you've been friends forever."

His grin was impish—part elf, part shaman. "I'm delivering invitations in person," he said. "We—my mother and I—are hosting a costume party and dinner this Thursday at five o'clock. We're counting on the Baird family joining us."

"I think RuthAnne and her husband will be here by then."

"The more the merrier," he said, the corners of his eyes creasing. "Costumes required," he added. "Without one, the gatekeeper will not allow anyone to cross over the moat."

She grinned, knowing the bridge they'd use was likely the simple wooden plank joining his dock to Falcon Island. "Is there a theme—or should I guess?"

"Lords and Ladies of the Middle Ages," he declared.

"What will you be? King Arthur with his magic sword?" she asked.

His eyes danced. "I had Merlin in mind."

She pointed at Lou, who had started furiously digging a hole, rear in the air, tail wagging. "May I bring my little dragon?"

He laughed, playing along. "Of course. As long as she promises not to breathe shafts of fire by my woodshed. I've worked too hard filling it. Maybe someday I'll try spending a winter on the island. But not this fall." His eyes flickered with energy. "I have other plans."

"Such as?"

"My photographs of moose have received a fair amount of attention. I've been invited to speak at a symposium this fall in London about my Hudson Bay expedition. So I figure, why not travel around and speak where I can?"

"I'll be in Paris by then," Trinity said, happy that his plan was still on. "We'll have to find a way to meet up."

He agreed. "We must!"

Then they chatted about how things were going for Victor and his efforts with a group of young lawyers in St. Paul, championing his uphill fight for wilderness.

"Well then, dear Trinity," he said and set off in his canoe.

"See you Thursday!" he called. The water flashed diamonds of sunlight in his wake.

She returned to her book and watched until he disappeared around the edge of the peninsula.

She felt so confused. Whenever she was around Victor, she was left wanting more. Hollow, in a way. As if part of her was gone when he left. They were woven out of the same fabric and shared the same deep loves.

Art.

Music.

Books.

Rainy Lake.

Unable to concentrate, she closed her novel.

What was this inner turmoil?

Was she always trying to fill the void her father left when he went away to war? And if so, what would having a boyfriend, a lover accomplish? She had always believed that it would make her more whole. But if she wasn't enough in herself, as she was, then maybe being in love, giving herself wholly to another, would leave her somehow diluted, less than her true essence.

She exhaled in frustration.

Someday, she mused, she'd be an old woman and she'd look back on this time of yearning, churning, and reeling—this time fraught with confusion—and she would see it with clarity.

But not now.

In such a mood, she would do better to paint.

10

AS SOON AS GEORGE LEFT the next morning for Ranier, Mother worried aloud, "Are you sure, Agatha, that we're ready for the Pennyfords? Their cabin is in tip-top shape?"

"Of course, Mrs. Baird," Agatha replied, before gathering empty breakfast dishes and disappearing through the swinging door into the kitchen.

"Honestly, Mother," Trinity said. "RuthAnne is family. You can relax."

Father cleared his throat, as if he were about to speak, then resumed reading the newspaper.

Mother whispered, "Lately, I'm wondering, well, if George and Agatha are giving us 100 percent. Who knows how they fill their hours when we're not here to supervise them?"

Father pushed back from the table. "Oh for God's sake," he said as he stood up and stepped out of the porch door and headed toward the boathouse, his newspaper tucked under his arm.

Clenching her white napkin, Mother rose from the table, left the porch, and let the door slam behind her—breaking her own rule. She headed in the opposite direction from Father, toward the cabin on the eastern cove.

As Trinity finished her coffee, a nameless tension gathered along her spine. "I'm sorry," she said to Max, who remained. "You've done a good job of staying invisible through all that."

"One learns," he said.

Mere moments later, Mother yelled, "Agatha!" Trinity spotted her standing outside the cabin door with a dark scowl across her face.

Agatha raced to the porch. "Oh my gosh, what is it?"

Trinity pointed through the screens.

"Mrs. Baird, what is it?" Agatha called through the screen.

"This!" Mother wielded a white cloth, now smudged gray with incriminating evidence of a job less than satisfactory. Trinity wouldn't be surprised if she had dirtied it in hearth ashes to make a point. Her mother's voice carried. "I ran this across the fireplace mantle and here's what I found. Hardly 'tip-top,' Agatha!"

Agatha turned to gather her bucket of cleaning supplies. "I must have missed a spot," she apologized, stepping off the porch and scurrying to where Mother stood. "I'll give it another going over before the Pennyfords arrive. I'm terribly sorry."

A HALF-HOUR LATER, as if for the arrival of royalty, her parents waited near the boathouse against a backdrop of wild roses in perfect pink plumage.

Trinity looked on from a nearby log bench with Lou on her lap. The knot in her belly tightened as the yacht rounded the peninsula. She watched as George expertly brought the yacht alongside the dock, hopped off, and tied off bow and stern.

Before RuthAnne stepped off the boat, her dark hair covered by a teal-colored cloche, Trinity knew something was amiss. It wasn't her drop-waist dress, a light mauve with teal embroidery, or the straight, knee-length style, which gave an impression of a box on two sturdy legs.

"Mrs. Pennyford," George said. "Allow me." He pushed the wooden step into place and RuthAnne stepped down.

Another woman—short strawberry blonde curls, navy skirt and white blouse, a few inches shorter and a few years younger than RuthAnne's thirty years—trailed behind, a suitcase in each hand.

"Everyone," RuthAnne declared, "this is my maid, Millie."

As RuthAnne stopped to kiss her parents, Trinity left her post with Lou and walked down the dock to meet them.

"You're home," RuthAnne said, in a tone that acknowledged her presence, without a hint of concern.

"I am," Trinity replied dutifully.

Father nodded toward the yacht. "And Emmett?"

"He always gets motion sickness," Mother said with an understanding nod. "He must be resting below, yes?"

"No," RuthAnne said. "He stayed back. He's not with us."

"Oh, a pity. Did something come up?" Mother said.

"Yes, you might say. Something called *divorce.*"

"What?!" Father swung his head like a threatened bear.

Trinity was stunned, not that her sister and brother-in-law had exhibited an ideal marriage, but that divorce rarely happened. Not in their social circles.

"Yes, you heard correctly. Emmett and I are recently divorced," she stated, not showing the least bit of anguish.

"Divorced!" Father's face contorted in anger and he spat the word out as if it were tobacco juice. "This is your little surprise?"

RuthAnne gave a simple nod. Behind her sister's usual caustic demeanor, she appeared almost . . . what was the word? Happy? Trinity guessed RuthAnne had found someone else back home.

"No one in this family gets divorced," Father said. "Not now, not ever."

Mother sniffed. "That's right."

RuthAnne crossed her arms and with a tilt of her head said matter-of-factly, "I knew you wouldn't like it. I knew you'd try to talk me out of it. And that's why it's done and over. Better to tell you straight away than wait for the perfect time."

Father stomped away, turned, stomped back. "This is temporary," he began, then his words flowed in a torrent. "It can still be voided. Nobody has to know. I forbid you from mentioning it to anyone beyond our immediate family. Give yourself a few days, you'll feel differently. As far as I'm concerned, you and Emmett are still married."

"Think what you like," RuthAnne replied. "But I'm here for the summer." Behind her a few steps, Millie waited, an uneasy crease forming between her brows.

"And then what?" Mother blurted. "You have no training for work. You didn't finish your college degree, which I never said anything about since I expected you would be tending to your own family someday."

RuthAnne leveled a look of scorn at Mother and Father.

Mother's face contorted. "This is the most horrible news. Positively unthinkable!"

Trinity felt as if she were watching a moving picture. Her sister had always been a bit of a tyrant, but Trinity had never seen her so openly defiant. Let the bright beam of Mother's cold eyes be focused on her sister for a change.

"While you digest that bit of news," RuthAnne said, "I'd like to get settled in my cabin. George, be a dear and give a hand." A statement, not a request. "I seem to have quite a pile of luggage on this trip. And remember, George, bring ice to my cabin, quick as a whip."

The windmill powered the island's DC batteries for electricity, but ice came from George's efforts in winter. He cut large blocks from the frozen lake and stored them under sawdust in the icehouse, a log structure built into an embankment.

"Of course," George replied with a nod.

Dumbstruck, her parents didn't say a word. Mother's mouth twitched, no doubt holding back her indignation and fury.

Trinity could scarcely believe how her sister had put them so easily in their place. If anything, RuthAnne was the embodiment of Mother, only magnified—her moods to be avoided at all costs.

RuthAnne lumbered up the stone path, with Millie following, to the cabin with its sleeping porch and matching twin beds. Of course, she needed a maid. RuthAnne was completely inept. Trinity knew she should be more generous given her sister's news of the end of her nearly ten-year marriage. She should show more empathy, but it was difficult when RuthAnne's caring took the form of Christmas cards. At Oak Hills, when Trinity sorely needed a word of encouragement or a personal letter, her sister's holiday cards arrived with only two penned words: *The Pennyfords.*

A FEW DAYS LATER, as Trinity and Max drank lemonade and played a game of cribbage in the cooling shade of a cedar, Father came to the picnic table. "Sorry to stop things short," he said and went on to explain that sudden design issues had cropped up at B&B. "Max and I need to catch today's train and get back to Davenport."

"Do we have time to finish our game?" Trinity asked.

Father glanced at his watch. "Sorry. Not if we're going to get to the depot in time." For a moment, Trinity met Max's eyes and wondered if this would be the last she'd ever see of him, until Father added, "We'll return as soon as we can."

No sooner had they left the island than Mother reclaimed her throne, a high-back wicker chair in the living room. A dusting of yellow pine pollen drifted through the screens, settling on the floor and tabletops. It was always the case in June, and always a contributor to Mother's increased headaches.

"Agatha," Mother said, "bring me every worn bed sheet, every frayed kitchen towel or piece of clothing beyond mending. I would love to make Margaret Guttenberg a hostess gift." Since RuthAnne's arrival, Mother had hooked rugs as if her life depended on it.

When Trinity passed through the porch that evening, a sketchbook in hand, she better understood her mother's obsession. Sweat beaded on Mother's brow. The more she concentrated, the more she clenched the tip of her tongue between her teeth. Her hands moved with the steady precision of a spider building an intricate web.

For that moment time stopped. Trinity committed her mother's intense expression to memory. As she did, it dawned on her that she and Mother shared something in common.

They had each found ways to keep their demons at bay.

With RuthAnne's abrasiveness and jarring news, Mother had turned immediately to her rug hooking with a vengeance, compulsively using every last little scrap of cloth available on the island. When things felt out of control, Mother always turned to rug hooking; she took pleasure in wrestling strips of worn, colorful fabric into something manageable.

Something sensible.

With equal intensity—*but Lord help her, never with her tongue between her teeth*—Trinity painted and sketched every single day. It amazed her how she could be in the foulest of moods, and no matter what she drew or painted— the face of the sunniest child or that of the most disturbed lunatic—she always felt better creating something than she had felt before she started.

She stepped to the west end of the porch and the screen door squeaked as she pushed it open.

"Where are you going?" Mother asked, startling Trinity out of her musings.

"To sketch," she replied.

As she followed the stone path, with her mother's face etched in her mind, a lovely pine scent drifted down, along with a golden haze of pollen. She let go of her earlier intention

of sketching seagulls and instead carried her mother's determined expression with her all the way down the path of the
sloping island to the granite peninsula facing west.

The massive rock was warm and bits of lichen crunched
beneath her sundress as she made herself comfortable. She
undid the leather pouch holding her pencils—something
she hadn't been allowed to use at the asylum where the
sharp pencils could too easily be turned on staff or self—and
brought her sketchbook to her knees.

On the blank page she started with the chin, square and
determined, and, in a flurry of lines that grew darker and
darker, committed her mother's image to paper. Brooding.
Unpredictable.

By the time she finished and looked out, the sun was
an orange atop a dark blue plate. In silhouette, a flock of
seagulls called as they flew. At a distance a boat drifted with
three fishermen . . . casting in a lake that seemed to stretch
on forever.

She smiled. Was she a fisherman, casting about in an
infinite universe . . . or was she a fish, on the lookout for an
unforgiving hook?

11

TRINITY'S FIRST MISTAKE was passing Victor's invitation along to RuthAnne, who was drinking before noon and tottering by 4:30.

The second was letting her board the yacht for the party at Falcon Island.

Mother had insisted that the women all wear the tall, pointed hats she'd fashioned out of wire and fabric, and RuthAnne wore her medieval hat fastened under her chin with a red ribbon. "I'm perfectly capable . . . handling myself," she said, a tumbler in hand as she boarded the yacht and wobbled down the gangway to the yacht's stern with Millie following close behind.

RuthAnne sang out, "Millie, Silly, Diddily-do!"

Lou dashed past as Trinity boarded after them.

The engine idled as George cast off lines, hopped back on, and reversed *Trinity* into the bay.

Mid-gangway, Trinity paused beside the overturned dinghy, waiting for the drama to play out at the stern before she continued.

"Careful now, dear," Millie said just ahead of her and reached for RuthAnne's hand protectively. It was a small, simple gesture. Simple, but filled with seeming affection. And it left Trinity wondering if there was something more between maid and mistress than met the eye. Not that it was her business, but if so it only added to the layers of confusion all around her.

RuthAnne aimed unsteadily for a wicker chair, but Millie steered her instead toward the hatchway. "Oh, perfect spot for a little rest! Maybe a little lie-down will be a g-good think. *Thing!*" She corrected herself, a little too loudly.

Millie started backwards down the hatchway ladder. "Let me go down first, just in case you stumble—"

"I'm not gonna goddam stumble!" RuthAnne bellowed.

"Your hats!" Mother shouted over her shoulder from the aft. "Don't damage them!"

RuthAnne yanked hers off and disappeared below deck after Millie.

Mother waved, beckoning Trinity. "Come, sit with me!" she called as the boat headed for the channel, its engine settling into a hum.

Trinity turned back to the wheelhouse, where Lou was already seated on one end of the bench seat, Mother on the other.

George turned his head from the wheel. "Mind your sister doesn't fall overboard."

Trinity nodded. "I'll try. At least Millie seems to know how to handle her when she's like this."

Mother added, "Better than her husband ever managed to do."

Trinity met Mother's eyes.

At last, something they could agree on.

Mother patted the space beside her. Trinity wasn't used to such a gesture. "Your sister," Mother began. "You must know, she gets anxious before gatherings and usually needs a drink ahead to calm herself."

"Or two," Trinity said. "Or six or seven."

"Trinity, stop."

"Mother, you don't need to make excuses for her. It's just . . . I'm not thrilled at the idea of arriving at Victor's with a sloshy sister."

"Excuse me?" Mother said, her voice sharp.

"Oh, please," Trinity said, recognizing for the umpteenth time that Mother would always kowtow to her eldest daughter. Still, she pressed on. "With any luck, she'll fall into a deep inebriated sleep and not wake up until we return."

"Don't be judging her," Mother snapped back in a whisper.

George kept his back turned toward them, his hands on the boat's wheel.

No matter the risk, Trinity thought. Some things needed to be said.

"Who said I'm judging? But I know a drunk when I see one. I met several who were admitted. And committed. It turns ugly when they can't get their booze. In time, denied it, they can dry out. Sometimes straighten out." She paused, knowing she should rein in what she wanted to say, but out it came. "Maybe RuthAnne would do well at Oak Hills for a time. You might consider sending her, you know, for her 'own good.'"

Mother put up her hand as if to stop oncoming traffic. "Trinity, don't be all high and mighty." Beneath her royal cloak—a bed covering of paisley reds and golds and fastened with a brooch at her throat—she started breathing harder, her chest heaving up and down. "She'll be fine after a little shut-eye, you'll see. She's not always this way."

"Mmm," Trinity said. No, it was always this way. Always the same utter denial of what was reality and a complete defense of Trinity's oldest sister. Why did she even try? She could see she wasn't going to get anywhere. "I'm going to the bow," she said, untying her hat and leaving it behind on the bench. Lou hopped off the cushioned passenger bench and followed her out of the wheelhouse, up the short hatchway steps, and onto the white deck.

Lou sat beside her as Trinity stretched her legs out and settled back on her elbows. Here she could escape. She loved the breeze that stilled the chatter of others as the vessel cut through the late afternoon's cobalt water. She loved the moist air on her face, even as she reminded herself that she'd applied theatrical circles on her cheeks with lipstick for the party. She had belted her bedsheet into a gown so it skimmed her knees.

Someone had to play the court jester.

AT THE NORTH EDGE OF FALCON ISLAND, they tied off to an overhanging cedar and an edge of the floating dock, solidly secured with heavy chains bolted into granite. The moment George turned off the engine, Lou zipped off the boat and disappeared on shore. She was quickly adapting to island hopping.

George, too, had his own plans while on the island. His fishing pole and tackle box were at the ready in the wheelhouse. "Okay, Mrs. Baird, if I try the west end of the island for walleye while you gather?"

Mother nodded slightly, which sent her hat flying toward the water, but George caught it. "Here you go."

"Ladies of yore, knights of old," Victor called, standing beyond the two-foot-wide plank. He wore a belted doeskin hide over red long underwear that hugged his calves and thighs. "You may cross! Though I just saw the dragon fly over without permission."

Mother looked confused, but Trinity laughed. "It's hard to stop an eager dragon."

Standing at Victor's elbow, Margaret Guttenberg, who was shorter than Trinity's mother but equally as stout, wore a black full-length dress with lace across the bust.

"Wherever did you find such a costume?" Mother asked, stepping across the plank and placing her latest cotton rug into Mrs. Guttenberg's hands.

Margaret grinned. "I have my secrets, fair lady of Baird Island. You certainly weren't required to bring anything. What an intricate design!"

"A hostess gift," Mother said, pleasure rising in her face.

When Victor announced dinner, Trinity and her mother

gathered near the firepit and grill with the other dozen guests, including the Larssons and Worthingtons.

Mrs. Worthington pulled Trinity aside. "Sadie Rose said to tell you hello and that she's terribly sorry not to be here. She said to picture her buried in lesson plans."

Trinity smiled. "She's dedicated. But tell her I miss her, too. I haven't seen her since we hopped off the train."

"I know," Mrs. Worthington said with a nod. "She's taking her tutoring work very seriously."

"Trinity!" She turned to the familiar voice. It was Henry Densch, who was a few years older than Victor, not much past forty.

"Hello, Henry," she said with a grin. She had met him on her week back last summer. It was his first trip to Rainy Lake, and he'd seemed to have a grand time. She knew little about him, other than like Victor and Father he was a Harvard alum, that he played a shrewd game of chess when they'd taken the yacht as a group to Kettle Falls, and that he claimed to own a chess set first owned by Marie Antoinette and later by Napoleon Bonaparte.

Now, his appearance made her chuckle. He wore a purple cape that looked suspiciously like a tablecloth over his white union suit, which was buttoned clear up to the hollow of his pale neck. He bowed in a dramatized greeting. "At your service."

Trinity quickly glanced behind her and saw no sign of her sister. She was relieved. She wouldn't have to introduce RuthAnne, who was still apparently on the boat with Millie.

A wooden table was set outside, laden with dishes, pots, and platters, including Margaret's homemade bread, baked beans, and double-layer chocolate cake.

"Your mother is such a good cook," Trinity had once said to Victor as a teenager, as they paddled together after sharing another scrumptious meal. Victor told her that when his mother first came to Rainy Lake she'd never cooked a meal in her life. She arrived with a fear of water, which she had had ever since she was a child and lost her uncle, and then later lost her own child, Victor's younger brother, to a drowning accident in the Mississippi River. Because of that, Victor admitted that he hadn't learned to swim until he was seventeen or eighteen. When they first came north, poor Margaret was so worried about losing him to drowning that he finally told her that "a person who is so timid about the lake shouldn't be up here." After that, Margaret stopped voicing her fears and worries about the lake. Instead she took up learning to cook over an outdoor fire and eventually a wood-fired oven.

Savory smells rose from a cast-iron pot on a grill over smoldering wood coals.

"Tonight's main course," Margaret pronounced, one hand on her ample hip and the other pointing to the kettle, "is Tantalizing Wizard's Turtle Soup."

The response was muted.

Turtle soup.

Trinity had always loved turtles. Since she was a little girl she'd watched baby turtles crawl out of leathery eggshells deposited in the sand on her island's shore. More than once she had helped a baby turtle escape a bothersome shell or had moved obstacles from its path so the little one could crawl from land into the safety of the water.

She eyed the cast-iron pot, the same kind used at logging camps or in floating kitchens, called wanigans. It bubbled with broth, carrots, celery, onions, and hunks of white meat. She inhaled the steamy broth. *Chicken,* she was sure of it.

"Before we dine," Victor said, pulling a book out from behind his back. "Every court needs a poet." He took an expansive bow with a swoop of his arm. "*The Canterbury Tales* of Chaucer come to mind, but I thought I would stray from such a well-known work and read something by Petrarch, translated from the Italian." He cleared his throat, drew himself taller to his modest height, and began to read:

> I have not seen you . . .
> leave off your veil in sun or shadow,

since you knew that great desire in myself
that all other wishes in the heart desert me.

Trinity watched him read, watched his lips move. When
he glanced up at his audience, he looked her way. Was it
meant for her? An ember burned in her chest, traveled up
her neck, and flamed across her face. She dropped her gaze
to the ground, studying tiny blue wildflowers on thin patches
of soil as she listened.

While I held the lovely thoughts concealed,
that make the mind desire death,
I saw your face adorned with pity:
but when Love made you wary of me,
then blonde hair was veiled,
and loving glances gathered to themselves.
That which I most desired in you is taken from me:
the veil so governs me
that to my death, and by heat and cold,
the sweet light of your lovely eyes is shadowed.

His words sent shivers dashing across her skin as she
clapped with the others. What did this poem mean? "Blonde
hair" could be hers, or his more sun-bleached version. Did
he see her as if behind a veil? Was it her time away, or did
he mean her unraveling before she was sent away? *The veil
so governs me / that to my death . . . / the sweet light of your
lovely eyes is shadowed.*

Or was it a simple love poem that had nothing to do with
her? A simple expression of something written in its time
that suited his fancy for this evening's revelry? But before
she could give it more thought, he reached for his violin atop
a wooden table, set with plates and loaves of bread. "And
now, something baroque, yes?"

Again, the guests clapped.

Taking in the scene, Trinity glanced over her shoulder
at Henry, who was standing close behind her. He pressed his
hand to his chest. "Quite moving."

Suddenly, the mood was broken by a heavy splash—*kaploosh!*—coming from the direction of the yacht. Millie shrieked, "Help! Help! She went under! Help!"

Victor stopped.

"Where?!" Henry shouted.

Trinity ran toward the yacht, moored thirty yards away.

Millie screeched from the stern, pointing frantically at the water. "She fell overboard! There! Oh please help! I can't swim!"

Afterward, what happened in seconds played over in slow motion in Trinity's mind. Trinity had raced toward the water, figuring that RuthAnne must have awakened, wobbled about, sat on the boat's railing, and tipped over backwards. She scrambled down the gangway to the stern.

"Save her!" Millie cried, hands to her face.

Trinity yanked off her belt and bedsheet down to her lace-trimmed silk undergarments. Damn decency. She jumped up to the boat's railing and balanced, hands clasped overhead. She knew to be careful. In a panic, any drowning swimmer might pull down her rescuer. She dove and sliced through cool water, searching with her hands, opening her eyes, hoping to find her sister.

In some northern lakes the water was so clear you could see twenty feet down, but Rainy Lake wasn't one of them. The water was pure, yet dark with minerals, and Trinity could barely see her own hands stretched in front of her. She swam in an ever-widening circle, but she touched nothing. When her lungs burned for oxygen, she pushed toward the amber light and surfaced.

"Where is she?" Henry called from the dock. He and Victor had dropped their capes, poised to jump in.

Millie shouted from the stern. "There!" and pointed to a spot somewhere between Trinity and the dock.

Victor dove in.

Trinity was about to dive under again when Henry jumped off feet first and started dog-paddling, sending up a flurry of white splashes. What on earth was he thinking? He could barely swim!

"Go back, Henry!" she shouted.

Henry paddled back, flailing, his head barely above water, and she was sure he would need rescuing next. But Millie met him at the dock, her hand extended, and he took it and climbed out.

A few yards away, Victor surfaced, hair plastered to his head. He looked around, and like a loon pulled under by a giant northern pike, he went under without a sound.

Not a sign of him—except a swirl of water.

"Victor!" she shouted. Had no one seen it but her? RuthAnne must have grabbed him as her lifeline and pulled him under.

"Toss the life ring!" she yelled.

In a flash, Henry was on the boat. "Where?"

"By the dinghy!"

With a toss, the white ring flew through the air and landed right beside Trinity. She grabbed it and swam to the spot where Victor had gone under. God Almighty, she couldn't lose him, too.

As she neared, two heads bobbed to the surface.

Sputtering, wheezing for air, Victor held RuthAnne in a headlock with his elbow, gripping her beneath her chin. She choked, flailed, and then went quiet, pale as a corpse.

Trinity pushed the life ring to Victor's free arm. When he held on, she grabbed the life ring's rope and tugged and swam with all her strength toward the dock.

Victor wheezed and coughed, but he kept his head above water, and RuthAnne's too, and soon they were at the dock.

Henry squatted at the edge and pulled RuthAnne up, hands under her shoulders.

Trinity and Victor climbed out.

RuthAnne was stretched out on her back, her head tilted to the side, staring at nothing.

12

THE DOCTOR ADVISED BED REST for a full ten days to avoid pneumonia. RuthAnne therefore spent the days that followed the incident in her cabin, tucked under a sheet and cotton blanket in one of the twin beds. Rather than rely on George to keep up with RuthAnne's demands for ice, Mother took on the task with saintly dedication.

"Trinity, I can only imagine," she declared while hooking rugs, "what the Densches are saying about us now. And to think I had entertained hopes about their son Henry. He comes from the right kind of family, and now you have ruined your chances!"

The scandal. Her daughter, scantily clad, was all Mother could talk about.

Four days later, to Trinity's relief, Father and Max returned.

"Bring that to your sister," Mother said as lunch came to an end. She pointed at the tray Agatha carried with a bowl of turkey wild rice soup and a small plate of crackers and sliced cucumbers. "It's the least you can do to make up for the scandal you've no doubt set in motion."

As Trinity rose from her chair, she met Max's supportive gaze across the table.

Father spoke up. "I think we've covered that ground. From what we've been told, Trinity helped. She dove in and risked her life. I understand Victor was in real trouble. You can't keep faulting her for that."

With a grimace Mother sniffed. She closed her eyes, inhaled audibly through her nostrils, as if imagining the worst, then opened her eyes with a dramatic exhale. "Easy for you to say. You weren't there in the middle of the nightmare."

"Oh, please," Trinity said with exasperation. "I did what I had to do."

But Mother acted oblivious to her comment and continued. "Trinity stood on the boat rail, as if she'd been waiting for the chance to show off her French silks. Left little to the imagination, if you must know."

Max's eyebrows rose and his mouth twitched, and Trinity knew he was trying hard to suppress a grin. But even in Max's presence, supposedly another possible suitor, Mother wouldn't be stopped. "And after Victor saved RuthAnne, I swear—wet to the skin, she looked almost naked—did Trinity rush for a towel or a sheet to cover herself?"

At that, Trinity rose and left with the tray for her sister's cabin. No matter what she did, Mother always turned it around, turned it against her.

Lou dashed up alongside her as she made her way down the path toward the white pine, its massive branches dwarfing RuthAnne's cabin. Two red squirrels chased each other round and round the tree, and Lou parked herself at its base. On duty.

"Lunch!" Trinity announced.

Millie appeared at the screen door before opening it. "Oh, thank you, Trinity. I could have gone up to get it."

"I know," Trinity replied, but Mother had insisted on posting Millie bedside around the clock in case RuthAnne took a sudden turn for the worse.

Millie stepped aside as Trinity stepped inside. Balmy, pine-fresh air drifted through the screen windows.

RuthAnne wiggled up from under her sheets to a sitting

position and adjusted pillows behind her. "You may put it here, on my lap."

Trinity noticed another smell. Sickeningly sweet. The pungent smell of booze.

※

THERE WAS SOMETHING DIFFERENT in her sister's green eyes. Eyes that only a few days earlier had stared at Trinity with such utter blankness that they spelled death. In those moments on the dock, Victor tried to help. He had turned RuthAnne's head to the side and water seeped out of her mouth. He lifted her limp arms up over her head. More water spilled out; still she appeared lifeless.

That's when Mother started wailing and dropped to her knees with a low and mournful cry like nothing Trinity had ever heard before. She flopped across RuthAnne's seemingly dead body.

"My poor baby girl! Where's your father? He should be here!"

"Mrs. Baird," Victor ordered, forcibly pulling her away, "move back, please!"

"I'm her mother and I'll hold my baby girl if I want to!"

Kneeling, he pressed his hands, one over the other, on RuthAnne's abdomen. Over and over. He stopped, rested on his haunches, and waited for a moment or two before starting again.

And that's when RuthAnne began to cough up water. She rolled to her side in a fetal position and then, rising on all fours, began to heave.

※

TRINITY SET THE TRAY on her sister's lap. "Enjoy," she said.

RuthAnne whispered, "Thanks, Trinity. For everything."

Something had shifted. A little less haughty. She had called Trinity by name.

"You're welcome," Trinity replied and stepped back outside, just as Mother was coming up the path with a silver ice bucket.

"How's she doing?" Mother asked.

"Alive and well," Trinity said without meeting her eyes and continued down the path, soaking in the soothing hum of cicadas.

From behind her, RuthAnne's voice leapt theatrically high. "Mother, how did you know? Cocktail hour!"

Cocktail hour this early in the afternoon? How was that supposed to help keep pneumonia away? Mother's behavior was so confounding, and at the thought Trinity's heart ached with each beat. She willed it to settle, to slow its rhythm with each droning pulse of the cicadas.

When whistling rose from the boathouse, she drew a fresh breath and kept walking. She knew that whistle. It was one thing she loved about her father. No matter the circumstance, he could whistle a tune as if he hadn't a care in the world. And for all Trinity knew, he didn't. He didn't seem to take on turmoil around him but let it slide off as easily as rain from a roof.

She needed a moment alone with him—especially since he had just returned that morning and Mother had given her one-sided interpretation of just about everything. She stepped into the amber shadows. "May I talk with you?"

In the fishing boat, peering into an open tackle box at his feet, Father looked up. "Of course."

As Lou jumped down into the boat, choosing her seat at the bow, Trinity sat down on the boathouse floor and dangled her feet over the water. A school of tiny minnows swarmed by through the shaft of light, then disappeared into shadows. "You should know she was drunk when she went overboard," she said. "Mother wants to make it sound like—"

"I figured so," he replied with a nonchalant wag of his

head, as if it were a joke. Though how he found it humorous, she had no idea, not after what she'd witnessed.

"So why am I always the one in trouble?" she asked. "I was only trying to help."

"Oh, this storm will pass," he said, examining a lure with multiple barbed hooks. He grabbed fingernail clippers and nipped off old fishing line.

"Father, RuthAnne drinks all day, every day."

"Ah, I wouldn't worry about it. Hey, it makes her more lovable!" he said with a chuckle.

Trinity didn't laugh.

He added, not looking up from his tackle: "You know, she's going through her own marriage difficulties. But things will get sorted out. You'll see."

"Father, why do you have to reframe everything? She's not just 'going through' difficulties. She's divorced." She had never challenged him so directly.

When he didn't look up, didn't say a word, she felt more emboldened. "Mother acts as if keeping her ice bucket filled is about keeping RuthAnne healthy. When in fact it's about keeping her—"

Father lifted his head abruptly and cut her off. "That's enough. Who's to say RuthAnne's drinking is all that bad? We all need a bit of help now and then. If you must know, the doctor prescribes Mother a bit of tincture so she can sleep. Without it, she'd be up all night long."

"Tincture? You mean . . . ?" This was news. She knew alcohol and opium were often blended into a concoction only recently regulated by prescription. "How long has she been—"

"Oh, I don't know. For years."

"But opium, Father! She's probably addicted!"

"I'm not saying that's what's in it. I don't know what's in it. I don't bother to read the fine print from the pharmacy. We do as the doctor advises—and to be precise, RuthAnne's business is none of your concern!"

Though familiar scents of cedar and water surrounded her, Trinity felt an odd dizziness. As if she might topple into the water from the swirl of it all.

No wonder her world had so often felt off center.

Mother had a habit of opium tincture.

RuthAnne was a drunk.

Father denied hard truths.

And no matter what Trinity said or did, she was always at fault.

As crazy making as the asylum.

And yet she was stuck with them all on the island for the next few months. How was she ever going to maintain a hold on her own sanity?

Thank God Max had returned.

Someone she could trust.

13

WHEN THEY RETURNED from the evening cruise and the yacht was secured, everyone headed straight for their cabins.

Except Trinity.

The night was exceedingly breathtaking, and she couldn't go to bed.

Not yet.

The moon was rising, framed above the bay by pine trees and scrub oaks, nearly full and haloed in misty white.

On the expansive bow, Trinity laid on her back under a smattering of emerging stars, a haze of Milky Way, and darkness stretching beyond.

Frogs sent up a symphony filled with thumping bass notes and high-pitched piccolos.

On the sand beach, Lou snuffled, probably discovering toads. It had been one of Trinity's favorite activities when she was little: catching brown toads, some the size of her pinky finger, others the size of her fist. She had learned quickly that catching and holding toads came at a price: they peed in self-defense. When Lou snatched one up in her mouth, she'd quickly learn her lesson.

Trinity inhaled pine-resin air, the waft of moving water, the spice of cedar, the clean sweet fragrance of summer flora and fauna. She was ten when she had first stepped on the island. Ever since, no other place in the world could compare.

She'd had a good day and had enjoyed Max's company. Though she felt a mutual attraction, she was in the middle of her own struggle to reclaim herself, a process that was far too important to get starry-eyed about anyone turning up on the island. Still, she wondered about him. As she gazed upward, a shooting star arced through the night sky, grew faint, and disappeared.

Two years ago, she was that star, soaring along a trajectory, before dimming into something she barely recognized. Where was the girl who stretched naked on the sofa in the lodge, waiting to surprise Victor when he walked in the door? Though she had waited for the moment when she thought she'd had the island to herself, her actions had been incredibly bold—and foolish, she realized later—but she'd stopped blaming herself. After summers of swimming, diving, and talking together, of Victor's mesmerizing storytelling and violin playing around campfires, she had grown impatient. Her crush had turned to frustration. Surely, he had to know there was something special between them. Yet he left her uncertain. She never knew what she meant to him. Had they grown to be the deepest of friends or something more?

Then that fateful summer afternoon, when he stepped into the lodge and spotted her—the world stopped turning, waiting for his reaction—and he simply walked out, rejecting her. After that, what young-woman-in-love *wouldn't* be a swirling tumult of shame, injured pride, and bewilderment? For several days she had gone without sleep, until the night her mind became so dark and jumbled that she'd thought she couldn't go on any longer.

It was late at night. She tried swimming away from the island to end it all but had turned back.

Drenched and chilled, with a silver knife from the galley, she made her way to the yacht's rooftop. And after that things blurred, filled in later by details from Sadie, who had apparently talked some sense into her, wrapped her in a quilt, and eased the knife out of her hand.

Trinity remembered how she felt waking in the lodge, strapped down to a bed. Bewildered, scared, confused.

Not long after, she was sent away for hysteria.

She caught herself holding her breath, her jaw tight and aching.

Breathe, breathe, breathe in.

Let it go, let it go, let it go.

She exhaled heavily.

As Northern Lights fanned across the sky, sending shafts of pale green and lavender toward the stars, two loons began calling back and forth, their plaintive wails exquisitely beautiful, exquisitely sad. She'd missed so much of this, this place where she felt at home.

Time passed.

A soft padding of steps sounded on the dock.

She glanced over. It was Max with a cardigan over his pajamas, his flashlight beam aimed downward, illuminating the beaded moccasins he had purchased at the trading post in Ranier. "Hey," he whispered. "May I join you?"

"Sure."

He boarded, climbed the wheelhouse steps onto the bow, and stretched out on his back beside her, hands clasped behind his head, gazing upward.

She was glad for his company.

"There are times," she said, keeping her voice low so she wouldn't wake others, "when I feel like my mind spins too fast and I get overwhelmed. But if I have a chance to be quiet and reflect, like this . . . I can get things settled in my head."

"Actually, I understand," Max whispered, not turning his gaze from the sky. "Back in Chicago, I go to museums and galleries when I need to think."

A comfortable silence fell. As the stars grew brighter, the bay reflected them more intensely. When Trinity turned her head and softened her gaze, the sky and water melded into one.

She was floating in a watery sky.

SHARP, HIGH-PITCHED barking erupted.

Max bolted upright. "Oh my god, oh my god! Is it a bear?!" He snapped on his flashlight, sending beams wildly back and forth in every direction.

In a shaft of moving light, Lou stood on the beach, her back hairs flagged, barking at the yacht. Then she dashed onto the dock, jumped on the boat, and scrambled around the gangway.

"She's after something," Trinity said. "Hand me your flashlight."

Max scooted closer, handing it to her.

She thought of the hors d'oeuvres they'd eaten earlier and decided an empty can of oysters must have attracted notice. "Lou!" she called, dreading that she might get tangled up with a raccoon or pine marten.

Lou barked at the overturned dinghy tied at the boat's center.

She raced through the wheelhouse, then back toward the stern again.

Trinity called for her, with no luck.

Finally, Lou stopped in the wheelhouse, legs braced in a defensive posture. Growling turned to shrill barking.

"What is it, girl?"

And then Trinity spotted it.

An otter sat on the dock near the minnow bucket, staring back at Lou.

When it slipped over the dock's edge, Lou jumped down after it, barking at the dark space between the dock and the boat.

Soon points of light flashed along the island paths.

And voices.

"Now look what you did," Trinity said as she scooped Lou in her arms. Struggling to get down, Lou wouldn't stop barking. "Shhh," Trinity said, and carried her back to the bow of the yacht and sat beside Max. "Just an otter," she said, sitting down. "They're always raiding the minnow buckets. Can't blame 'em. It's an easy meal."

In seconds, a rush of voices, robes, and pajamas gathered on the dock: Father, Mother, George, and Agatha.

Mother gasped. "What's going on down here?" she asked, gazing from the dock to the bow of the yacht. "Mr. Bern, it's a bit late for architectural sketching."

Jumping to his feet, Max said, "I thought a bear might be causing trouble—and I came to help."

Trinity set Lou down and stood up. "I was enjoying watching the stars when Lou went crazy. An otter must have smelled leftovers from our cruise. George, you'll want to check your minnow bucket before you head out fishing tomorrow."

Max glanced around nervously. "So, um, looks like everything's okay."

"Yes," Father added coolly. "Thanks for checking."

"Trinity," Mother said, "I still don't understand your being up at this hour."

Trinity stepped back toward the hatchway ladder. "Mother, I've told you, and I don't have anything more to add." Then she made her way off the boat. "C'mon, Lou," she said.

Water had a way of carrying sounds for incredible distances. With each step toward the beach, she heard their conversation.

Father's voice was almost jovial. "Well, Mr. Bern, from here on, George and I will handle any rabid dogs, wild otters, or lascivious women who find their way onto this island."

Max laughed, as if cornered. "Yes, Mr. Baird."

Under the milky swath of stars, with her little dog at her side, Trinity headed along the strip of beach and up the slope.

14

WITH EACH PASSING DAY OF JUNE, the sun had a way of popping up in the east, long before anyone was ready to wake up, sending blazing rays of dazzling light through cabin windows. Well before Trinity was fully awake, birds welcomed the dawn with jubilant, raucous singing. Outside her window screen, mosquitoes stirred and hummed.

Lou nudged Trinity, who grudgingly opened her eyes and glanced at her alarm clock. "It's four-bloody-thirty in the morning!" She pulled a pillow over her head.

She later woke up in a sweat.

"Seven-forty. Better," she said. Before heading to breakfast, she filled her white porcelain pitcher with lake water. She emptied it into the washbasin, cleaned up, and brushed her teeth.

Lou waited for her beside the door.

"Okay, let's go," Trinity said.

The moment Lou stepped out, she began barking her head off and flew up the slope past the granite boulder.

"Not again!" She couldn't let Lou wake up the others before they were ready. That was not a good way to make friends.

Trinity followed after her and stopped at the beach, where she found Lou barking incessantly at two men. "Lou, quiet down."

One was Father, who dropped his robe and waded into the water in his dark wool bathing suit. Trinity wasn't surprised at his swimming so early. It was his morning ritual. A half-hour swim each morning before breakfast, no matter the weather.

The other was Max, who held a towel around his shoulders and bathing suit, his pale legs bare and covered in gooseflesh.

"Come on in, Max!" Father called as water reached his waist. "Water's fine!" he shouted, then he turned and began to swim.

Trinity picked up Lou, who quieted, and walked up to Max. "You don't have to," she said.

He groaned softly. "Yes, I do. I'm his guest. Plus I work for him."

"Get in here, Mr. Bern!" Father called again.

"I'm not that great of a swimmer!" Max called back.

Not everyone had the opportunity to spend entire summers on an island or had a father who deemed swimming as necessary as breathing. Years ago, Trinity had learned to be comfortable in water and had mastered the crawl, backstroke, sidestroke, and breaststroke. Rather than fearing water, she took comfort in it. Though, unlike Father, she waited until it was hotter outside. Midafternoon was usually the best time. But you never could wait for the lake to feel warm. It was always predictably cool.

"You'll never get better standing there on shore!" Father bellowed.

"See?" Max said under his breath.

"Mm-hmm." She enjoyed standing beside Max. And she didn't want to see anything bad happen to him. "Stay where you can touch bottom."

He nodded, drew a breath, and dropped his towel. "Here goes!"

With a charge, he dashed across the sandy beach into the shallows. When the water reached his thighs, he plunged under. He surfaced, wiping water and hair out of his eyes. "Methuselah!!"

"Methuselah?" Trinity repeated with a laugh. "Why?"

"It's better than what I want to say!"

"A little chilly?" she called.

"Nothing survives this kind of cold! If I ever wanted a family, this puts an end to that dream."

She laughed, happy that Mother hadn't overheard. It would have been an inappropriate joke for a young man to tell in a young woman's company.

"Bern, follow me!" Father called, treading water. "Stay close." With his usual military momentum—always forward, never retreat—he set off doing the crawl with precision. His normal routine was to stay in the bay, swimming from point to point and back again. What was it with men? Why couldn't Max just stay on shore where he was safe? Why must he feel goaded to keep up with Father?

When Max tried the crawl, his motions were awkward, and he slapped the water more than he scooped it. He barely inched forward.

Trinity watched, her stomach tight.

Changing his method, Max settled on the dog paddle, but he held his neck and head high, throwing his balance off. His lower back seemed to arch under him rather than float on the water behind him.

He was, in truth, a terrible swimmer.

He flailed and flailed, then stopped to catch his breath, feet apparently touching bottom, his head above water. He needed instruction. Trinity wanted to give him suggestions, but she held her tongue. She didn't want to embarrass him. Perhaps later that day she could meet him at the beach and give him a few tips.

Hand above her eyes, blocking the sun, Trinity watched.

Father swam toward the end of the nearest boat dock.

Max, she thought, would be smart and stay close to shore.

But he didn't. He glanced back at Trinity, smiled, and waved. "Told you!"

Then he returned to dog-paddling, thrashing his arms and moving ever so slowly forward, but now his torso seemed a little more relaxed, his legs flutter kicked. It was progress.

Still, she kept her eyes peeled in case he went under. She glanced at the round life ring hanging on the side of the boathouse. If she needed to, she could toss it his way, but already he was a good distance from shore.

She set Lou down and hurried along the beach to the dock, then casually strolled out to the end of its length as Father went past. Max followed in a self-made froth of churning water, alarm in his eyes. He was swimming. He was above water, but just barely.

Damn that father of hers.

She ran to the boathouse, pulled off the life ring, and as Max neared the end of the dock, tossed it to him. Her second near-rescue of the summer. He grabbed it. "I was doing okay," he said, resting his arms on the edge of the ring.

"And you'll do better if you hang on to that—at least today. Swim after him if you must, but now you'll survive it. Work on kicking your legs harder. Swimming takes practice. You have to build up to Father's kind of endurance swimming."

Max grinned. "Thanks." He set off again, the life ring leading his way.

It was at that moment that Father glanced back. "Oh for God's sake," he said, half-scolding and half-laughing.

"Not everyone is you, Father."

At that, Father boomed, "I'll say not!"

Now that she believed Max would survive, she turned away and headed back to her studio. She would rather get dressed for breakfast than watch Father prove his prowess at someone else's expense.

To Trinity's astonishment, after that Max showed up every morning to swim with Father. And with each day that passed, he improved.

DURING THE DAY, she found time to wander with Max, showing him her favorite places as they scouted out building sites. She showed him her favorite spot to watch sunsets on the west-facing slope of rock. She showed him her favorite cove: shallow and wind-protected, it was also a favorite for great blue herons, mallards, goldeneyes, mergansers, and cormorants. Beyond the sandy-bottomed cove, she showed him the tiny island that sat a stone's throw away from the northern peninsula.

She told him about when they'd first bought the island and started camping. "We set up here," she said, gesturing to the semicircle stone hearth and grill that still sat there, rarely used. Not until they had spent time on this end of the island did they realize that though it commanded great vistas, it was too exposed to the elements; the winds were unforgiving on the north point, and when one storm blew an empty tent off into the lake, they packed up and moved to the shelter of the east side. Experience, unfortunately, was sometimes the only way to learn.

Water swept over the rocky inlet. "Look, it's the whales and dolphins, just below the surface," she said. "Or at least that's what I like to imagine."

"You're a dreamer," he said. "So what, may I ask, are your dreams for your future?"

"You sure ask direct questions, Mr. Bern."

He sat down on a half-log bench beside the hearth of stones and cooking grate. "Forgive me. I lost my mother when I was quite young, and ever since I live with a constant awareness that time is fleeting. I don't like to beat around the bush."

She wasn't ready to sit, so she paced. "Well, for starters, I'm happiest here, on the island. So I can't imagine a future without it. I need to leave, to stretch myself as an artist, to continue my education, and yet I know I'll always return. To keep this part of my life somehow."

He nodded, listening.

She knew she wasn't giving expected answers and added as an afterthought, "Maybe children someday. Maybe marriage."

"In that order?" he teased.

"No, ideally not. But I'm not in a rush for either."

"Mmm."

It might be polite to ask the same question to him in return, but Trinity worried she'd be bringing up a matter that was more serious than she cared to discuss. She felt wonderfully cozy in his company, but she wasn't ready to go beyond being friends, especially when her parents were always a short distance away.

She changed the subject.

"Max, it's important that we choose sites close enough to the lake to hear the water lapping against the shore when you fall asleep," she said.

"It's an island, Trinity. I imagine you can hear the water from *every* spot," he said with a laugh, tapping his clipboard with the end of his pencil.

"I'm serious," she said. "Every spot is different. You'll see, once you sit for a moment and listen. C'mon."

They walked along the shoreline beside the mammoth winter boathouse and crossed the steel rails that helped launch *Trinity* every May. She explained how every Labor Day, Father and George would start up the truck motor on one end, and with the use of steel cables the Elco would be pulled from the water where she belonged to dry out for the winter months ahead under the protective walls of the boathouse. It always made Trinity feel sad, because it signaled an end to the season she loved more than anything else in the world—summer on the island.

When they headed to her side of the island, they skirted the eastern path toward a simple log cabin built into a hill. It looked across the water toward the beach and boathouse. "A perfect spot for watching the comings and goings," Trinity said. "This is the caretakers' cabin. George and Agatha's."

Then she motioned to a spot beyond juniper bushes—a lichen-covered slab of granite. Perfect for sitting and watching.

Water rolled in and out against the rocky shoreline. *Swish, swash. Swish, swash.*

Max rested on his elbows and closed his eyes. "You're right. It's a different music here, too."

Knees bent, he crossed his right foot against his left knee. The sun had tinged his face a shade of pink. Trinity had a sudden urge to lean over and kiss him. But it could only complicate things, and she needed to focus all her energy on keeping her life manageable, her life in control. She knew all too well how passion could get in the way of sound judgment. After a few moments, she hopped up, dusted off her trousers, and said, "Let's follow this path along the channel. I'll show you my studio."

She led the way down the winding trail, past the massive boulder, and finally to the square log structure by the water.

"Oh, a cabin," he said. "I was picturing a French flat with tall windows, high ceilings, an enormous stream of light coming in . . ."

"No, not a cabin. My studio." She placed her hand on the doorknob and turned, feeling the risk of being alone with Max. She needed to keep her wits about her. How could she trust herself? Only a few days earlier, Victor was the only person on her mind. She couldn't follow every impulse that came along; she needed to make choices that were good for her own well-being.

She paused. His breath was warm on the back of her neck. He stood too close, trapping the air between them.

"I'd very much like to see it—and your work," he said. His hand lighted on her waist, not in a demanding or insistent way, but soft as a butterfly to a flower.

She wanted to let him in, to share her art and herself with him. She stopped herself. Not yet. She couldn't risk it. If she were found alone with him in her studio in any kind of compromising situation, she risked being labeled *promis-cuous.* That one word was enough to send her away. And that raised a glaring question. Why would her parents bring a handsome young man for an extended stay on this small island, unless . . . unless they intentionally hoped something would start up between them. Mother had been quick when they'd first arrived to point out that Max came from a good family. She bristled at the thought.

She pivoted to face him, almost nose to nose. He moved closer, but she flinched, avoiding his intended kiss and pushed past him. "I'm sorry. This was a mistake. I'm not ready to show my work . . . to be that vulnerable—to you, to anyone."

"But we have *something . . .*" He looked away toward the water, then turned back again. "Tell me you don't feel it, too."

She met his eyes briefly. How could she put it into words? Maybe in the past she would have acted on a whim, but she couldn't do that now. Things had changed. She had changed. She'd learned in spades: she had to look out for herself.

I can't, she thought. *And unfortunately, it's not negotiable.*

He stepped back, eyes downcast like a child unexpectedly reprimanded, then he glanced up from under his hat's brim.

The kitchen bell clanged from the other side of the island.

"I enjoy your company," she said. "Nothing more."

"Okay," he replied, looking knocked back on his heels. "Whatever you say."

She turned and led the way to the island's highest point where the windmill was anchored. "From here you can see in every direction," she said. "I think a guest cabin here would make perfect sense."

He tilted his head. "But it's farther from the water. You keep saying—"

"Except here. This should be the future cabin site for my sister. RuthAnne wears earplugs when she's here. Says she sleeps fine in a city, but wilderness keeps her awake all night."

He grinned. "I think I may suffer from the same condition."

15

THE TABLE WAS SET TO PERFECTION with shimmery crystal wine glasses, polished silver, and fresh-cut flowers. Candlelight poured through four suspended iron grates, each tossing lacey patterns of light across the dining room. Mother had invited the Guttenbergs over for a "quiet little dinner," as she had explained it, "after all that we put them through a few weeks ago."

The scandal. Trinity wondered when Mother would get over it. All had turned out well in the end. RuthAnne had survived the scare of pneumonia and was no longer banished to her cabin; she and Millie joined them at every meal.

Seated across from Victor and Margaret, Max gazed around the room. "I find these light fixtures unique in an antiquated way. Charming."

"They're from France," Father replied from his end of the table. "Old floor grates I found at the end of the war."

"Ah, yes. The war," Max said, as if putting the pieces together. "Is that why they call you the Major at B&B? Were you?"

Father nodded. "Yes. When the Army discovered I knew five languages, they quickly put me to use. See, the military's logistics still relied on nineteenth-century technology, and they were struggling to keep up with the demand for supplies." He went on to explain how his experience in manufacturing and shipping came in handy. "When horse-drawn wagons and trains failed to get supplies to the soldiers in what became trench warfare, we had to come up with a new plan."

"What did you do?" Max asked, and Trinity shot Victor a knowing glance as they'd both heard this story countless times before.

"Hell of a mess. Hell of a mess," Father said. He waved his hand as if orchestrating the next notes. "We had to improvise. Figured out how to build special narrow-gauge trench railways to extend the rail network to the front lines. Hell of a war."

"'The war to end all wars,'" RuthAnne said, repeating the familiar phrase.

Mother cleared her throat, followed by her habitual sniff. "Well, staying home alone with children was a different kind of war. That's a story no one talks about."

"Mrs. Baird," Max said, his face softening toward her. "I'm sure. How did you cope? You must have worried?"

Trinity caught a gleam in her mother's eyes, sharing the realization that Max Bern was proving to be a fine conversationalist, a trait always admired in their guests.

"Summers were spent here on the island," Mother began, "and thanks to Victor and his mother—" She nodded at Victor and he returned her acknowledgment with a nod. "They stayed here with us, always a comfort. Margaret, you took up cooking."

"I did," she replied.

"And Victor was always around in the event of trouble. Downed trees after storms, motor problems, a need for the doctor, whatever the emergency . . ."

As she talked, Trinity's mind drifted. Her family would never have traveled north had it not been for Victor. She'd first known him as a musician, playing his violin at gatherings at their nine-bedroom home in Davenport. But when he returned from his travels and described the wilderness he had found, it sparked something not only in Father but in her, too. She'd been awestruck as Victor shared about paddling a vast lake once traveled by French voyageurs—a lake dotted with island jewels. He talked about the Ojibwe people of the area, and how he wanted to learn their language and their stories. At Father's request, he had scouted out land for sale on Rainy Lake; long before he obtained an island of his own, he returned to her family with the announcement, "I found your island."

Victor bought it on Father's behalf for $500. From the moment she learned the news, Trinity couldn't wait to see it for herself.

She packed up with her family that first summer, not knowing what life would truly look like on the island. They rode the passenger train to a little blink-of-a-town called Ranier on the edge of an immense lake that shared a border with Minnesota and Canada. With their crates and trunks, they waited at the dock, along with a few women carrying parasols and wearing ankle-length dresses with corset-tiny waists. Unless they were laborers, men wore three-piece suits or suspenders over shirt and trousers. All waited for the steamboat to carry them to their destinations on Rainy Lake.

Victor showed them the island, and Father insisted on naming it after Victor, since he had found the "jewel" for them. But Victor protested, "Oh no. Baird Island."

For two summers Trinity's family camped in baker's tents, no more than canvas walls hoisted above a wooden platform, "getting to know the lay of the island" before Father started construction. Then came the log lodge built around its centerpiece, the towering stone hearth, and an adjoining bedroom.

Over the summers, Trinity went from admiring Victor to developing a strange and terrible crush on him. Especially when the war broke out and Father was gone for two years. It had baffled her, this overpowering yearning to be with Victor, to lean on his every word and gesture as if he were a god.

She'd never forget the summer when she was fifteen, and the day Victor was struggling to start a boat motor. Over and over he pulled on the cord, until his whole body buckled and collapsed. His body hung over the edge of the boat, face-down. If Trinity hadn't been there to pull his head out of the water, he would have drowned. Their lives were intertwined. When he came around, he was sent to the local doctor, then shipped by train to see his heart specialist; he only returned north again after he claimed to "shamelessly plead" with his doctor to allow him to return.

She pulled her attention back to the conversation at the table. Mother was saying, "Many of us women looked wher-ever we could for support. I studied the occult and found it especially helpful during that time to frequent a clairvoyant."

"We all know seeing a fortune-teller helps sometimes," RuthAnne said flippantly.

With a push back from the table, Mother nodded unapologetically. "I did. And it helped. Madame LaBelle calmed my nerves whenever I visited her, and I always left with the confidence that my dear husband would return to us, safe and sound."

Father lifted his glass of wine. "To the brave and the fall-en," he said. "And those who fought their own battles on the home front. We salute you."

Everyone toasted and drank.

And then Victor added another toast. "To the Major."

"To the Major!"

Before dinner was over, Father joked about how he used to offer to pay each of his daughters if they could swim from one point of the island to the other.

"Did they?" Max asked, who no doubt appreciated the distance of such a swim.

Father laughed. "Only this one," he said, extending his arm toward Trinity. "I don't think she cared about the money as much as she couldn't pass up a dare."

"True?" asked Max, with a grin.

Trinity glanced at her empty glass, then looked up. "I can't deny it."

"That's why you're a strong swimmer to this day," Father said, pushing his chair back from the table, his signal that dinner had come to an end.

"Before we move to the living room, one more toast." This time Father toasted Paris. "For without that city of light," he went on, taking a half-bow toward the other end of the table and lifting his glass high, "I would never have met my lovely wife, who had been traveling there at the same time with her family. But somehow, in the heavenly balm of that radiant city, I convinced her to trade her life on Prince Edward Island for a life together with me. *Salut!*"

Everyone toasted and drank. And then Mother asked, "Max, have you ever been there? Paris?"

He grinned, and turning his head slightly toward Trinity added, "No, but it sounds like I should visit soon."

AS WAS OFTEN THE CASE when they gathered, Mrs. Guttenberg played the piano after dinner in the living room. Victor stood nearby, violin pressed under his chin, filling the room with music.

Though Trinity could not match the concert quality of either Victor's or his mother's music, she sat in a chair and strummed her mandolin. And it didn't matter that she was still learning the instrument. Everyone seemed happy to simply gather together.

As she strummed, she caught a view of Victor. Eyes closed, fully absorbed in the music, he played, elbow raised, his bow flying across the strings. As his music had always done, it sent tremors of emotion through her. She imagined herself in her younger years, listening to his violin music and superb storytelling in the amber light of many bonfires.

When Victor and Margaret started on "The Blue Danube"

by Strauss, Max jumped up from the sofa. "I propose dancing!" He swept across the carpet to Trinity and bowed. "May I have the pleasure . . . ?" He extended his hand.

"Of course," she said with a smile and set aside her round-backed instrument, smoothed her sundress, and soon was dancing around the room, his hand on her waist, her hand to his shoulder. They glided—one, two, three, one, two, three—around and around the living room. Max was a splendid dancer, leading without pushing, perfectly moving to the lilt of the melody and its rhythm.

When her parents started to dance, Trinity was shocked. She hadn't seen them dance in years. Following their lead, RuthAnne and Millie joined in, too.

As she twirled in Max's arms, she remembered her dream. The recurring one of Victor piloting a plane. He would land briefly on the island's sand beach, props spinning, and always in her dream she became frantic. Desperate. She had to climb into the plane and hide, become a stowaway, before he set off again into the sky, leaving her behind. Strange. It always left her feeling confused. As she danced, it dawned on her: the recurring dream of him was intertwined somehow with Father. In the dream, she'd worried about never seeing the pilot again. But it wasn't Victor who went off to war, it was her father. Major Baird. He was the one she should have been most worried about during those uncertain years. In Father's absence, Victor proved to be a better listener and storyteller; he laughed easily and was always generous with words of encouragement and praise. She hated to admit it, but it was hard to miss someone who ran a family like a military machine. Father had always seemed more concerned with his empire building than with the individuals around him.

No wonder Victor was the one she had feared losing.

She didn't understand why, but it felt important, as if she'd just discovered a missing puzzle piece. And she understood that her crush on Victor was a thing of the past—a treasured part of growing up, especially when her Father had gone to war.

All she knew was that for this dance, swaying in the arms of Max, she felt lighter. Serenaded by Victor's violin and Margaret's piano playing, she felt more at ease in her own skin than she had in a long, long time.

When Max later walked her to her side of the island, thunder crackled in the distance and flashes of lightning lit the sky. Before she stepped into her studio, he clasped her arm above her elbow and drew her close. "Do you want to know what I see?"

She met his eyes, but then felt herself pulling away.

"You. You're talented. You're beautiful. And I see the struggles you go through and how you need someone to be your advocate."

She pulled back to discourage him from saying anything more.

"Well, more than that," he said. "I love it up here, and I enjoy everything about being around you. I loved dancing with you this evening. By now, I think you know I'm growing quite fond of you."

"I'm not ready to get involved with anyone," she said.

"And I'm not finished," he replied. "What I feel for you is much more than wanting to get into bed with you. My hope is that we can take time to see where things might go between us. I would hate to rush something so promising."

"Yes," she said and kissed him. His mouth was warm and sweet, but she stopped just as suddenly and pressed her forehead against his.

Everything in her wanted to pull him into the studio, to spend the whole night together. They would kiss and undress and climb under the sheets, skin against skin. A medicine for her past months and the toll they'd taken on her confidence. Now, she had to force herself to take her time. He was right. She didn't want to rush things either. She had no idea what the future held, no idea of what she even truly wanted, but if she and Max had any possible future together, then they could take time to get to know each other before falling into bed together. She laughed at herself, because a little carnal knowledge could be a dangerous thing, and as far as her parents knew she was still a virgin. She wondered if Max would care about her past experience. Would he appreciate that she knew a thing or two already? Or was he like many men who expected women to remain virgins until married? And why, for God's sake, was this social restriction placed only on women?

Fat and heavy raindrops began to fall. *Plink. Plunk.*

Max stretched out his palms. "I better hurry, before it's a downpour."

"Probably too late for that," Trinity said, leaning closer and kissing his earlobe, then shooing him away.

16

A WHITE-THROATED SPARROW sang flutelike outside the porch screens—an exquisite serenade—as everyone gathered at the table for breakfast.

Mother cleared her throat.

Trinity realized she had missed what Mother had been saying. "I'm sorry, what was that?" She looked up from eating her last bite of poached egg.

Mother replied, "If you'd *listen* when I'm speaking, dear. We'll pick up Sadie and her parents on the mainland, then make a day of it today to Kettle Falls. We're taking rooms at the hotel and you and Sadie can sleep onboard."

"Oh, good!" Trinity replied. "Max, I can't wait to introduce you to my good friend Sadie."

"Another time, I'm afraid," Max said, lifting his hands. "I have drafting to finish that must get in tomorrow's mail."

"Ah, too bad," Trinity said. But she was no less thrilled at the idea of seeing Sadie and introducing her to Lou. She would be forever grateful to Sadie for her visits to Oak Hills, when they walked the mowed greens, visited the livery stable, and pretended that nothing had changed. But now that Trinity was released, she looked forward to being together in a more normal setting and falling asleep to the roar of Kettle Falls.

Trinity packed a duffel bag, pulled the shoulder strap over her shoulder, and with Lou in her arms boarded the yacht.

※ ※

THEY FIRST TRAVELED WEST to Ranier to pick up the Worthingtons. As Sadie and her parents stood at the pier waiting to board, Trinity held Lou in her arms. "Guess what?" she called as the boat eased alongside them.

"Yours?" Sadie asked with a smile, her bobbed waves extra curly in the high humidity. Her linen dress with capped sleeves matched the pale blue sky. "What's its name?"

"Lou," Trinity said, kissing the top of the dog's head.

The senator—Mr. Worthington—lifted his fedora in greeting. Mrs. Worthington was a vision of ivory from head to toe in a satin brocade dress, matching shoes, and parasol. She looked up. "Hello, dear Trinity!"

Trinity beamed as she stepped aboard. "I was so looking forward to this day!"

"Trinity, you look amazing!" Sadie said. "And it's not just the haircut or clothes. You're feeling better, aren't you?"

"I am," Trinity replied, leading the way down the short steps to the stateroom at the stern. Morning light from stateroom windows spilled across two berth beds and a four-drawer dresser and mirror. "Pick your bed. Guests first."

Sadie sat on the starboard berth and began unpacking her tote into cubbyholes.

"Then I'll take this one," Trinity said, stretching out on the port side. Lou leapt from her arms across to Sadie's bed and greeted Sadie with chin licks.

"She's not shy!"

"She was at first," Trinity said. "Didn't last long."

※ ※

MIDDAY, as they dropped anchor off a sand beach on the lake's Canadian side, two loons swam away from the shore, one with a baby tucked safely into its back feathers.

The sun bore down, warm and sizzling. Trinity and Sadie changed into bathing suits and dove off the stern.

The top layer of the water was almost warm, but with each layer down it grew colder. "My legs are freezing!" Trinity exclaimed.

"I worry," Sadie Rose said, "that a giant snapping turtle will eat my toes." She floated on her back, sculling with her arms, her feet at the surface.

When they finished swimming and climbed the ladder, they wrapped up in warm, cotton towels.

For a moment, drying in the sun on the bow, Trinity had the odd sense she was a dragonfly. She'd arrived on the island in a nymph stage in the gray beetle-like hull of her old self, and with each swim underwent some deep kind of transformation. She had stopped the life she had known the day she entered Oak Hills . . . where everything in her molecular being, every small way in which she'd defined herself, had been altered. Her thinking. Her way of seeing the world. At a cellular level, she guessed she was made of the same genetic elements, but she had been completely rearranged into a new version of herself.

A metamorphosis.

After changing in the stateroom, she and Sadie climbed into the dinghy and George rowed them to shore, where their parents were settled on blankets. George handed out bag lunches of ham and cheese sandwiches with pickle slices wrapped in wax paper, pretzels, candied mints, peanut butter cookies, and lemonade.

As they ate, Father shaded his eyes and motioned to the water. "We have visitors."

An Ojibwe family approached by canoe. The man paddled at the stern, the woman at the bow, and the young child rode in the middle. They were perfectly balanced, and the birchbark canoe moved across the water with the ease of birds crossing sky.

"'Tis the season," Father said.

The man lifted the rounded end of his paddle in greeting. "*Boozhoo!*"

"*Boozhoo* to you!" Father called back.

The woman reached toward her feet and lifted a basket and tilted it, just enough to show its sapphire jewels—the first of the season.

"Blueberries," Trinity said.

"How much?" Father yelled.

"One dollar," the man called back.

"You're kidding me," Father replied. "Too damn expensive!"

The canoe touched shore, but the family stayed in their canoe, waiting.

"We could use a few gallons," Mother whispered. "You know Agatha's blueberry pies are the best in the world, and her blueberry jam . . ."

Trinity added, "Blueberry pancakes and blueberry muffins." Her taste buds conjured up the flavors. She knew they would go blueberry picking on their own soon, but you could never have too many on hand.

"One dollar. Okay?" the man called.

But Father waved back. "No, not okay. That's way too much!" Then he turned his back to the shoreline, trying to contain his grin, and whispered. "I'll give him to the count of three. Watch. One. Two. Three."

"Seventy-five cents!" the man in the canoe countered.

"Way too much!" Father flung up his arms in mock frustration, then turned his back again to the man. His grin grew. "Watch and learn, girls." Then he held his hand close to his chest, three fingers extended, and this time counted silently.

One.

Two.

Three.

"Fifty cents!" called the man. "Good price."

"That's more like it," Father said under his breath, facing everyone, "but you can't act desperate." Then he stood up and, as if he were commanding a troop of soldiers, said loudly, "Let's pack up and head to Kettle Falls. I bet we can get a better price there for berries."

Trinity glanced across the beach at the Ojibwe man and his family. For thousands of years, their people had lived off this land and its seasons of blueberries, wild rice, sturgeon, and venison. It would take such an intimate knowledge of nature, a mastery of so many skills.

Lost in the woods, she'd be lucky to last a week on her own.

She imagined it had taken this family many, many hours to gather several gallons of berries. Now Father was turning their livelihood into another one of his games. A game he always won. Somebody had to stop him.

She hopped up, tucked herself under Father's shoulder, and pleaded quietly, "Father, just pay what he was originally asking. Please."

But he only chuckled. "Business is business," he said quietly, ruffling the top of her head as if she were a toddler. "Let's head back!"

Soon everyone was climbing into the rowboat and squeezing onto its wooden seats. As George rowed to the anchored yacht, a quiet conversation in Ojibwe floated back and forth between the man and woman in the canoe. Though Trinity couldn't understand what they were saying, their melodic voices carried across the water.

Mother's eyes were half-closed and she trailed her fingers in the water, as if she were floating in another world. And perhaps, Trinity thought, she was.

Across from Trinity, Mrs. Worthington leaned into her husband. "Dear," she began, "I have no problem paying full price." But her husband shook his head. "This is the Major's negotiation," he said. "Not ours."

Once everyone was back onboard the yacht, George raised the dinghy and swung it back into position. With Lou on her lap, Trinity settled on the bench seat beside Sadie.

With a turn of the key, George started the Elco's engine and it rumbled to life. At the push of a button, he began pulling up anchor, bow and stern. The yacht was state-of-the-art;

there was no other vessel quite like it on the whole lake. "Next stop, Kettle Falls," he announced.

But before George shifted gears, Father bellowed from the stern. "Hold up, George!" And under his breath he added, "Here they come! I knew I could jew him down."

Trinity glared at Father. *What a terrible, prejudiced thing to say!* But he was oblivious to her repulsion, his attention instead fixed on the Ojibwe family paddling closer and closer, until they pulled up alongside the yacht and its rumbling engine.

From the canoe, the man cupped his hands around his mouth: "Twenty-five cents."

Father stepped closer to the railing, smiling ear to ear. "Twenty-five cents, not a penny more!" Soon he was exchanging money and receiving basket after basket. He handed them to Trinity and Sadie, who stowed them at their feet.

As the family set off, paddling in unison, Father called, "Handsome blueberries! We thank you!"

Trinity studied the abundance at her feet. Four baskets, she calculated, for half the price of one. *It was criminal.*

17

AS GEORGE PUSHED DOWN the throttle beside the wheel, and they set off toward Kempton Channel, Trinity felt a heaviness set in. The weight of being the Major's daughter. A Baird. On both sides, she was born into massive wealth. A truth she couldn't avoid. But that didn't mean she agreed with treating others—no matter their social status—as anything less than human and deserving of respect. Of basic fairness. But what was fair?

For the first time, she felt the burden of her name scrolled letter by letter across the boat's stern. It was always there, christening her father's pride and glory, his fifty-foot Elco yacht. Her name, synonymous with Major Baird and his ever-growing empire, with Mother's arrogance, and with Father's business strengths, flaws, and faults.

She bent her head into Lou's and inhaled the earthy scent of dog fur, uneasily aware of her lofty place in the world. The burden of responsibility that came with it. She was a product of bloodlines and generations of ambition, but she didn't have to perpetuate her parents' shortcomings—the kind she'd just witnessed by Father. She was better than that.

How had she escaped inheriting their prejudices? she sometimes wondered. The answer was always there, waiting for her to discover it.

From her first trip north, it was Victor who had shown her another way. He had spoken only with respect about the Ojibwe peoples he had met on his expeditions; he spoke only with gratitude for the skills, knowledge, and companionship of his Ojibwe guide. Indeed, he was always quick to admit that he wouldn't have made it to Hudson Bay on his own and he wouldn't have survived the near-winter return either. Though he'd been Harvard educated, same as Father, he'd helped her see the world from another perspective. Not from an elevated position of social class, but from being part of the natural world.

Wilderness was its own university.

Nature, its teacher.

THE LAST FEW MILES to the Kettle Falls hotel, winding through a narrowing waterway, the sky turned from dove gray to ash and thickened to a dark mud. By the time they arrived at the bay below the roaring dam, the wind had picked up in gusts and rain hammered down in blinding sheets along the docks and boardwalk leading to the white-washed two-story hotel.

"We can wait it out here," Father said to Mr. Worthington, as everyone clustered under the roof in the wheelhouse.

But when a horse and carriage appeared at the end of the dock, its horse prancing in place, the driver waved them over with urgency. Father declared it held precisely four passengers. "We'll send him back for you girls!" he said.

"Don't bother," Trinity said. "We want to stay here. We might join you later if the rain lets up."

She watched from the wheelhouse as the parents hurried into the carriage. Once inside, the driver flicked the horse's reins and it bolted forward.

George was suited up in rain wear.

"You don't mind the rain," Trinity said.

He laughed. "I'm told there's a bed for me in the workers' cabins."

"Because we're sleeping onboard?" Trinity knew his narrow bunk was in the belly of the boat, wedged near the engine and bilge pump.

"You girls have fun," he said, and headed off into the storm.

When he was out of hearing, Trinity said, "Whoop-dee-doo! Time to ourselves! Let's go below."

She and Sadie headed backwards down the steep ladder. In the *V* of the bow, the small galley held a tiny cookstove, tiny sink, and shelves with dishes—every amenity you would need to live aboard. A dining table was secured between two berths, which served as narrow sofas. Above one end sat a shelf, secured by an extra strip of wood trim, which displayed an array of glass decanters.

Trinity pulled down the bottle with a square silver top. "This is one of Father's favorites."

"Whiskey?" Sadie asked, who wasn't one who often drank.

"From Canada," Trinity replied, removing the bottle and setting it on the galley table. Something about the rain and the coziness of being tucked away in the boat . . . the vanishing parents . . . made the forbidden all the more enticing.

She found two small crystal goblets, poured one finger of whiskey each, and handed a glass to Sadie. "Join me?"

As the rain pounded on deck, Sadie grinned. "After this past week, what with tutoring and giving piano lessons, why not?" She talked about working with students from different economic backgrounds and a variety of ages. "It's challenging, but I can always find something good in every kiddo."

They each stretched on a berth among velvet pillows as the rain turned to a deafening assault.

"I still can't believe it. Twenty-five cents per basket," Trinity said, her father's actions still grating against her skin. "What would it have hurt him to simply pay their asking price? He has enough money, and yet every chance that comes along he bargains for the lowest price possible. You know, I don't even like to go for groceries in Ranier. It's embarrassing. He haggles with the butcher over every single piece of meat. He makes Henry cut off all the fat before he weighs the meat. And did you know, he used to steal peanuts out of the barrels?"

Sadie looked surprised. "You're kidding! Is that why they bag them now?"

Trinity gave a nod. "It's a game to him. Some say that's how you get wealthy, but I don't like it."

Sadie cupped her chin in her hand. "Mrs. Worthington, I mean my mother, comes from money, too. But she is always donating to good causes and being generous at every turn with anyone in need."

"Yeah, the Major is a world unto himself," Trinity said. "He's one of the wealthiest and gets away with being the cheapest. It's all about winning, no matter how it affects others."

"Through my father's work in the legislature," Sadie said, "I'm starting to believe that things only work when everyone wins. It's all about negotiation and compromise. They keep at it until everyone gets something they want. One side can't have it all their way—at least not forever—before things topple."

"Exactly. Like France, Russia," Trinity said, thinking of her family as she pulled a pack of cigarettes off the top shelf. *Sometimes a revolution is in order.*

When Sadie formed a *V* with two fingers, Trinity gave her a cigarette, then lit one for herself. Before she was sent away, she liked to smoke on occasion. This seemed like a perfect moment.

Sadie drew her first puff and started violently hacking and coughing. "Oh, I'm not good at this." She made a face and then put out her cigarette in an ashtray of green glass.

Smoking was fashionable these days, but Trinity had to admit it had been a long time since she'd tried it. Now her mouth tasted like campfire ashes. She snubbed out her cigarette, too. "Thought it was a good idea."

Sadie asked, "Have you seen Victor since you've been home?"

"A few times," Trinity said, "but I've been waiting to tell you about someone else." She described every detail, including the one of Max carrying Lou under his arm on his arrival. "I feel so at ease with him. I think he'd like things to move ahead between us, but I'm just not ready for anyone else in my life right now. Not in that kind of serious, all-consuming way." She gave Lou a smooch on the top of her head, curled up beside her. "Except for this little girl." And then she remembered. "Oh, but I almost forgot. Victor has some news," she said.

Sadie's eyebrows lifted.

"England in the fall. Some kind of speaking tour about his expedition. He seems quite excited about it."

But Sadie was staring at the galley ceiling, as if she had stopped listening a few sentences earlier. "Sadie. Something's bothering you."

Sadie shrugged, her lips sealed.

When Owen hadn't bothered to greet Sadie on their arrival at the Ranier depot, Trinity knew something was off-kilter between them. "It's Owen, isn't it? Have you seen him?"

"That's just it," Sadie said, her chin trembling. "It's like he's disappeared. I've seen him, spoken a word or two at the creamery, but honestly, Trinity, he seems like a different person. I'm not sure what happened since I left here after last Christmas. I think he's lost interest in me." And then tears budded in Sadie's eyes until she blinked them away. In one big gulp, she tipped back the whiskey and swallowed. She sputtered and managed, "I'm not going to cry," but her shoulders heaved up and down, and soon she was weeping.

Trinity found a dishtowel in the galley. She sat beside her, shoulder to shoulder, and handed her the towel, its edge monogrammed—like everything else onboard from napkins to silverware, whether stitched or engraved—with the letter *T*.

"Let's have another," Sadie said at last, her voice wavering as she sat up straight.

"If you insist. But I warn you, we're being decadent." Trinity filled their glasses again. "But we better have something to eat or it will go straight to our heads." She rummaged in the galley and found smoked trout, two kinds of cheese, crackers, pecans, and pickles. She set out a platter. "*Voilà, mademoiselle,*" she said. "*Bon appétit!*"

"*Merci!*" Sadie replied, lifting her glass.

BY THE TIME THEY SETTLED in the stateroom for the night, the rain had stopped. In the distance the sound of the nickelodeon, the coin-operated player piano in the hotel's adjoining tavern, drifted through the night air.

It was after midnight when footsteps sounded up the gangway. The boat swayed as someone stepped onboard. "Think they went to bed already?" Mr. Worthington asked.

"Girls?" Father called near the stateroom's hatchway, now firmly closed and locked. "Are you okay down there?"

Trinity tried as clearly as she could to form the words "We're fine."

Across from her in the other berth, Sadie clamped her hand over her mouth but began to giggle. Rising to her elbow, Trinity put her forefinger to her lips. "Shhhh."

Once they both started laughing, they couldn't stop. They were tipsy, and if Mother had come to check on them, she would have given them a stern lecture. But Trinity was pretty sure Mother had retired at the hotel for the evening. No doubt, Father and Mr. Worthington would soon trek back to close down the Kettle Falls blind pig.

She had visited a few of the speakeasies in Ranier, which

locals called "blind pigs." They were small operations tucked behind the legal facade of a shop selling sodas. Father had hinted more than once that with bootlegging booming on the border, right under the noses of the federal agents, it was a tempting business opportunity—if he didn't have his hands full with B&B, and if he were a less honest man.

"We'll see you two in the morning," Father said.

"Goodnight, girls," Mr. Worthington said. "Ladies," he said with extra emphasis, as if to remind them that they should act like nothing less.

As their footsteps retreated, Trinity cracked up. It felt wonderful to be with Sadie again, to be able to laugh for no good reason at all, swayed by the boat's gentle motion on water and perhaps by a little whiskey.

18

IN THE WEEK leading up to their gala lake party, Mother had marched around frantically, trying to make sure everything was perfect, setting everyone, including Trinity, on edge. *Finally, the day had come,* Trinity thought, as she set a small vase of freshly picked bluebells on her studio's fireplace mantel.

She could count on Father to give tours, something he did whenever guests showed up, and she gave the maple floors one more sweep with the dust broom. Then she stepped outside. Sunshine kissed her face, arms, and calves. She enjoyed the swish of her silk sleeveless dress and hated to admit it, but Mother had been right: she had needed a dress for such an occasion. "C'mon, Lou. Let's try to have some fun."

By late afternoon, the sun loomed high in the sky, and Prohibition didn't keep booze from flowing on Baird Island. Extra staff had been hired from the mainland to serve drinks and hors d'oeuvres, while those with islands and money—or with an island and a Harvard education in lieu of money, as was Victor's case—milled about, creating a buzz of conversation on the veranda of granite slabs joining the docks and boathouse with the shore.

Trinity glanced around for Max.

A few children of guests carried buckets of water to the sand beach, filling the moat around their multitowered sandcastle. A teenage boy did a backflip from the end of the dock, followed by cheering from a cluster of adults, who lifted their drinks in salute.

Max was nowhere to be seen.

Halfway between the boathouse and the lodge, she spotted Victor on the path, deep in conversation with E. W. Ennis. Victor was her height, five and a half feet, and in khaki pants and his usual rumpled white shirt and moccasins, he was forced to look up when speaking to Mr. Ennis, who, broad-shouldered as an ox, towered well over six feet. Despite temperatures in the eighties, the lumber tycoon wore a pinstriped suit, tie, and fedora. Trinity had never seen him otherwise. He flicked his cigar, and as she stepped closer, his ashes nearly fell on top of the tip of her shoe.

"Hello, Victor. Hello, Mr. Ennis," she called.

"Trinity," Victor said, leaning closer and giving her a light kiss on the cheek. "So good to see you!"

Lou immediately jumped up and put her paws on the knees of Victor's trousers.

"I'm sorry," Trinity said. "Down, Lou. Good girl."

"Miss Baird," Mr. Ennis said, lifting his ice-filled glass toward her. At the asylum, when she'd asked for ice, she'd been ridiculed. She had learned to get along fine without it, but some things she'd once given little thought to she now saw with new eyes.

"Young lady," he continued, "we were just discussing for the umpteenth time who determines the future of this vast and untamed watershed. Should it be harnessed for more dams and hydropower to help put International Falls and this whole region on the map—or be protected for the few individuals who consider it their backyard? Should not these resources be shared with everyone?"

She knew he didn't give a damn about her opinion. She wasn't going to waste her words on him.

"Edward," Victor said. "You know my plan is to share it by keeping it wild for everyone, for future generations to enjoy. If you turn it all into a giant reservoir, you'll destroy natural habitat."

A loon called from somewhere on the water.

Ennis laughed. "Loons! Hear that?" He shot a glance at Trinity. "Now in the big picture of this advancing country, I'd call that loony thinking. Wouldn't you agree, Miss Baird?"

She looked to Victor, who had crossed his arms across his chest, a sign he was formulating his next point. She would wait for a better time to visit with him.

"Excuse me," she said. "I'll let you two debate."

Victor grabbed her hand lightly as she turned to go. "A bonfire here this evening?"

"Of course," she said, then left, feeling the warmth of his skin lingering on her hand. Stop, she told herself. Her feelings ran crosscurrent with logic.

AN HOUR OR TWO INTO THE PARTY, nearly every guest had met Lou, who was quickly learning to move from cluster to cluster to see what tidbits might fall from the table. A bit of deviled egg, a slice of cheese or ham, a baked bean, or perhaps a stray bread crumb.

"Brought the dog back as a gift for Trinity," she overheard Father say to Bruno Larsson, the middle-aged man who had recently built a towering home directly across from the island owned by Mr. Ennis.

"Gustavus Adolphus College," Bruno said, nodding his head in approval. "So she's been attending there with the Worthingtons' girl . . . or, rather, adopted daughter."

Father didn't steer Bruno toward the truth. "Indeed! So good to have them back north for the summer." He had a knack for redirecting any conversation.

So this would be the rumor, Trinity thought. She'd been away to college.

Bruno's new wife, Gizelle, his second, was only ten years

older than Trinity. Her platinum hair fell fashionably over her left eye, her lips were attention-demanding red, and her lithe body swayed beneath her thin-strapped dress as she talked. The sheer silk layers shimmered in the sun. Spotting Trinity she called out, "Kiddo, darling! It's been a woefully long time since I've seen you!"

"Trinity dear, I hear you've been away making something of yourself," said Bruno.

Or *unmaking,* Trinity wanted to joke. "Good to see you again, Gizelle!" They weren't friends exactly, but Trinity had enjoyed a frank conversation with her in the past about the difference between boys and men.

When Gizelle clenched Trinity's wrist, it was clear she was wallpapered, needing support to keep from tipping over. "Here, sweetie, hold this." She handed Trinity her gimlet.

Gizelle was a Hollywood actress, but her best role seemed playing *herself* all summer long on the lake. It was rumored that she said she couldn't stay on an island unless she had a butler; now she kept their poor butler running like a dog after a jackrabbit. She dug in her handbag and produced a cigarette and stiletto holder, lit it, and after one deep draw exhaled.

"Any new Hollywood roles?" Trinity asked.

"Oh, I'm waiting to hear back from Paramount Pictures. They have a part that's perfectly made for me! Oh, and kiddo, have you heard? I think our island is about to become the hub of all things artsy and literary! Sinclair Lewis took us up on our offer to host him while he writes."

"You're kidding! I just finished *Main Street.*" A thrill of excitement shot through her. "It was fabulous."

Gizelle beamed. "Yes, but writers are always working on something new. He has a dazzling novel that he told me all about, something with a corrupt preacher, but he needed time to work on it. And I told him we have the perfect haven for him and he's welcome to stay here a week, a month, all summer if he cares!"

Trinity felt Mother's sturdy hand cupping her elbow. "Gizelle, you won't mind if I borrow my daughter for a moment?"

Gizelle puffed on her cigarette. "Not at all. As long as Trinity returns my gimlet. Besides, I was just looking to freshen it." The moment Trinity handed her the cocktail, Gizelle raised her hand. "Over here, young man!"

Mother steered Trinity toward the dock where George was catching the bowline of an incoming Chris-Craft. Both long docks on either side of the boathouse were lined with boats small and large. But George found a spot for the speedboat.

"Trinity," Mother said, "I want you to meet Henry's parents."

Henry steered toward the space, looking more suited to his soft gray fedora and matching suit than his purple cape. He turned off the motor and jumped up from the wheel and to the dock. "Trinity," he said, sweeping closer and grasping her hands. "I was hoping you'd be here!"

"Hello, Henry," she replied.

Mother brought her hands together, almost in prayer. "Wonderful! You already know each other!" It was an odd statement, because they'd all recently been on Falcon Island the night RuthAnne fell off the boat.

"We do," Trinity said, trying to read what might be going on behind Mother's eyes. She added, just to see if it triggered Mother's memory, "And last year, remember, when we took that day cruise to Kettle Falls? Henry came along."

Henry's tailored suit made his shoulders appear broader than they were. She remembered feeling almost sorry for him last summer when they had all gone swimming. Next to Victor, Henry was scrawny, his skin pale as the belly of a fish.

Mother motioned to the couple stepping onto the dock. "And surely you know Henry's parents, Mr. and Mrs. Densch from Davenport?"

Trinity nodded at them politely. "Welcome. I'm sure we

met somewhere along the way in Davenport, though it must have been when I was much younger."

Everyone exchanged pleasantries, and then Mother added, "I hear that you all just bought an island!"

Mr. Densch laughed. "Not quite sure how it happened," he said with a chuckle. "But Henry was keen on the idea, and what Henry wants, Henry usually gets."

"Now, that's not entirely true," Henry said, looking from Trinity toward the gathering. She guessed he was hoping for a drink.

As Mother steered the Densch family toward the veranda, a boat motor buzzed to life inside the boathouse.

Curious, Trinity stepped through the doorway and under the building's open beams, letting her eyes adjust to its shadows.

Hints of cedar, lake water, oil, and fish filled the air. Water danced with golden light between the two boats— the Garwood speedboat and the eighteen-foot fishing boat where Max sat as a passenger, his suitcase at his feet. George sat in the stern, his hand on the motor's tiller. What? Where were they going in the middle of the party?

"Max?" Trinity called, but he faced the stern, his back to her. She called again, but her words were lost to the motor's rumble as George backed up and turned the bow away. Picking up speed and leaving a frothy wake behind, the boat disappeared around the peninsula.

Without saying a word to her as to why, just like that, Max was gone?

She felt the wind knocked out of her, much the way she felt as a child when she fell off a swing at St. Katharine's Episcopal School. She willed her chest to rise and fall.

Sketching together . . .

Exploring the island together . . .

Talking under the stars . . .

Dancing . . .

It was all still new.

Filled with possibility.

These past nights, she'd fallen asleep with him on her mind.

Though her feet were planted firmly on wooden planks, she had the overwhelming sense that the boathouse roof was falling down around her.

19

HURRYING PAST a couple playing backgammon, past guests toasting with a clink of glasses, Trinity swept inside the lodge kitchen.

Agatha and a few helpers were busy at the long marble counter and large cookstove beneath its massive copper hood.

"I'm looking for my parents," Trinity said in a rush of words.

Eyes downcast, Agatha pointed toward the adjoining dining room.

"Agatha," Trinity said, pleading. "You know, tell me."

But Agatha wagged her head. "Not my place."

Candlesticks, silver, pewter, and crystal—the dining room table glowed.

"Mother? Father?" she called, storming into the living room. She looked beyond the towering stone fireplace, mounted moose head, couches, overstuffed chairs, and coffee tables. The doors to the adjoining bedroom were open, bed made, no one visible.

Trinity turned and crossed the room through French doors onto the long screen porch to the north, also called the Green Porch. At its far end, seated in four wicker chairs, her parents and Mr. and Mrs. Worthington chatted, drinks in hand.

"Hello, Trinity," Mrs. Worthington called, waving her petite hand. Compared to her tall husband, the senator, Mrs. Worthington seemed as if she might fit in a thimble. "You're probably looking for Sadie Rose, but as you might know, she's taken on several tutoring jobs this summer and wasn't able to join us on the lake today. She said to tell you hello."

"Thanks, Mrs. Worthington," she said. "Please tell her hello. I would love to see her soon." Then she cleared her throat, trying to hold back her growing suspicion and anger. "Mother, Father. What happened to Max? He just left the island with George without a word."

Pushing himself forward and off the chair, Mr. Worthington stood up, his head nearly grazing the low ceiling. "Darling," he said, helping his wife up. "Let's go see what is happening out there."

"Something must be terribly wrong, because I thought he was staying a few more weeks," Trinity said. "Do you have any idea?"

Mother fingered the white piping of her gray dress.

Father finally said, "I sent him away."

Trinity felt nauseous. "You what? Why?"

"Because he lied," Father replied, standing up. "We really should get back to our guests."

"No, Father," Trinity said, hooking her hand in the crook of his elbow. "Please, I need to know. Were you worried we were getting too close? Is that it? Because nothing happened between us, if that's your concern. But do we like each other? Yes, that seemed pretty evident, no doubt. If that was your concern, please bring him back. It's only a few more weeks."

"He lied to us," Father repeated. "I learned when I hired him that he came from a wealthy family, but he didn't disclose everything."

Incredulous, Trinity demanded, "Like what? He's a felon, a murderer? What? Tell me."

Mother stood and ironed the front of her dress with her

hands. "Worthingtons, forgive us. Trinity, we should wait and have this conversation at another time."

"Now is perfectly fine," Trinity said, not to be put off.

Head high, shoulders back, Mother said, "If you insist. I asked him about his family, and he told us that his family comes from Germany."

"Yes," Trinity said, "so he told me."

Mother's brows scrunched together with concern. "And then I learned . . ."

"He's Jewish," Father stated, as if it was a bold, hard, damning fact.

"You sent Max away because he's *Jewish*?" Trinity was unable to keep the anger out of her voice.

"It's for the best," Father said, glancing at Mother, who nodded in return, her lips tight. Then he continued. "Trinity just doesn't understand how the world works, and, anyway, it's not acceptable to intermarry, especially in our circles. This has nothing to do with his bloodlines and everything to do with his not telling us before bringing him out here. Mother asked about his family, and he told her. But he should have told me the moment I hired him. You know we could never let you get serious with someone of his background. We should never have brought him here."

Fists clenched at her sides, Trinity didn't move. "Be honest. Listen to yourselves! You sent him away because he's Jewish. And not only that, but you sent him away without talking to me."

"Business is business," Father said.

"How is a person's race or ethnicity *business*?"

"Don't get uppity with us," Mother said. Her eyes flashed and she lifted her arm. For a second, Trinity wondered if she was about to be slapped. "You're out of line, young lady. *Everything* is our business."

"We might be a little old-fashioned," Father began with a good-natured tone as he guided Trinity by the elbow from the porch to the living room.

But she couldn't bear to hear another word and broke free, fleeing ahead of him.

She bolted from the lodge, and though she wanted to run, she willed herself to take one ladylike step, then another, as if she felt no rush at all.

She swept past Victor and Henry, gleaning bits of Harvard this-and-that, and headed straight for the sandy beach beyond, intending to hole up in her studio for the rest of the party.

BUT AS SHE NEARED THE BOATHOUSE, she had another idea. She didn't want anyone tracking her down, convincing her to join the party. Rattled by the conversation, she needed some time alone to gather her thoughts. She headed inside.

The speedboat Father had purchased last summer awaited her, its key still in the dash. The boat smelled of new leather and polished mahogany. With its sleek shape and lightning speed, it was a thing of beauty.

As she untied the front line from its cleat, a voice startled her.

"Let me help."

She looked up. It was Henry Densch.

"All right," she said, seeing no reason to protest. She climbed into the boat's wide front seat as Henry untied the boat's stern.

But before he tossed the stern line into the boat, he coiled the line in a large loop and held it as an offering. "Actually, I'm dying to escape. Would you mind too terribly if I jumped in with you?"

Trinity appreciated his directness. She had come to have little patience with people who didn't say plainly what they meant. Like her parents, who were always scrambling as far as possible from the truth.

"I need time alone," she said. "One rule: No talking." Too upset to argue, she motioned him to jump in.

Henry, whose sandy hair was trimmed tight on the sides and long on top, settled himself on the seat beside her, almost touching her shoulder. "Thanks."

Without a reply, Trinity turned the key, and the motor roared to life before she throttled it back to a rumbling hum. Shifting into reverse, she looked over her shoulder and carefully backed out between the two long docks and numerous guest boats.

Once into the bay, she turned the boat until it faced forward, pushed the throttle down, and sped around the peninsula in a wide arc, heading west through the channel into the expansive waters of Sand Bay. She aimed for Ranier at the source of Rainy River, zipping along a few quick miles until they reached the lift bridge.

She slowed the boat.

Above and beyond them, a passenger train clattered across the bridge from Canada into the United States. The train that would take Max away—without a chance to say goodbye.

It galled her. It wasn't that she was in love with him. She'd barely had time to get to know him. But he didn't deserve to be fired and sent away early. Her parents liked to think of themselves as so broad-minded, worldly, and cultivated. But this was unthinkable.

She turned the boat around and headed to the village pier, hoping she might still get a chance. Was there time? Could she catch Max before he boarded the train?

As they drew closer, she spotted George in his fishing boat, pulling away from the dock. He was the only passenger and he pointed the bow toward home.

For a brief second, gazing between Erickson's Fine Grocery and the trading post, she glimpsed the train. From a stop, it started up again and rolled forward along the rails. She had missed her chance. She cut the motor and they drifted. Seagulls lifted from the docks and flew toward them.

When she found herself clenching the polished wheel, white-knuckled, she drew her hands back. She interlaced her fingers and stretched her palms over her head, then brought her arms to her sides. "I will never become my parents. They're so arrogant. They think they always know what's best for everyone else." She was so lost in her thoughts that she wasn't sure she'd spoken aloud until Henry answered.

"If I may . . . you're not like them," he said, "or anyone else I've ever met." He swept his arm toward the water. "For instance, I like this about you."

"What?" She didn't understand. "'No talking?'"

"This. You want to do something—you just do it."

She glanced at him. Maybe at some other time she would appreciate his words. But she felt too sore, too emotionally bruised. She didn't need flattery or his opinion about her, nor did she wish for conversation. She'd needed time alone and should have demanded it.

Henry continued, irritating her.

"You seem so brave. A truly modern woman. I feel as if I'm really lucky getting to know you—or the *real* you. Not just the pretty gal I met last summer with a yacht named after her."

"Your father said you get whatever you want."

Henry shrugged.

She'd figured last summer that Henry Densch was nothing more than an overgrown spoiled child who thought that whatever he wanted his wealth could buy.

He grinned. "I do love it here. That trip to Kettle Falls and back, the five of us. You, Victor, me, Owen, and—what was her name again?"

"Sadie," she replied. "The Worthingtons are at the party, but she couldn't make it."

"Who could be too busy for a party on Baird Island?"

"She's giving music lessons and tutoring this summer." For a moment, Trinity envied her friend and her work toward becoming a music teacher. "She's actually doing something *useful* with her life. And what am I doing?" she said aloud. "Out here floating, escaping."

"Ah, the life of the bourgeoisie," Henry teased, then turned more serious. "Unless you're in Russia these days."

She bristled at his light-hearted scolding but knew he was right. Only a few years earlier, the czar and his family had been murdered at the start of the Marxist revolution. "True," she said.

"Think about it, Trinity. People like us make contributions that are different from working, say, at a creamery day in and day out."

Trinity knew he was referring to Owen Jensen, who was indeed working at a creamery, but Owen was one of the smartest people she'd ever met. He was always reading something and stretching himself beyond his humble beginnings. She had come to appreciate authenticity in people, no matter their social status. She'd seen it in Owen as well as Sadie. Rather than present themselves with pretense, trying to act or dress or speak in a way to gain status, authentic people meet your eyes and say, without a word, *Here I am. And there you are.* Seeing themselves as worthy. Seeing others as equally worthy, just for being.

Henry talked on. "Not that I need to toot my own horn, but I'm glad to give sizable donations to institutions that are trying to help those in need. Orphanages, children's homes, hospitals back home in Iowa."

She closed her eyes, wanting nothing more than to be alone and away from Henry Densch. "Maybe at heart I am a commoner," she said.

At that, Henry laughed out loud.

She challenged him by not joining in.

He went on. "You think Andrew Carnegie isn't doing something with his life—with his money? I mean—he's only single-handedly building a brick-and-mortar public library system across this country, town by town, dollar by dollar."

He'd made a good point, but she didn't want to debate.

Max had been banished. The last thing she needed was to talk.

She started up the speedboat and cruised back into the bay's open waters.

She tasted the bitterness of loss. She hated the way her parents had treated him, the way they wielded power over the lives of others, yanking strings as if they were puppeteers. Max may be banished, but she was determined to write to him at her first opportunity. They'd connected at a meaningful level, and that wasn't something to throw away without care.

She throttled forward and steered the bow into wide, arcing circles. She formed figure eights, back and forth, cutting over the boat's own choppy wake.

Henry laughed. "This is nuts!"

"Hang on!" she called, feeling a devil-may-care attitude.

After several minutes of churning up the water and feeling the wind on her skin, the power of the motor running the length of the Garwood, Trinity straightened out the wheel and eased down to a comfortable speed.

"You're a wild cat," Henry said with a laugh, as he unclenched his hand from the boat's gunwale.

She didn't answer. When he'd asked to come along, she should have refused.

They traveled east and reached the channel marker on their right, and her red-trimmed cabin on the left, perched at the edge of the water. The boat buzzed around the southern peninsula of the island, and then Trinity steered for the docks. She throttled back and the boat slowed, matching her own reluctance to return.

As they drifted from the bright sunshine into the shade of the boathouse, Trinity made out the unmistakable silhouette of her mother.

Straight and stiff.

A little black terrier strained and yipped at the end of the leash.

20

TRINITY SHUT OFF THE MOTOR. "Is Lou all right? Did something happen?"

"Did something happen?!" Mother's voice bounced off the boathouse walls with accusation. "Well, if you count Gizelle's dress getting ripped, another guest tipping a glass of red wine down his wife's back after tripping over this dog, and causing one of our servers to trip, sending a platter of drinks and crystal goblets flying and breaking across the veranda—I suppose you might say something happened. All the work that has gone into this party, and you allow this dog to ruin it all."

As Henry secured the lines, Trinity climbed out of the boat and squatted beside Lou, whose tail was tucked under her bum. "I'm sorry," she said, scooping the little dog into her arms. "I should have taken you along," and added silently, *but my mind was distracted.*

"Mrs. Baird, hello," Henry said, joining them.

"Do you two know how brazen this looks?" Mother exclaimed. "You leave the party without any explanation. Henry, your parents asked me where you were. How was I to know? And when others asked about Trinity, what was I to say?"

"I took the Garwood for a spin," Trinity said, then kissed the top of Lou's head, who in turn licked her chin.

"You could have at least taken your dog with you," Mother said. "Or locked her in your studio."

"I didn't think—"

"Of course you didn't think," Mother interrupted. "You *never* think." Then spinning on the toes of her sensible shoes, Mother walked away, but stopped at the open boathouse door. With a glance back, she added, "There's nothing that says we can't find that dog another home."

A searing threat.

Trinity wouldn't put it past Mother to carry it out.

"I thought the dog was a gift," Trinity replied, keeping her voice calm. "I thought she was *my* dog."

With a humph, Mother turned and strode away into the glaring light.

"Ouch," Henry said. "That whole encounter was . . ."

"Horrific," Trinity said.

"I'm sorry for you."

Her eyes burned. "It's the way she is. And she's getting worse."

"What are you going to do?"

Trinity held Lou fast, determined not to lose her. She'd be more watchful, keep an eye on her at all times. And she'd make things right.

"I'm going to apologize to each and every guest," she said, heading out.

"I'll go with you," Henry said. "Time for a drink."

* * *

A SERVER OFFERED TRINITY a glass of punch and she drank it down, feeling the warmth of whatever had been added. Rum, she guessed. In the past she would have gone on to the second glass, and over the hours and into the evening perhaps the third and even a fourth. But now she would stop at one. She needed her wits about her more than ever. She'd be sincere, charming, witty, and utterly convincing that she was the same young woman everyone expected and knew—but she'd do it without extra booze. Mother was at the helm and summer was far from over.

A screech, high-pitched and sharp, sounded overhead. Trinity followed the sound with her eyes as an eagle lifted from a tall and slanted pine. She gripped Lou a little tighter, wishing they could leave that very moment together on a steamship from New York across the Atlantic.

In Paris, little dogs were as ubiquitous as baguettes. Lou would fit right in.

AFTER THE LAST BOAT LEFT, and the staff was busy cleaning up, Trinity slipped away with Lou to her studio. At her writing table, she pulled out a fresh piece of stationery and addressed it to Max. She didn't know his home address, but she knew the address of B&B back in Davenport and would send it there. She began:

Dear Max,

By the time you receive this letter you will be, I hope, back at work at B&B. If not, I will have lost touch with you completely, and that thought makes me quite sad.

I cannot explain how stunned and angry I am that my parents sent you away! I cannot excuse their narrow thinking. They say it has nothing to do with your being Jewish, but there's only one word for their ill behavior toward you. Prejudiced. And I am ashamed of how they have treated you.

I am extra despairing, because I had the most wonderful times with you here on the island.

She went on to enumerate the many things they seemed to share in common, and how she admired his determination to become a better swimmer, which he indeed had accomplished. And then she paused, holding the pen in mid-air, because what she wanted to say was almost impossible to put into words. She'd thought she would have more time on the island with Max. She'd been cautious, not risking going beyond the threshold of their kiss. And why? Because after being locked away, she knew how desperate she was for touch and affection. She was like someone found starving who couldn't eat a big meal but, rather, had to regain the capacity for food bit by bit. So, too, she had enjoyed Max's voice, the brush of his hand across hers, his sense of humor.

But instead of expressing this, she kept the letter short.

Please write back. I already miss your company.
Yours truly,
Trinity

P.S. Other than RuthAnne's, always site cabins close
to the water.

P.P.S. I do hope someday you might return to
Rainy Lake and fall asleep to the sound of water
on these shores.

She tucked the letter in an envelope.

The next day, she insisted on joining George on his errand run to Ranier. While he picked up fresh cuts of meat from the grocer's, she walked with Lou to the post office. From her leather satchel, she pulled out the letter and set it on the counter.

The postmaster scrunched up his wiry brows as he picked up the letter addressed to Max Bern. "B&B is the Major's company. Why not just send this with the package Mr. Baird sends out each week? Save yourself a stamp." Then he chuckled. "But who worries about a single stamp, eh, when you got a yacht named after you, eh?"

It felt like an accusation. Having a yacht wasn't good or bad or nice or terrible. It represented the life she was born into. His comment didn't deserve a response, but saying nothing would also make her seem more rude than she felt. "It's a work of art," she said with a faint smile. Then she plunked down her coins. "Please, I want it to go out separately."

He gathered her money and applied a stamp to her letter. Then she left to find Lou where she'd been leashed, her tail wagging—*thump, thump, thump*—against the flagpole.

21

THE SUN BURNED THROUGH the weave of Trinity's straw hat as she squatted next to foot-high, lacy green blueberry plants. This year's crop was especially good, and the picking season had lasted longer than usual. Deep blue berries needed only a little nudging from her fingers to be separated from their plants and drop—*plunk, plop*—into her metal bucket, which was already half-full. Though they could have purchased more blueberries from Ojibwe traders, there was something important about her family taking time each year to pick some of their own. A tradition. Since she could remember, she had enjoyed picking berries and later cleaning them by rolling them across towels to pick out twigs, bugs, and debris.

She glanced around. At the base of a rock ridge, Lou was busy snuffling around the ground. Patches of blueberry plants grew out of thin soil in sunlight between the undergrowth. Ahead, Trinity spotted George, standing and stretching.

Trinity smiled to herself, wondering what they thought about the earlier talk at breakfast about employment. Agatha had been coming and going from the kitchen, while George was outside on the porch, sweeping pine needles off the wooden steps and cobwebs from the eaves.

From the newspaper, Trinity had read aloud a posting of jobs available through the Northern Pacific Railway Company. It began "MEN WANTED" and listed machinists, blacksmiths, sheet metal workers, electricians, boilermakers, passenger car men, freight car men, helpers. Wages varied from seventy cents per hour down to forty-seven cents per hour.

And then, a column over, she read another notice. "Then there's this one. It says, 'Help Wanted: Ten Sales Ladies at Burton's Department Store at once for Midsummer Madness Sale.' Guess how much it pays?" she asked.

"Thirty-nine cents an hour," RuthAnne guessed.

"No, not that high," Millie said.

"A mere seven cents per hour," Trinity said. "It makes my blood rise. I mean, how can any young woman become independent with such pitiful wages?"

Father almost choked on his coffee. "You're not seriously thinking of applying, are you?"

Guarding herself from saying too much, Trinity simply said, "Perhaps." But what options did she have, short of marrying into another wealthy family, to ever fledge the ever-smaller nest of her family? Did they prefer she work as a prostitute at Kettle Falls? Become a housekeeper or a governess? Sooner or later she needed to find a way to live on her own rather than be controlled through their golden handcuffs.

"I dare hope," Mother said, leveling her gaze at Trinity, "that we did *not* pay for private schools for you to take some menial job. And what does that communicate to a man who wants to provide for you? That you don't need him? Do you want to become a spinster?"

RuthAnne chuckled. "What's worse? A spinster," she said, her voice tart, "or a divorcée, like me?"

"RuthAnne," Mother said. "This is serious. Our daughters will never take menial jobs and diminish their chances of being married off well, even if it is the second time, if they want to enjoy the benefits of the Baird name."

Trinity seethed and lifted the paper, but the print blurred before her eyes. Her parents were living in a bygone era! The passing of the Nineteenth Amendment was about more than women getting the right to vote: it was also about seeing women as equal not less than or inferior to men. If it carried any weight at all, it had to mean that she had the right to live as she chose, no matter the family she'd been born into. Perhaps the answer was to run away.

RuthAnne laughed. "Ha! Trinity, did you see the front page? Hold still so I can read it better."

Trinity held the paper still and gazed over its top at her sister, who was clearly amused.

"This year," RuthAnne said, "Governor Preus is giving prizes and a total of $90 at the State Fair for the cleanest, best teeth! There'll be demonstrations on proper care of teeth. Ah, but—too bad, Trinity." She tilted her head and made a pouty expression. "It says it's only for ages two to sixteen. You could have made some money with those perfect teeth of yours."

SHE HAD BEEN PICKING BERRIES for well over an hour, maybe two, when she gazed down the hill toward the yacht, tied up to tree trunks at the edge of the deep cove.

Overhead, the sky was sun-drenched, but since they'd started picking berries, the sky toward the west—and Baird Island—had formed a black, dense wall of ominous clouds. A jolt of alarm coursed through her and she shuddered. These were not ordinary clouds that come with a typical rainy day, when there's nothing more blissful than curling up under blankets and reading a good book while rain patters like music on the rooftop. No, this was the curtain rise of something far more threatening. And in the next moment, a cool wind struck, roaring across the lake and turning its surface into a rumpled bed sheet.

"A storm!" Trinity yelled. "We need to leave!"

She dashed to George, who glanced at the western sky.

It churned and billowed, changing with alarming swiftness.

George yelled, "C'mon! Everyone back to the boat! We don't have much time before it gets here!"

Carrying metal buckets, Father and Mother hurried down the slope. "We can't keep *Trinity* where she is!" Father shouted. "She'll get busted to pieces when that hits!"

George shouted back, "We'll head east and find a spot out of the wind!"

Soon Mother, Father, and George were scrambling with Trinity down the slope of the uninhabited island to board the boat. Trinity slipped, skinning her knee, but caught herself and saved her berries by grabbing stalks of ferns as she went down. She held up her bucket proudly. "Saved 'em!"

The waves climbed higher by the second, building into swells that rolled and crashed into the cove. As Trinity climbed aboard, the boat swayed back and forth. The lines threatened to break as the yacht rolled in the slosh of waves, inching closer and closer to the boulder-strewn cove. As waves hit the boat, giant sprays of water shot into the air, spewing across the boat.

"Life jackets on!" George ordered, wiping his face. Everyone scrambled along the gangway, grabbing life jackets from under the overturned dinghy before taking cover in the wheelhouse. Grabbing the wheel, George shouted, "Hang on! I'm gonna gun it!"

Trinity knew something was wrong, and not until she spun around did she figure out the problem. "Lou's still on the island! I have to find her!"

"There isn't time!" George barked, hand on the throttle. "She's a dog! She'll find shelter!"

Trinity had an idea. "Let's head to the other side of this island!"

With a shake of his head, George said, "Too shallow.

Can't get close enough. Now. You and Mr. Baird, stand ready to cast off when I say so, and not a moment before!"

"We'll come back for her when this is over!" Father called, heading to the stern.

Keeping her center of gravity low, her footing wide, Trinity raced to the bow. She didn't want to be blown into the water. But what would happen to Lou if they left her? Black clouds churned closer, driven by increasing wind. If she left Lou behind, she might be eaten by a bear or wolf or fox. An eagle might spot her. Or she might be swept off the island into the water and driven by the waves until she drowned.

Trinity did her best to keep from sliding under the railing and into the water as waves sprayed the bow.

"One, two, three—now!" George yelled, though his booming voice was nearly swallowed by the storm.

She couldn't leave Lou to fend for herself.

She wouldn't.

With a yank, she pulled the quick-release knot free and then leapt from the deck and onto the closest boulder. Her feet slipped and she fell to her life-jacketed belly as waves crashed behind her and sent a shower of water over her entire body.

"Trinity!"

She ignored the calls of concern and clawed at tree roots and pulled herself onto shore, jumping to her feet and glancing back. But the storm was pushing harder, pushing the boat closer to the rocks despite George's efforts at the throttle. Sheets of water began to fall, and she couldn't make out any faces in the wheelhouse as they moved away from the dangerous shoreline.

She waved them away and shouted, "Go! I'll be here when it's over!" hoping that would be true and knowing they couldn't hear a word she had said.

As the boat churned away from the island, lightning crackled. Clouds danced with ominous arcs of bright light. Seconds later, a deafening drumroll sounded, erupting into low rolls and booming claps of thunder.

Trinity dashed headlong through leafy ferns and under-brush. "Lou!" she shouted as the wind iced her drenched skin. "Lou! Come here, Lou!"

As she reached a midway point on the slope, she glanced back over her shoulder.

Riding the waves, the yacht looked like a bathtub toy, nearly swallowed by deep troughs. At last the boat turned eastward, wind at its stern, and to Trinity's relief it found purchase among the whitecaps.

Trinity called "Lou!" over and over as she headed to the island's leeward side. She picked her path between moss-covered boulders and slippery rocks.

And then she heard something faint.

So slight she thought she had imagined it.

There, it came again.

A whiff . . . no, an inkling . . . and then her ears caught it.

Somewhere off to the right, a faint whining.

22

WIND BENT TREETOPS as easily as paper straws. A crack of gunshot, then another. Not gunfire, but trees breaking. Trinity ducked as the forest seemed to crash down around her. She dropped to the ground in a ball, covering her head with her arms. Something hit her back, enough to hurt and burn, but she could still move. She wasn't dead. *This was nuts!*

When the wind paused for a moment, Trinity crawled out from the hovel of downed birch branches and looked around her. Lengths of thick pine trunks and heaps of broken branches covered the ground.

Unnervingly close.

She'd been lucky.

In a moment of quiet, she heard Lou's whining again, fainter now. She followed the sound toward shore, pushed through a thicket as thorns poked her skin, and stumbled on a small sandy inlet and gasped. "Lou!"

Lou's soaked black body was being tugged into the water.

It was as if something had caught her right paw, tugging her deeper, while with the other paw Lou was trying to twist her body and haunches under her, clawing at sand.

Something strong had her. The jaws of a large snapping turtle? What else could have enough strength?

Trinity grabbed a stick from shore and rushed in. "Lou!"

At that moment, the dog slid back into the water and her ears, then eyes, then nose went under.

Trinity screamed, "No! No! No!"

Lurching into the water up to her knees, she reached straight down, finding Lou's body in her hands. When she tried to lift, she felt the sleek edge of something at her wrist. Not a turtle but a fishing line!

Trinity pulled at the descending end of fishing line, trying to break it free. When that didn't work, she bit down hard on the line, chewing at the filament until it finally gave way. As the waves rolled in, she scrambled back to higher ground with Lou in her arms.

On shore, Lou wheezed and yelped.

A metal fishing lure was stuck in Lou's right paw.

"Poor girl!" Trinity gripped Lou tighter as she squirmed to get free.

"I'm not going to hurt you," she said. But she also didn't want to get ensnared by the treble hook lure.

She remembered something Sadie had once told her about a time she had cast a line with a lure right into Owen's arm. Because of the barbs, she couldn't pull it out. She had to push it through.

Trinity studied this lure. Its barb was sunk deep, and she would need the help of a pliers to push it through. There was nothing she could do now.

Lou looked up with round, pleading eyes.

"We have to wait to get help."

THE WIND HIT AGAIN and gathered in greater force, and Trinity wondered if a tornado was about to drop from the clouds. Frantic, with Lou in her arms, she looked for shelter. A towering white pine, at least a hundred or more years old—as she considered it, the tree bent and with a loud *snap* broke halfway up and dropped. The ground shook as it struck, leaving a sprawl of rock-bound roots exposed when it toppled.

"Oh my God! Oh my God!"

She had to find a safe place to sit out the storm, but where?

Scanning the island's mix of barren rock, underbrush, and steep rise, she headed toward the top of the granite ridge, then slipped on a smooth rock slab covered with slick, pale green lichen. She landed several yards down from the top, but she was out of the wind.

A few more steps and she found what she was looking for. The granite face jutted up and away from the earth, forming an overhang of protection from the rain, with a three-foot-wide indentation at its base. As another shaft of lightning lit up the sky, she dove for it.

It was perfect.

It offered them protection until the storm passed—which it seemed to have no intention of doing anytime soon. She set Lou down and used her hands to rake dry leaves into a small bed. She checked herself for injuries, and other than a few scrapes and some soreness, she was in one piece.

"But you," she said, sitting cross-legged and lifting Lou into her lap, the injured paw outstretched.

Another tree broke with a loud crack, then another, and the wind refused to let up.

Trinity buried her nose in the wet fur of Lou's neck. They had to wait it out.

"If I'd left you—" she began, but the pain of nearly losing Lou lodged in her throat.

A wave of relief and emotion filled her. She wanted to let loose and cry, but she held back. And then it dawned on her: there was no one to hear her, no one to accuse her of hysteria.

She almost laughed with relief as tears sprang to her eyes and fell down her face. She had made the right decision to return to the island. If she hadn't, Lou would have been tugged into the water and growing waves.

She had saved her.

The thought touched a wound. Who, Trinity thought, had come to save her when she was locked away?

If Sadie hadn't been nearby and making regular visits, Trinity was sure she would have lost her mind. This time, as her chest felt weighted with pressure, she allowed the feelings she'd worked so hard to contain to surface.

Rejected.

Abandoned.

Bewildered.

Anguished.

Confused.

Powerless.

Lonely.

Hopeless.

Angry.

While locked away, she had stayed strong—refused to be pulled under by the swirling tumult of her emotions.

When weeks and then months went by and her parents didn't visit, she felt sorry for herself and believed that the thing she needed most was their love. She nursed feeling rejected by them, and by Victor, until she felt almost numb at the thought of him. But eventually, she came to understand that her survival had nothing to do with him or her parents. She had to survive on her own, despite feeling the deepest despair.

Everything was stripped from her—the freedom to eat what she wanted and when, the freedom to stay in her room or be with others, the freedom to be alone with her thoughts and away from the tormented shrieks and ramblings of other patients . . . The more she lost outwardly, the more she sank her roots into the nourishing soil of her deeper self.

In her worst moments she would imagine the island, as if she were an eagle, circling above it. She'd imagine every cove, every tree, down to the icy-blue forget-me-nots. In her mind she would paint, brushstroke after brushstroke. Detail after detail. And as she imagined painting, fully concentrating, she was nearly transported to the island, inhaling its crisp, sweet air with each breath.

The attendant with the twitching eye would come to

their dorm room in the wee hours of night, his breath rank with alcohol, his words vile and slithering, his buck knife unsheathed. In those times, she went away to the island. She let herself drift beyond, setting down tap roots that protected her from toppling.

As she cried—wringing out the memories, shame, and pain from every corner of her mind, body, and heart—her jaw ached and her teeth hurt. Her chest and throat tightened, making breathing difficult, but she allowed herself to feel.

When her breathing slowed . . . when Lou licked her cheek . . . when the flood of emotion was at last spent . . . she felt cleansed.

Beyond her patch of dry earth, however, the storm continued as if there were no end to its source. All she could do was wait it out in the safety of the rock that had been there, unchanging, for eons. A hill of rock that had been there forever. She ran her hand on the granite above her, to either side of her.

A patch of lichen here.

A crack there from a winter's freeze and thaw.

She ran her finger along the stone's outer edge, wet with rain and moss.

What was she thinking? Rock changes over time. Where she now sat must have once been part of a greater whole that had broken away.

Everything changes . . . in its own time.

The air temperature dropped.

Shivering, Trinity rubbed her arms and legs, trying to warm up.

But nothing helped.

She thought of warm-water treatment. The first time she was ordered to have treatment, Trinity had resisted with all her strength. After she'd been admitted, she'd been too upset to sleep the first few nights. She worried another patient would harm her while she slept, or that she would never be released. She questioned her own sanity, landing in such a place. But after not sleeping for most of a week, nerves frayed, she demanded to be released. She imagined things. Finally, attendants took hold of her and brought her to the hospital ward and a room that held several deep ceramic tubs. Stripped of her gown and forced into the tub, thrashing and kicking, she yelled and screamed. A lid was fastened to the tub so that only her head protruded. When she saw that she was stuck, she quieted and allowed the warmth of the bath to soak into her chilled toes, fingers, legs, arms, and torso. "It will help calm your hysteria," she was told. The water treatments worked. Took the piss and vinegar right out of a person.

In the small refuge between the rock and the storm, she felt something she hadn't felt in years. There was no one watching, no one monitoring her movements, telling her how to behave, what to become.

No parents, no staff . . .

Huddled with Lou to her chest, soaking wet and chilled, she felt something strangely delicious coursing through her.

Rain poured off the rock, carried east by wind slipping over the top of the ridge. The water rolled off in a steady gush—a tiny waterfall—and she was sitting behind it, safe from its trajectory, observing droplets of jade. She wanted her paints. She wanted to capture the image of water backlit by pines, the feeling it conjured from her place of shelter. She laughed at herself, because here she was thinking like an artist when she should be more worried about surviving the night ahead.

And then it came to her.

She knew—as surely as she knew she needed oxygen.

She was her truest self when she was creating.

To her core, she *was* an artist.

She refused to be pulled under by her family.

As surely as she had saved Lou . . . as surely as light left the sky . . . as surely as darkness descended . . . she was *determined* to save herself.

23

THE HORN WOKE HER FIRST, followed by the boat's familiar thrum.

"Trinity!" Father called, his voice distant. "Where are you?"

Aching with cold, she pushed herself up from her fetal position, waking up Lou who was still curled in a ball. She'd tried to stay awake after the storm lost its full fury, wondering if the yacht would return for her in the middle of the night. But now the sun was up, peeking through a cool morning fog as water dripped from every leaf and branch.

Mosquitoes buzzed and Trinity smacked one on her forehead, only to withdraw her blood-splattered hand.

Lou whined and licked her wounded paw, now twice the size of the other. "Hey, girl," she said. "You're going to be okay. Hang in there, little one."

Scooping up Lou in a careful hold, Trinity headed down the opposite slope to the cove where the yacht floated in a soft haze, its hull lemon-colored in the early light.

"Trinity!" Father called again, standing on the bow as a mourning dove cooed nearby. The boat eased into the quiet cove, and he beamed with relief. "Thank God, thank God!"

The yacht's engine and bilge pump rumbled and glugged, the most reassuring sounds Trinity had ever heard. George emerged from the wheelhouse, jumped from the bow to land with the line in his hand, glancing at her. "Oh, you're hurt!"

"A mosquito bite," she said.

"Okay then," he said, patting her back where the limb had struck.

She winced. "Except right there."

He pulled away. "Sorry."

"Poor little pup," Father said from the bow as he held out his hand. "Here, Trinity. Hand her over. George will help you aboard."

When Mother climbed up from below deck, her hair askew and her clothes unchanged from blueberry picking, Trinity realized that her parents hadn't stayed somewhere with friends on the lake but were onboard all night. The experience had taken its toll—Mother's eyes were darting and anxious as if unable to rest in their sockets. She seemed too upset to say a word.

Once they were under way, Trinity settled on the bench seat with Lou curled on her lap under a striped wool blanket. Careful not to jostle or bump her dog's paw, Trinity gently stroked Lou's ears and gazed out.

A morning mist hung in the air, creating an eyes-half-closed effect, a Monet softness across the water. The boat hummed along, cutting through water and sending a tiny spray of wet beads into the warming air. Trinity filled her lungs with crisp and minty air as an eagle, its white head brilliant in the light, lifted from its thatched nest of sticks in an old-growth pine.

Mother joined Trinity on the bench, bowing her head over her hands as she shaped her cuticles with her thumbnail. "Father wanted to come get you in the middle of the night, but I said better to wait until morning."

"I understand," Trinity said. "It was no time to be on the lake."

Mother sniffed. "I told him you need to start learning that there are consequences to your actions."

"Consequences," Trinity repeated, glancing at the wheel-house ceiling. "Honestly! As if I haven't already?" She would never understand the woman she called her mother.

"I'm glad you're okay," Mother said, looking to the water.

A pain danced on Trinity's back and she shifted uncomfortably. "Trees were falling everywhere. Would you take a look at my back?"

"Dear! Blood stains on your shirt!" Mother scoffed. "Good Lord!"

Trinity felt Mother's cool fingers lifting the back of her blouse. "Scrapes, mostly," she said. "Nothing deep. But I'll go find the emergency bag and put on some salve."

As Mother stepped down the boat ladder to the galley, Trinity almost laughed at herself. It was such a ridiculously small thing, having a tiny bit of attention from Mother, but she decided to accept it, no matter how meager the drop of kindness. And then she realized: her moments of feeling any sort of closeness with her mother were when she'd taken ill. Measles, as a toddler. She remembered Mother sitting bedside, cool palm to Trinity's feverish forehead. At their home in Davenport, when any kind of influenza kept Trinity in bed, Mother herself always carried the tray to Trinity's room. She hadn't needed to, as their mansion was always brimming with enough staff, but by choice she entered the room bearing a silver tray of soup and crackers, always with a single flower in a small vase.

When Mother returned, she gently applied salve, her hands trembling. "There," she said. "Now the sooner we get back, the better for everyone."

"Thank you," Trinity said, that small gesture of kindness helping her see things in a new light. Trinity watched as Mother began pacing about the wheelhouse. It struck her that for many years Mother had been religious about taking her medicine before bed. Because of yesterday's storm, she'd missed last night's tincture.

When they reached a wide expanse of water, George put

the boat in neutral and left the wheel. The yacht drifted as he returned with a toolbox, knelt in front of Trinity on the bench, and studied Lou's paw.

"George!" Mother shouted. Her eyes darted anxiously. "We need to get back. I can't stand being in these dirty clothes one more second!"

"Mother, try to be patient," Trinity said.

"It will take just a moment," George added, wire cutter in hand. "Trinity, hold her firmly." Then slowly reaching for Lou's ballooned paw, he clipped off the hook's other barbs, placed the lure in his toolbox, and returned with a pliers to deal with the one barb sunk deep, with a long metal tail. He grabbed it with the end of his pliers. "This is going to hurt like hell, but I'll be quick as I can."

Then he worked the hook through.

Lou struggled and yelped. She snarled, teeth bared, and Trinity worried she might bite, but then it was over. Settling into Trinity's lap with a sigh, she began licking her paw.

George handed Trinity a clean rag. "Let it bleed a little and then keep pressure on it."

Trinity did as George instructed, letting the spot flow for a few seconds and then stanching it with the cloth. "George," she asked. "Any ice left onboard?"

"You bet," he said, quickly disappearing into the galley and returning with an ice-filled teacup, which Trinity held on top of Lou's swollen paw.

"Oh—for God's sake!" Mother paced, pushing at her cuticles and licking her dry lips. "George, may we go now?!"

It was unsettling, and Trinity had to look away. She was grateful when George stood behind the wheel and pushed the throttle forward.

"George, I must get back to check on RuthAnne," Mother said. "She's probably worried sick. Can't you go any faster?"

George edged the throttle forward again and the boat picked up speed, its soft purr turning to a deafening rumble.

Mother, Trinity realized, was going through withdrawal.

And as Dr. Stratton had tried to help Trinity understand, this wasn't her mother's true self. Not that Trinity
would recognize Mother's truest self anyway, but it was her
addiction, hungry to be fed. Trinity wanted to understand.
Mother had grown up in the late 1800s, when laudanum was
used for nearly every ailment and called the "poor person's
nursemaid," so trusted it was even given to quiet teething
babies. Back then, people thought nothing of it. But learning about Mother's tincture of opium was disturbing. Trinity
wondered how long her habit had been going on, how it had
started in the first place, how much of her behavior was driv-
en by her habit. Mothers were supposed to be stronger than
that—the hens who safely tucked their chicks under wing.

But that wasn't her mother.

Hadn't been for as long as Trinity could remember.

An image of an Oak Hills patient surfaced. The one with
silver hair, cut short. She stopped to tell anyone who passed
how she'd taken a terrible fall from a horse as a teenager that
left her limping. To cope, she had lived on laudanum, purchased cheaply to deal with her hip and knee pain. After laws
changed, she had to get her medicine through a doctor's prescription. Then the Harrison Narcotic Act passed in 1914,
and it stamped out many doctors' practice of prescribing
opiates to "maintain" an addict's habit. "If I'd been born with
a silver spoon," the woman said, her teeth brown and rotten,
"I might have gone to one of them clinics that helped addicts.
But by then, I didn't want help. I was too far gone. I did anything to get what I needed. Shameful things," she said, always
finishing with a wag of her finger. "Don't you ever start."

Though Mother wasn't as far gone as some, Trinity
replayed scenes of opium addicts: at Oak Hills they would
arrive agitated and wild-eyed and then go to the hospital
ward with days of chills, fever, and vomiting. Eventually the
physical symptoms passed; recovered patients joined others
in the dorm, often bringing their dark moods and cravings
with them.

The yacht cut through a light chop toward the dock, where Agatha, RuthAnne, and Millie waited.

"I was worried sick!" RuthAnne called. "I was sure you'd crashed into rocks and sunk! Thank God you're back."

"Welcome back!" Millie waved.

"You're home and all in one piece," Agatha said, crossing her arms over her aproned chest.

George waved in greeting and hopped off to secure lines. As soon as he finished, Agatha was at his side. She took his face in both hands and kissed him, right on the lips—clearly relieved to have her husband back.

He gave her a quick kiss on her forehead. "Quite a storm. But we're all fine."

"That's what matters," Agatha said. "Coffee's on and cinnamon rolls are still warm. Fresh from the oven." She glanced at RuthAnne and Millie. "Told you they'd be back."

"Whad'ya say I get the sauna stoked up?" George said, loud enough for everyone to hear, and motioning toward the squat building. At the south end of the sand beach, the sauna building sat on a rock ledge, its dock perched over the water for easy diving into deeper water.

"Perfect!" Trinity answered, stepping off the boat with Lou in her arms. As she set her down gently on the dock, Lou lifted her injured paw. Trinity picked her up again. It would take some time before she would put weight on all four paws.

"I must have a lie-down," Mother said. "What a perfectly dreadful night!" With a flutter of her hands and not another word, she ambled off toward her cabin.

Until the sun burned off last night's rainfall, the island's rocky slopes and granite steps were slippery. Trinity watched her footing. First, she fed Lou from the kitchen, and then made her way back across the sand beach. At the sight of mallard ducklings resting on the edge of shore, Lou struggled to escape Trinity's arms. "Sorry, girl. Not yet." As they drew closer, the ducklings, bigger now since the last time Trinity had seen them, popped up on yellow feet and scuttled into the lake.

Lou whined, then yipped.

"You're not the boss," Trinity joked. "C'mon."

She scaled the stone steps to the other half of the island, reached its top, and glanced down, relieved to spot her studio unscathed.

When Trinity stepped into her studio, she set Lou on the twin bed, and then looked in the mirror. She laughed at her smudged face, rumpled and dirty blouse, and untamed hair.

"It's a mop!" she said aloud. "A sauna—that's what I need."

She donned her red-and-gray-striped bathing suit, gathered a towel, shampoo, and soap, and headed over the slope to the beach. Food would have to wait.

A soft gray smoke swirled up toward the blue sky from the sauna's chimney pipe. The sauna's door faced the lake and a small length of dock. Trinity knocked and no one answered. She stepped into semidarkness, glad to have some time to herself. Engulfed by warm, cedar-scented air, her body relaxed. It was pleasantly warm, but not hot. She glanced at the wall thermometer, which read 137 degrees. Certainly not warm enough for taking a sauna.

Lou whined as she stepped back out. "You can't go in," she said, setting Lou on the dock.

From the small woodshed nearby, Trinity gathered a supply of dry logs. With an armful of birch and pine, she knelt beside the exterior cast-iron loading door and opened it with the edge of a log. George had started the fire, and it was burning, but it needed more fuel. She added more, piece by piece. When she closed the door, the fire roared within.

She returned inside to the top bench, watching the mercury climb bit by bit in the thermometer toward 180 degrees.

How often she had imagined herself in this very place during those moments when she needed to escape the damp chill of Oak Hills and its icy floors made of concrete. Its showers were one vast room, offering no privacy and chilly no matter the season. When the furnaces pumped heat through the brick building, there was never enough to reach her side of the dorm or take the cold out of her bones.

From the wooden bucket on the bench, she scooped out a ladle of water and tossed it on the hot stones at the top of the woodstove. The droplets spat and sizzled, transforming into hot steam that filled the room. The intense heat sent a shiver through her skin. She tried to relax into the high temperature, letting the air penetrate her muscles and tendons and ease every joint in her body.

When sweat beaded on her forehead and ran down her chest and spine, she was driven out. She gently descended from the top bench, careful not to trip into the perilously hot cast-iron woodstove.

Outside, she hurried to the end of the short dock, hands overhead, clasped, and pointed. She angled herself into a shallow dive like an arrow, well-aimed and sure. Slicing through dark water, she felt her body temperature cool from fingertips to scalp, from torso to toes. There was nothing like it.

She surfaced with a yelp.

On round two, the heat had shot up, and she added more water to create steam. Then she lathered up with shampoo and soap. When she couldn't take the heat a second longer, she raced out and dived in.

This time she swam as far as she could underwater, letting the water rinse her body.

When she surfaced, tilting her head to let her hair fall back from her face, she felt alive.

Almost free.

24

ONE MILE EAST OF BAIRD ISLAND, the Larssons' mansion towered above the water on its island's highest slope. Trinity half-listened to drifting conversation as she gazed out over the veranda's stone wall, which prevented guests with one too many drinks from slipping down the sheer thirty-foot cliff into the lake below. And what a guest list it was, complete with the son of a famed Egyptologist, a Spanish princess, and an author: Charles Breasted, Maria Sophia de Bourbon, and Sinclair Lewis.

The afternoon was warm and the lake was unusually calm as it stretched east under giant mushroom clouds of white. The nearest island, owned by E. W. Ennis, appeared in miniature with its lodge and surrounding cabins.

Gizelle swished close to Trinity in layers of beaded silk, knee-skimming fringe, her arms adorned with gold bracelets. A rogue deerfly landed on her apricot shoulder strap, but she slapped it away before it could bite, then nodded toward the island. "This is exactly what my husband had in mind. We can always *look down* on his former employer."

Trinity had heard this explanation before. Mr. Larsson had gone on to start his own successful manufacturing business and wasn't about to let E. W. Ennis forget it.

Gizelle winked. "Your dress is the cat's pajamas. Fashion, right in the middle of wilderness!"

"Thanks," Trinity said. She'd picked it up at Irene's, plus the matching floral scarf she wore around her forehead. "I like getting dressed up now and then, but today, honestly, we should all be cooling off in the lake."

With theatrical flair, Gizelle motioned toward their beach and boathouse. "That's where you'll find my husband. Oh, but I see your glass is empty." She raised her hand high and snapped her fingers. "Jedrek," she called, first sweetly. The second time, her voice was more demanding.

In seconds, the butler appeared. He was a lithe man, said to be from India, whose every motion, fluid and precise, reminded Trinity of a great blue heron.

"Jedrek, Miss Baird needs another drink," Gizelle said.

"Yes, ma'am," he replied, spinning away.

"I'm not sure that I need—" Trinity began.

"Nonsense!" Gizelle said with a sweep of her arm. "It's not the booze we need. It's the ice we need to keep us cool!"

Trinity laughed.

"On my last trip to town I spotted a flyer for the circus. This year, I think we should go together, yes?"

"Sure," Trinity replied, flattered by the suggestion.

Gizelle peered over the wall. "At least they're an interesting lot, circus performers. Something to at least spark the curiosity! Well, any sign of the paddlers yet?" she asked, motioning toward the water.

"Not a sign," Trinity replied. She'd been waiting for the two canoes to appear from the west. Earlier, Henry and Victor had taken on a challenge to race two teens around the island. But that was an hour ago, and after two hours at the party, Trinity was ready to leave. But Mother was deep in conversation with two other women; Father was smoking cigars with other businessmen; RuthAnne and her maid were playing croquet on a patch of mowed grass.

"Oh, there he is," Gizelle said, pointing beyond to the east.

At first Trinity thought she had meant Victor, but Gizelle

was looking in the opposite direction toward the cove. Mr. Larsson was strutting around in a red bathing suit, just a small bit of fabric below his mildly protruding tan belly.

"Whenever my husband puts on that Italian bathing suit, he thinks he's a Greek or Roman god," Gizelle hooted. "Bet he won't take it off until everyone else is fully dressed and he's covered in gooseflesh." Then she laughed. "Here's a secret," she whispered. "Sometimes he wears it to bed."

"Oh," Trinity replied and tried not to imagine what came after that.

As she watched, Mr. Larsson put down his drink and started chasing the young girls, who squealed as they ran. If he caught them, he kissed them, a game he'd been playing as long as Trinity could remember. A wet kiss with the overly sweet smell of too much booze? *Horrid!* A few mothers sat nearby on chaise lounges, smoking and chatting, seemingly oblivious to his antics.

"Does he think girls actually like that game?" Trinity asked.

Gizelle lit up another cigarette and held the silver holder high, so the smoke drifted over Trinity's head. "Boys will be boys."

"Yeah, that's the expression that somehow gives them permission to get away with anything, doesn't it?" Trinity said. "But girls will be girls? We're still expected to be pretty, smile, and not be too outspoken."

Gizelle nodded, taking another drag. "When we push boundaries, we're considered a threat."

"Well, to hell with that!" Trinity said, a little louder than she intended, drawing the attention of three women, standing outside the lodge's French doors.

Including Mother, who sent her a warning glance.

Trinity wasn't sure if it was what was in her drink or if she'd suddenly become immune to caring what Mother—or anyone, for that matter—thought. "These heels are killing me," she added. "I'm going barefoot." She sensed eyes on her as she freed her feet from the T-strap shoes.

Gizelle didn't seem offended and hooked her arm in Trinity's, whisking her away. "Come with me. I want you to meet our elusive author! And wait till you see our new tepee! First, have I given you a tour of our home?"

Gizelle made it sound like the author was another exotic piece of furniture she had acquired. Trinity knew that some painters were supported by wealthy patrons. Each served the other's needs in some way, whether it was a need for money, recognition, or status. This author fell into the latter category for Gizelle. Still, Trinity was interested in meeting Sinclair Lewis, who had turned a simple premise—a gifted young woman married to a dull doctor in a small town—into a masterpiece.

Gizelle steered past urns overflowing with white geraniums, through the terrace doors and into the living room with its vaulted dome ceiling.

Trinity toured the kitchen, butler's pantry, dining room (with its own attached breakfast room), plus a music room, a corridor with five bedrooms, and three full bathrooms. "The only heat is from our three fireplaces," Gizelle concluded as she stepped out a side door. "Hence, we stay on only from Memorial Day to Labor Day."

The warm air was heavy with the scent of sap and resin.

Gizelle followed a path of flat stones between birch trees, spruce, and pine. She paused and turned to whisper, "I overheard Mr. Lewis say he wanted to write someday in a *circular* house, so I had one built for him—twenty feet in diameter and thirty feet high!"

Trinity padded along barefoot. When she glanced up, the tepee rose from its mammoth round base to the treetops— far bigger than she'd imagined. Unlike an Ojibwe tepee constructed of leather hides or canvas, this was a carpenter's creation of wood, nails, white paint, and decorative strips of birchbark.

"Incredible," she said. And *awfully strange,* she wanted to add.

"The workers finished building it one day before he

arrived," Gizelle said, dropping her voice in a proud whisper. "We had just enough time to get it ready for him. I know he has his work, but honestly, we'd hoped he'd be a little more social. People want to get to *know* him."

"Artists and writers. We're a peculiar sort," Trinity agreed.

"Yes, far quieter than actors!" Gizelle said, her voice rising back to its loud normal. She stepped to the screen door and the sound of someone pounding away on typewriter keys.

She knocked twice and silenced the typing.

"What now?" The man's voice sounded tired, resigned to his fate.

Trinity expected something different when she entered. Something far more rustic. Beneath the towering ceiling sat a circular white fireplace and a mahogany baby grand piano accented with golden dragons. Turkish tasseled rugs covered much of the honey-colored, freshly varnished maple floor. Countless red cushions of silk and velvet were strewn about. It was a space fit for a sultan.

At a small black table, a lanky man turned from a typewriter and a half-typed sheet of paper. Parted in the middle, his hair was brown, thin, and flattened to his head. His long neck protruded from the open collar of his linen shirt. He studied them from probing eyes under ponderous brows—a turtle peering up from its rather drab shell.

"Terribly sorry to disturb you," Gizelle said, clearly not sorry at all. "I want you to meet another creative soul. This is Trinity Baird. She's a fine painter. She's studied in Paris and more recently at Gustavus Adolphus College in St. Peter!"

At the half-truth, Trinity felt a wave of heat climb her cheeks. She could correct her, but she let it go. For Gizelle, pretense was everything.

The man extended his hand, grasped Trinity's, and brought it to his lips. "The pleasure is mine." She met his eyes, as if he were in that instant taking in the whole of her past and future in one glance. Then he let go of her hand, not lingering a second longer than was proper. She knew he was a best-selling author with a national name. She had read two of his novels, and the words and stories soared, taking her to worlds she'd never traveled before. She had enjoyed them immensely. But here he was, just a man. The person behind the work. For a moment she felt disappointed. When he turned back to his chair, she reminded herself that the creation—the work—is the manifestation of all that's best in its creator. The work had the ability to surpass the mundane, the ordinary, even the insanity of its creator. Van Gogh came to mind. She'd felt that illogical yearning, the desire to create something beyond herself. But she didn't know how to express such thoughts to someone she had just met.

"I appreciate your writing," she said. "I loved *Main Street*."

"Thank you," he said, nodding once. "I'm honored."

With a tiny wiggle of her shoulders, Gizelle swished her dress with impatience. "Mr. Lewis, *please* come and visit our guests. I know everyone would simply love to get to know you better. If you wouldn't mind, we have another round of—"

He lifted his forefinger, stopping her. "The first hour, I made myself available," he said, looking up at her. "But I'm here to write, not to be anyone's social trinket."

Gizelle pursed her red, rounded lips in a pout. "Oh."

His chair creaked as he crossed his arms and lifted his glasses from his nose to the top of his head. "I'd gladly join in if someone else wanted to finish this novel for me. I have a deadline."

"Even on such a lovely day as this?" Gizelle pressed, bringing her hands together beneath her chin. Trinity half-expected her to pretend to faint, if it would help her cause.

"He has to write," Trinity said.

"Finally, someone understands," he said, lowering his glasses and turning to his typewriter. *Tat-tat-tat.*

"We'll go," Gizelle said, taking the strong hint.

"Sorry to disturb you," Trinity added, just before stepping out, but Mr. Lewis stopped her. "It's true? You've studied in Paris?"

She nodded.

"You two talk," Gizelle said, waving to Trinity from outside. "I'm going to check on my other guests."

Trinity pivoted toward the dim interior.

"Sit," he said, motioning to pillows on a chaise lounge. She sat down, looking around, and said, "Our cabins are more rustic than this."

"A white man's tepee," he said with a glance upward. "It's peculiar, but apparently this is the only place I can escape that woman."

Tucking her legs beside her, Trinity asked, "How did you meet Gizelle and her husband?"

"Not sure I recall. Some event in St. Paul? A friend of a friend? She insisted I come to write on their island. But honestly, such airs! I mean, every little thing they do—including supposedly building this *atrocity* for me to write in—seems to be done to impress others and themselves."

Trinity didn't want to say anything against Gizelle, one of the only people she had been able to talk to since she returned.

"Will you return to, let me guess, the Sorbonne?" he asked, glancing back to the typewriter keys.

"I hope to."

"Hope to? So you're not sure you're really an artist? Not sure you're committed to doing the hard work of studying at that level?" He sounded cranky, as if he'd heard too many people talk about their dreams without ever acting on them.

But she sat up straighter. "No! And yes, I'm serious," she said. "I'd be there this moment, if I could."

"And why there? Why not New York? Why not create from here?" His questions were fair enough, but his tone was brittle.

She stood up quickly. "I better leave. I'm clearly bothering you."

"I'm sorry. Maybe it's the heat or that woman. Sit. I'm just saying, what are you waiting for? What are you doing here if you need to be in Paris with its renowned writers and artists?"

She took a moment, considering him. His eyes looked tired, and an empty tumbler sat on his desk. She'd probably never see him again. If he wanted to know the truth, she'd tell him. "Through no real fault of my own, I was sent away to the asylum in St. Peter. I spent nearly two years there." The words rolled off her tongue, surprising her. But his honesty begat honesty. And she felt a freedom of communication with this person who had spent his life creating.

"I'm listening." He nodded for her to continue.

She told him everything, and he didn't say a word or turn away. He nodded here and there, allowing her to tell her story. When she finished, she said, "I'm as sane as the next artist, but now I'm being carefully watched all summer. If I cause my parents the slightest alarm, they won't let me return to Paris—or worse still, they'll ship me back to St. Peter." She winced at raising her voice on the veranda and deciding to go barefoot. She had to be more careful.

"That's awful!" His laugh came out as a snort.

"Which part?" she asked. "And why do you laugh?"

"You *should* be causing your parents 'alarm.' That's the new trend, isn't it? On campuses it's kids with their own music, own styles, own ways of thinking. It's their job these days—and an important one at that—to upend convention."

"Maybe. But that's a luxury I can't afford," she said.

As he stretched his arms behind his head and leaned back in his chair, she added, "I can't be locked away again."

"But aren't you locked away now?" His words hung in the air.

Her throat grew hot as a wave of anger threatened to break over her. She knew he was right. She was released from physical walls but still felt the crush of her parents' boundaries, which could spring up on a whim.

"You're the scapegoat," he said matter-of-factly.

"I don't follow."

"Oh, you know, Old Testament stuff. Through some kind of symbolism and ritual, a goat was burdened with the sins of others and then driven away. Cast into the desert. Carrying away the community's sins."

She couldn't quite grasp the comparison, but she felt a pang of empathy for the castaway goat. That part she understood, and the truth of it scalded the back of her throat.

"Considering what you've told me," Mr. Lewis continued, "and believe me, I've heard every word you've said, I have a proposal for you. Now you might think it strange."

She waited.

"You need a project."

"Yes," she said, cautiously.

"So paint me a portrait."

"A portrait." She gave her head a shake, not understanding. "Of you?" She thought he might want a portrait of himself creating his next best-selling novel.

"Boring! No." He glared at her. "I want you to paint a portrait of yourself. Not as others see you. You are a lovely young lady, but paint yourself as *you* see yourself. You do that, and . . . I'll pay you for it. Enough to get you back to Paris."

"What?" She tried to absorb the weight of his offer. "But why? You don't even know if you'd like what I paint. Why would you do that for me?" Here was an author almost old enough to be her father, though not quite. She liked him and his directness, but was he after something more from her? There had to be a catch. Kisses that would lead to more complicated favors? Everything came at a price, didn't it? She was desperate to return to school, but she wouldn't stoop to using her body as payment. "I'm not a child, Mr. Lewis. So please don't play games. Do you have an agenda?"

"No, no agenda," he said directly. "You're authentic. I felt an affinity with you from the moment you stepped in. The more I write, the less patience I have for anything less. I see a kindred spirit in you."

A warmth spread through her chest, and it was so foreign she didn't recognize what it was. But as she met his kind eyes, she knew. This was what she was needing. To be seen, heard, and known. Her lips trembled as she smiled.

He formed a chapel with his fingers. "I know how families work. How small towns work. Well meaning . . . but they can destroy you."

He kept talking, his words measured. "There are moments in our lives . . ." He let the words hang in the air and turned back to his typewriter, fingers resting on its keys. This was a man who had set his course to write, and neither the weather nor Gizelle's efforts would dissuade him.

She could almost see the rest of his sentence, scrolled in cursive in perfect calligraphy: *when we must choose.*

"I leave in one week," he said. "Can you have it for me by then?"

"One week," she said. "Yes, I can."

She thanked him and said goodbye. The *tat-tat-tat* sound of typing followed her as she stepped out.

Beneath a canopy of green leaves, the light and shadows had shifted. The world felt different, more open to possibility. Even her favorite songbird, the white-throated sparrow, seemed to chorus a more urgent song: YOU MUST LEAVE, *you-must-leave, you-must-leave, you-must-leave . . .*

25

AS MR. LEWIS HAD REQUESTED, Trinity tried to paint an image of herself as she saw herself. It was harder than she'd expected.

A light mist fell outside as she studied herself in her studio mirror. She pivoted from the mirror on the wall to the canvas, back and forth. But the more she studied her own image, the more sides she saw of herself. If she painted herself smiling, which is exactly what she did when she imagined the feeling of diving, or jumping off the cliffs in Anderson Bay with Victor, the light she saw in her own eyes was real. It was. But she guessed Mr. Lewis would dismiss the smile as what she hoped others would see.

After several false starts, she gazed out her window. Light skittered across the water with the shifting breeze, leaving sparkling prints. Inspired, she turned back to her oils. If she could somehow capture that same sparkle in the eyes—but every stroke seemed wrong. She was forcing it, as if she were trying to recapture a place she had been in the past and where she wanted to be in the future. Not where she was—here and now.

She gazed through the leafy branches to the breeze-ruffled waters of the channel, always moving, never staying the same. On the island she was surrounded by water at every turn. Whatever her concern, water had a way of softening sharp edges. In its presence she felt calmer, more serene. But when she tried to capture that feeling, she could see that she'd only painted an idealized version of herself.

When stray clouds drifted across the sun, blocking its rays and changing its mood, the channel turned slate gray. The breeze through the windows dropped a few degrees. She closed the windows, then returned to her task.

She shifted her chair, easel, and paints and tried from the other angle. Outside the north window, the massive gray boulder caught her eye, reminding her of another time.

"The back of the elephant," she said, remembering the boulder's rough, sun-warmed surface. Tail wagging, Lou took her words as an invitation to clamber onto her lap.

"When I was a girl," she told her, scratching Lou under her chin, to which the dog stretched her head skyward, "I played a game . . . First, I'd always ask the elephant permission to climb up on its back. Of course, the elephant always lowered his head, his way of saying 'Yes,' and then I'd pretend I was climbing its rough and leathery skin to a dizzying height." She laughed, because though the boulder was six feet at its peak, it didn't seem nearly so high now. "We crossed parched deserts and explored mysterious continents." She smiled at the memory.

Lou looked up and gave Trinity's chin one quick lick.

Riding the back of the elephant, she had felt powerful.

Wisps of her short hair tickled her cheeks. She had changed. She saw life differently now.

Beyond her screen window, a chickadee flitted from one branch to the next, its movements quick and precise. She was a creature, too, both insignificant and vital in the mysterious whole. She was human, breathing in and out . . . as important as the mighty elephant making its way through an impenetrable jungle. But she no longer needed to ride the back of anything to feel powerful. She was enough on her own. And she didn't need anyone's permission to move forward with her life.

Beat, beat. Beat, beat. She caught a glimpse as a half-dozen Canada geese flew over her studio, wings beating the air and then fading away.

Her heart drummed in her ears.

Beat, beat. Beat, beat.

She drew a deep breath of fresh, clean air.

And again, she began.

Time slipped by, and she stopped only to glance out the window.

Patches of lichen on the boulder caught her attention—not green, not gray—the color hovered between the vibrancy of life and the pallor of death.

The color of the asylum walls.

Her chest shuddered and a sob caught in her throat. She allowed herself to grieve, no longer needing to hold every ounce of energy to maintain her own sanity.

Lou hopped off the bed, favoring her paw, head cocked, watching.

"It's okay," Trinity said. "I'm okay. But I had a friend . . . in fact, I named you after her, because . . . because she made me smile. Like you." Half-laughing, half-choking on tears, she added, "She was incredible."

The day of her release from Oak Hills, Trinity had visited the asylum's cemetery. Searching through the grassy expanse for the right brick, she felt overwhelmed by the numbers. Over the years, hundreds had died there. She looked for where the earth had recently been disturbed and found a brick etched with only a number—673. Running her forefinger along the grooves of each number, deep and crisp, not yet worn by the elements, Trinity felt a crushing weight of guilt.

She hadn't suffered with epilepsy.

She hadn't been committed for life.

She hadn't died at the asylum.

She was alive.

She had survived.

━∗━

NOW SHE STOPPED PAINTING. "Goodbye, Lou," she whispered.

With a whine, her dog looked up from the base of the chair, head tilted, as if questioning if something was wrong.

"No, not goodbye to *you!*" Trinity said with a soft laugh.

She combed her fingers gently through the dog's black fur. "*That* Lou was incredibly brave. You would have liked her."

She cleaned the bristles of her paintbrush on old newspaper pages and began again, switching to a darker palette.

This time she painted herself, not with her hair bobbed and infused with sunlight, but pulled back. Not in her painting smock, but in a simple charcoal dress that blended into a background the color of stone and weathered boards.

The portrait she painted could be from any decade—out of time and place—from any number of countries.

She was Louise.

She was Marta, sent home only if she remained silent.

She was every young woman not heard, not seen for who she was.

She painted herself, a survivor.

If eyes were the window to the soul, then she would make them her focal point.

Eyes large and unflinching, fierce with determination.

26

TRINITY EASED THE FISHING BOAT into the cove at Lars-sons' island, shutting off the motor and gliding into the space behind *Gizelle*, a yacht four feet short of *Trinity*, as Father liked to frequently point out.

Earlier, she'd told Mother she was heading off with her supplies and canvas for a morning of painting. She didn't want to explain the self-portrait, dried to the touch and safely tucked in her portfolio.

It was midmorning, and Trinity felt assured she would interrupt neither breakfast nor lunch, or miss the author before he left by boat for the train depot in Ranier. The thought of showing Mr. Lewis her work filled her with dread and anticipation. She steeled herself for whatever he might have to say about it. It was raw and honest, and she had given it her utmost best.

The dockhand, a boy no more than fifteen, met her and tied up her boat. She thanked him and tipped him, something Father didn't believe in. "They'll come to expect it every time," he'd warned. "Their reward should be in a job well done." She might be his daughter, but she could be a different kind of Baird.

With her portrait tucked under her arm, she strolled up the gravel path between swaths of dew-tipped grass. Air rushed overhead, shushing through the tops of pines and fluttering aspen leaves, exposing pale green underbellies.

In the distance, she spotted the tip of the tepee. She wanted more than anything to go directly to Mr. Lewis. If he actually bought her painting, as he said he'd do . . . It was such an amazing opportunity, but she could scarcely allow herself to imagine. Better to take things one footstep at a time. Still, a painting in exchange for a transatlantic crossing? It seemed too good to be true. The possibility sent a shiver of hope through her fingers and toes, and she picked up her pace, despite the uphill slope.

It was proper to first stop and greet the hostess at the chateau-like home. She reached the massive oak door, framed with stone planters overflowing with orange and yellow nasturtiums. She lifted the cast-iron knocker and let it drop with a *thunk*.

Jedrek opened the door wide, half-bowing to Trinity. "Good morning, Miss Baird," he said. "What may we do for you today?"

She cleared her throat. "I'm here to see—um . . ." She couldn't just come right out and say "the author" or "Sinclair Lewis," as it would be wholly scandalous. And that kind of scandal wouldn't serve her goals. She must first see her hostess. "To see Mrs. Larsson."

"Wait one moment, please."

When the butler returned, he opened the door fully and swept his arm wide, inviting her inside. "She is happy to take visitors. Or shall I say, she said she is happy to see you. This way." He led her down the hallway, door after door, and knocked on the door with a small gold star. "Trinity Baird, ma'am."

Gizelle's voice floated from inside. "Oh, do come in!"

Trinity expected to see bright light streaming through sheer curtains and Gizelle in an exquisite dress, perhaps penning a request to one of her directors in Hollywood. But she stepped into a darkened room, the only glow coming from a bedside lamp. Propped up with several pillows, wearing a silk sleeping jacket, Gizelle set her fork down on her breakfast tray.

"I'm sorry to bother you," Trinity said. "You're not well?"

Gizelle waved away her assumption. "Applesauce! I'm just waking up, doll."

Trinity gazed around the room. The hands of the gilded clock read 10:55. "I try to get my beauty sleep," Gizelle said. "That's why Bruno has his own bedroom. We both sleep better that way. Be a doll and throw open those curtains, will you?"

She swept back the thick, brocade-trimmed curtains, allowing light to come through the sheers. When she turned back to Gizelle, she almost jumped. Her face looked so different. Trinity had never seen her without makeup, her face now naked except for the remaining high sheen of night cream. Gizelle always had the large, dramatic eyes of a starlet, extra heavy on the eyeliner, pencil, and shadow. Now her eyes looked small and ordinary, with puffs beneath her lower lashes. Her lips were round, but without lipstick they were a pale pink that blended with the rest of her petite face. To create her usual, spectacular curls, she'd rolled her hair up in "rag-rollers" with strips of floral fabric.

Gizelle tilted her head back with a laugh. "Pretty scary, huh?"

"No. Well, kind of." Trinity couldn't keep a straight face and burst out laughing. "I was thinking something alien— from *The War of the Worlds*." Then she tried to recover some form of politeness. "Forgive me."

"Balderdash! Consider yourself a friend. I never let anyone see me this way." Gizelle picked up her porcelain cup of coffee. "You better not hold it against me."

"Never," Trinity answered. "I brought a painting for . . ."

"A gift, for me?" Gizelle said, sitting up a little straighter. She reminded Trinity of a little girl at Christmas.

She saw that Gizelle knew nothing of her agreement with Mr. Lewis. "Sorry, no, I came to bring it to Mr. Lewis. He asked for a self-portrait in—"

"But, darling, he left the morning after the party."

"He what?" Trinity couldn't believe what she was hearing. All her effort, her anticipation, her hope . . . fell to the floor in a heap.

Gizelle went on. "Yes, a telegram arrived and apparently there was a death in his family. I'm sorry for his loss, but we had planned two more dinner parties, and I can't tell you how disappointing . . ."

When Gizelle finished, Trinity braved one question. "Did he leave any message for me?"

She bit the inside of her lip, waiting.

Gizelle grinned and wagged her finger with accusation. "Don't tell me you're sweet on the author? I should never have left you two alone, I can see that now."

Trinity shook her head slowly. "No, nothing like that. I just thought I'd show him what I painted."

"Well, I'm here and he's—who knows where he is. Show me!"

Reluctantly, Trinity opened her portfolio and revealed her self-portrait. Oil on stretched canvas.

"Oh," Gizelle said with a careful tilt of her head. "Oh my."

Trinity braced herself, not sure if Gizelle's reaction was one of awe or . . .

Gizelle dispelled all doubt, blurting, "Oh dear. Better he left on his own than to show him something so . . . so dark . . . moody . . . dreary . . . and frankly unsettling." Then she glanced from the canvas to Trinity. "Oh, I'm sorry for being so direct. But I've learned—you'll never get anywhere with false praise. She's not smiling or even very pretty. I mean, who *is* she?"

Trinity paused, caught off guard by her reaction.

"Sorry. You wouldn't know her."

27

WHEN TRINITY CLIMBED into her fishing boat, hand on the motor's tiller, she felt utterly deflated. She had been moving forward with such certainty, with a sense of purpose, of momentum, of inevitability that her trajectory was toward something positive. She'd almost dared to believe that her meeting Sinclair Lewis had been orchestrated, a predetermined thread in the tapestry of her destiny.

Now all she felt was foolish.

Second-guessing herself.

Uncertain of everything.

It had been a mistake to share the painting with Gizelle, but she was determined to redeem her morning. Somehow. She pointed the bow to the nearby island and steered southwest across choppy water a short distance to Falcon Island, one of several small islands lined up like naval ships, side by side.

Water flowed through the tiny channel like liquid through a funnel. Along the rocky shoreline, sentries of blue flag iris greeted her as she entered the tiny harbor created between two granite islands.

Honeysuckle filled the air as she neared the little building beside the dock—Victor's library. Who, other than Victor Guttenberg, had gathered a floor-to-ceiling book collection in the middle of the wilderness? In a short time, he had purchased books on geography, history, literature, exploration, language, Indian lore . . . anything of interest to him, including rare and first edition books. Every year he wrote personal and detailed correspondence to booksellers around the world, requesting this particular book or that. And the books came to him by the boxful. More than once, Trinity had helped him sort and shelve books as they arrived.

She cut the motor and glided in behind the Guttenbergs' fishing boat. The dock was moored lengthwise, tied to massive steel loops sunk into granite. Victor's birchbark canoe waited, turned over on the dock to protect it from the elements. A good sign. He was home.

As she hopped out, a pileated woodpecker called, then pounded at a tree—*tat-tat-a-tat-tat*—reminding her of typewriter keys.

She winced, secured lines, and grabbed her portfolio from the boat.

She followed the island's winding path, her senses dulled by pain. Still, ferns welcomed her with outstretched fronds. Wood smoke spiced the fresh air. Two hummingbirds zoomed past the top of her head, one chasing the other.

Situated on the eastern point, the cabin had grown from one room to include two additional wings and a second story. Sawhorses sat outside amid piles of sawdust.

She stepped under the porch roof and knocked on the screen door. "Hello?"

"Victor, I'm elbow-deep in dough," Mrs. Guttenberg said. "See who it is?" Then she called out. "Hello! Whoever it is!"

"It's me, Mrs. Guttenberg. Trinity!"

Smells of bacon, yeast, and something delicious baking in the oven drifted her way. She peered in and caught a glimpse of Victor as he set his book aside: head of sandy hair, trousers rolled up midcalf, white button-down shirt wrinkled and untucked.

Victor, always a family friend, confounded her. Why was she so often drawn to him when she was upset? He felt like an older brother or a favorite uncle, though they were hardly related. After his father abandoned his family, Victor grew up at his grandparents' stately home in Davenport. As far as Trinity knew, though he had ambitions of landscape architecture, becoming an author, and taking more expeditions, Victor's only real job had been as foreman to the work crew that built the Larssons' mansion. Not a go-to-work-and-get-paid job.

Now he padded barefoot across the floor.

Tan face, sunburned nose, he smiled and glanced curiously at what she carried. "You're not here to sell us something, are you?" he joked.

"Well, yes, sir, I am. Just a moment of your time," she replied, mimicking salesmen who showed up in Davenport trying to sell the latest gadget. "Perhaps you need a new dustpan and broom set, or stain remover, or shoe polish. But I see, you don't wear shoes, sir. Maybe shoes would be of interest? If I may just step into your foyer . . ."

He laughed. "C'mon in!"

"I hope you don't mind my popping by unannounced," Trinity said as she stepped in and glanced into the adjoining kitchen.

Warmth rolled from the chrome-and-butter-colored wood-fired oven. Mrs. Guttenberg turned from the Hoosier cabinet and a mound of dough on the flour-dusted pullout. "You're always welcome here," she declared, her dark hair secured in a braided bun. "Besides, Trinity, you're like a daughter."

Trinity smiled. "Thank you!"

"And you've brought something to show us?" Victor asked. "A new piece of art?"

Trinity tilted her head for him to follow, and they settled in rocking chairs on the front porch. Victor worked a toothpick between his lips, looking on, as Trinity opened her leather portfolio.

"I wanted to show you my recent painting," she said.

As he studied the canvas, a frown formed between his eyebrows. He tilted his head this way and that.

Trinity braced herself. Too dark. Too dreary. She didn't need his approval, but she hadn't prepared herself for a second rejection either. She waited, trying not to fidget, reminding herself she hadn't created it for the approval of anyone beside herself. Not even Mr. Lewis.

"It's something new," he finally said, leaning back in the rocking chair, gaze fixed on the canvas. "It's intense . . . filled with secrets . . . speaks to me of someone who has experienced hardship . . . it's dark, yes, but the eyes . . . they're spellbinding. Challenging." He removed his toothpick and with a flick of his fingers sent it flying into the underbrush. He met her eyes. "It captures the spirit of someone who refuses to give up."

A warmth filled her chest. No wonder she returned to Victor again and again. He understood what she had tried to convey.

"Yes." In one long exhale, she emptied her lungs. "Thank you."

Then she ventured ahead and explained her hopes regarding Sinclair Lewis and his offer and that he left early. "At first, I did this so he'd be a patron and he'd send me to Europe. But then, when I took his challenge seriously, I painted it as honestly as possible."

Victor gave his head a slow shake. "Trinity, it's a reflection of you and what you're capable of."

"Yes, though I admit I am disappointed."

"You'll get to Europe," he said, tapping her knee with his forefinger. "One way or another."

"Victor, excuse me for being direct, but you don't have a paying job so I have to ask—"

He sat back. "I just sent three stories to *Boys' Life*. It's just a matter of time before I start getting published."

"Yes, that's great. I'm sure you will. But I have to ask. How are you going to Europe? I mean, the transatlantic voyage, lodging, and food. It adds up quickly. Do your grandparents fund your expeditions—this next trip?"

Victor crossed his arms and looked away toward the water.

She'd hit a nerve.

"Victor, I'm sorry. 'Money and religion.' The two things I've been taught to never bring up in conversation, but here I am, stranded in a family of wealth. I'm . . . I feel desperate to find a way forward. I thought if I knew how you managed it, then maybe . . ."

"I have a generous benefactor," he finally said. "Someone who believes in my mission. I'd tell you, but I'm sworn to secrecy."

"You're joking, right?"

"Not at all," he said, his tone serious, his eyes convincing.

"Bully for you," she said and meant it. If only she were so lucky.

He grasped her hands in his own. Warm and firm. He met her eyes. "To avoid any misunderstanding, there's something I have to say."

"Okay . . ." She swallowed. An infinity passed. As she waited for him to speak, old feelings flickered.

He squeezed her hands. "Trinity, I want you to know that I love you and have always loved you—as a friend. That's all I can offer you."

Heat rose up her neck to her cheeks.

Of course, she knew this.

She had always known this.

His words erased any measure of misguided hope or confusion.

She had struggled for so long with her feelings—she expected to burst into tears. But she didn't. To her surprise, she felt peaceful. Relieved. Clear about what she was to him, and what he was to her. In his presence she felt seen and heard. She always had. No wonder she'd wanted to share her self-portrait with him. No wonder she felt she could be vulnerable with him. He'd always accepted her as she was.

A safe harbor.

"Thank you," she said. She kissed him lightly on his cheek. "I needed you to be honest. That's more than enough."

28

THEY ARRIVED MIDAFTERNOON in the Larssons' speedboat, cut their speed, and drifted into a wall of hot, humid
air. Trinity hopped out after Gizelle and joined her on the
Ranier dock.

With each step away from the lake and into the village,
Trinity's stomach tightened. She felt a nameless sort of dread
and didn't know why. *Breathe,* she told herself. She was out
of practice being in public, that was all. Circuses were meant
to be fun. Besides, Gizelle had begged her to join them. And
now she took comfort in knowing she had made plans to
meet up with Sadie, too, at the big show.

As Bruno strutted down the dock ahead of them in
his straw fedora and ivory suit, he called over his shoulder,
"Meet you gals at the show! I have a little business to attend
to first."

"That's code," Gizelle said, linking her arm with Trinity's,
"for finding himself a stiff drink."

"I figured," Trinity replied.

Every year, the Robinsons' Touring Circus train arrived
at night and was miraculously set up the next day like mush-
rooms after a rain.

Nickelodeon music played in the distance, the smell of
grilled sausages floated on the air, and one voice climbed
high and squeaky above all others: "Popcorn! Get your salted
popcorn!"

Locals glanced or stared as Trinity and Gizelle strode past Erickson's Fine Grocery and the trading post. At the extra attention, Trinity noticed a change in Gizelle, who pushed her shoulders back and slowed her stride to a saunter. She walked more slowly, one pointed shoe in front of the other, her hips swaying.

"All the world's a stage . . . ." Lines from Shakespeare popped into Trinity's head. It had been several years since she had memorized them in high school.

> *All the world's a stage,*
> *And all the men and women merely players;*
> *They have their exits and their entrances;*
> *And one man in his time plays many parts . . . .*

Gizelle took her starlet role quite seriously. And what of herself? What role was she playing now? Wealthy daughter of Major Baird? Artist? Recovering asylum inmate?

"Did you forget your hat?" Interrupting Trinity's thoughts, Gizelle wagged her forefinger at her own cloche hat, perfectly matched with her sequin-covered violet dress.

"Intentionally, yes," Trinity replied, grateful to be *sans* hat and that she'd chosen her featherweight sleeveless sheath. Mother would approve of the buttercup yellow color, but she would be aghast to see one of her daughters in public without a hat or stockings. On a hot, sticky, steamy day in July, it seemed to Trinity the only sane way to dress.

In the field beyond the train depot, small tents and wagons flanked a huge tent. The towering expanse of white canvas soared into a deep blue sky, tethered to the earth by ropes and wooden spikes.

"It's a marvel!" Trinity laughed, remembering her family's early tent-raising disasters on the island. "How on earth do they hoist up that monstrosity?"

"Elephants!" Gizelle said with a clap of her hands. "Oh, I love it! A little city has shot up overnight! Honestly, it's not so very different from a Hollywood set!" Then she sashayed her way to a circus wagon displaying colorful silk scarves, feathered boas, and dazzling costume jewelry.

Trinity joined her, but she was more keen on seeing Sadie than buying trinkets.

After Gizelle paid for a gold-fringed scarf and wrapped it around her waist, they roamed the circus oddities, paying pennies to enter freak show tents: the Hairiest Man, the Fattest Woman, the Tallest Man, the Genius Boy (who could add in his head any numbers the audience shouted to him), the One-Eyed Cyclops.

One girl no older than twelve sat in a chair, barefooted, with her legs extended. On closer examination, she had six toes on each foot and six fingers on each hand. The banner above her stated Spider Girl. She read a book the whole time and never looked up.

Oddest of all—the Siamese Twins. Ageless, somewhere between eighteen and thirty-eight, they wore one big dress and sat in a faded loveseat. Four legs and four feet in sandals. But where they should have been separate, their shoulders merged grotesquely.

Trinity raised her hand.

"Yes?" said one twin, with a raspy voice, her hair dyed bright red.

"What do you do when you need a break from each other?" She knew it sounded wrong, like a joke, but she hadn't meant it that way at all. She'd imagined sharing a body with RuthAnne—and the thought made her skin crawl. "You must get in fights sometimes, yes?"

The other's voice was softer and seemed to match her mousy brown pigtails. "Never," she said.

"Always!" said the redhead.

Then they went into a rapid-fire act, and Trinity realized they had heard this question countless times before.

"My favorite color is blue," said one.

"Horsefeathers!" said the other. "No, no, no. Yellow!"

"I prefer hot dogs with mustard, no ketchup."

"Yuck! Bluck! I hate ketchup. Mustard and relish, thank you very much!"

Gizelle laughed and Trinity winced. She knew too well what it was like to wake up as one patient in a room with a hundred white beds, never to open your eyes and find yourself alone.

"But there's one thing we agree should be changed," Pigtails said, turning serious, and whispered, "The 'Ugly Laws.' Anyone with deformities is required to stay home, hidden away from public view—except in cases such as this. Entertainment."

Trinity raised her hand again. "That's wrong. What if you refuse to stay hidden at home?"

Pigtails replied, "Then off to the poor farm or workhouse. Never to be seen again."

"That's right," Redhead added. "Folks, away from the circus, my sister and I would be thrown in jail and fined for showing up in public."

"Makes sense to me!" shouted a teenager behind Trinity. "You make me want to puke!" He and his friends laughed.

Redhead pushed on as if she hadn't heard. "Maybe those laws should be changed. But that's all we dare say," she said quietly, then belted out, "because—the show must go on!"

Trinity clapped the loudest of all. The twins were funny *and* serious. They were malformed, and they were brave and determined.

When Trinity left their small tent, she felt deeply moved as she walked alongside Gizelle. Humbled. More aware of her own two healthy legs that carried her step by step, wherever she wanted to go. More aware that she'd been born with a fair face and a physically able body, though she'd done nothing to earn her physical form, any more than the two sisters had earned being joined inexplicably together. More aware that she'd been born into a wealthy, educated family—and all that came with it—but could have, with an equal roll of fate's dice, been born into poverty. Before, like many, she had mistaken who she was for those outward trappings. But when everything was stripped away at Oak Hills—not all at once, but day by day—she had come to understand she was none of those outward things.

She was a wisp of energy.

A soul.

A flickering light.

She drew air deeply into her lungs. If those sisters could speak out for their rights, she most certainly could fight for her own.

The sun burned hot as a crowd formed into a line outside the big tent. Trinity waited, keeping a lookout for Sadie. Light danced on the bay beyond the lift bridge, where Rainy Lake flowed into Rainy River. With no plans of setting soon, the sun hung high to the west above the Canadian shore.

"Trinity! Over here!" In a summery straw hat, Sadie waved from beside a lemonade stand.

When Sadie eased into the line, the Larssons turned around to greet her. "Ah, Sadie Worthington!" Bruno said, his breath boozy. "The more the merrier!"

Trinity noticed a certain fatigue behind Sadie's gray eyes and asked, "How are you?"

"Other than tired—" she replied, inching forward with the moving line. "I mean, all morning and into the afternoon I tried to teach kids who just wanted to escape my efforts and go outside to play. Can't blame them on a hot summer day."

"Owen?" Trinity asked under her breath.

"Oh, it's still so strange with him." Sadie looked away with a sigh, then turned and whispered in Trinity's ear. "I can barely get him to speak to me when I go to buy butter and eggs. When I stop at the creamery, he hurries into the backroom. Lets his mother wait on me instead. It hurts!" She inhaled sharply. "I guess things change."

"Come out to the island when you can," Trinity said. She gave Sadie's fingers a squeeze. "You could swim and sun for a change."

"I'd like that."

When the line began to move again, Sadie linked her arm in Trinity's. "What would I do without you?"

Trinity smiled. "I'm the one forever indebted to you!"

Soon, they entered through the wide flaps of the big tent, leaving the ordinary world behind.

29

THEY SAT FRONT ROW, almost at the feet of the circus ring-master, his megaphone in hand. His black handlebar mustache was at sharp odds with his snowy white curls beneath his top hat. In polished black boots, black tails, and brocaded collar, he introduced trapeze artists and dog trainers, bareback horse riders, jugglers and clown acts. Sometimes there was one act, center show ring, and other times all three rings were filled with dizzying entertainment at the same time.

Through the show, Trinity shared appreciative glances with Sadie and Gizelle. Such a simple thing, being together, united by entertainment.

"Ladies and gentlemen," the ringmaster announced next. "Lion taming isn't for the faint of heart."

Trinity felt her enthusiasm wane, replaced by a sense of dread as the audience quieted down, and five lions and their trainer entered the center ring. At the command of his long whip, the trainer—a man in a buttoned vest, bowler hat, and mustache—sent the large cats trotting a wide circle around him.

"Please, everyone," the ringmaster said, his tone deathly serious. "Please be very quiet, and very, very still."

The audience hushed.

When a child's whimpers turned to wailing, the ring-master held up his hand, stopping the show. "Ma'am, for the safety of everyone, I ask that you step outside with your little one. No need to rush. Take your time. Come on back after the lions are safely returned to their cages."

A murmur of delighted worry floated up from the audience.

As the baby's cries faded away, the ringmaster continued, his voice lowered. "Now folks, these lions are from the wilds of Africa. They're as dangerous as they come. They're not your tame little house cat. No sir, good folks of Ranier, these lions are extremely unpredictable animals, and they'd just as soon eat you as entertain you."

Gasps filled the air. Then, with the ringmaster signaling toward the ring, the show resumed.

The lion tamer sent the lions into motion again, this time in the opposite direction. When he lifted his whip straight in the air, they all stopped and sat. With another flick of his wrist, the trainer motioned the lions to stretch out on their sides.

A hushed exclamation of marvel floated from the focused audience.

"But fear not," the ringmaster announced, "for we have with us today our highly skilled lion trainer, the one and only Edvard Ottofeldt the Third."

The man lifted his hat but kept his eyes fixed on the waiting lions.

Trinity wondered what kind of training it had taken to bend the will of these lions. She guessed they started with them as cubs, maybe from the wild, or, more likely, born on a circus train. They probably never had the chance to test their strength, to know how powerful they were. Why else would they submit? She watched the lions, wondering at what point they might fight back.

What would it take for them to snap—to refuse?

A three-foot round metal ring stood upright near the trainer. He touched the ring and it turned into a flaming circle of fire. At the command of his whip, he sent the lions walking around again and then stopped them on voice command. He pointed to the male with its shaggy mane, almost twice as large as the females.

The lion approached, its mighty head swaying with each step. Trinity realized that everyone was spellbound not by what was happening but by what they imagined might happen. What if the lion charged and ripped its trainer to shreds? It would be such a terrible sight, and yet . . . yet it could happen. It might happen. The powerful was under the control of the weaker creature. She guessed that she wasn't the only one in the audience, at some primitive level, who wanted to see the lion rise up and take down its trainer. There would be some justice in it for robbing these wild creatures of their dignity, their willpower. But in reality, what good would such a tragic event serve? The lions wouldn't run off into the wild. They'd be shot on the spot.

And then it came to her. She had never truly known her own power until she left the asylum. The unwanted late-night visits to her edge of the women's wing had forever changed her. She'd felt powerless when Twitchy Eye woke her with his hand pressed over her mouth. Some nights she didn't sleep at all, expecting every footstep or creaking door to be him. The first time she'd tried to stop him from touching beautiful Marta: Trinity had flown to his back, arms around his neck trying to pull him away. But he'd swiftly grabbed and twisted her hands, dropped her to the floor, and pressed his pocket-knife to her throat. "Patients that attack staff," he whispered in her ear, "they *never* get out. Think about it. Your friend might be released soon, but not if I claim that she attacked *me.* So this is our secret. I'm not going to hurt her. I only want to touch her tits."

Their beds were side by side and next to the closest door. When he took weekly liberties with Marta, Trinity coped by focusing her imagination on every cove and mossy crag of the island. Stroke by stroke. Breath by breath. With each motion at Marta's bedside, one hand fondling her breasts, the other down his pants. Trinity wanted to kill him. But he held all the power, and she could not do something that might commit herself or Marta to a guaranteed life sentence. Enraged, she smoldered beneath the surface, day after day, week after week.

The day of Marta's release, just as Trinity was looking on, Twitchy Eye had the nerve to wish Marta well, clasping her hand in his own. Trinity wanted to knee him between the legs. Would have, if she could have gotten away with it, to prevent him from molesting others. But she wouldn't serve time for attacking him. No, on the day of her own release, papers in hand, she delivered a sealed letter to the superintendent detailing the assaults and dates. Whether justice was served, she would never know. But she vowed to never, ever again be victim to someone else's power, no matter its form.

IN THE CENTER RING, at the trainer's command, the lion loped the outer ring, flicking the end of its long, tasseled tail in protest, fear, or, Trinity guessed, both. The lion approached the burning ring—the very thing its instincts told it to avoid and flee, the very thing that might end its life. It slowed its approach for a moment, and Trinity cheered silently that it would refuse. But she knew this was its routine, performed show after show. She watched as the lion gathered its legs and bounded through the ring of flames, outwardly unscathed.

As the audience broke into wild applause at the feat, her heart broke for the creature as the lion trainer sent it and the other lions one more time around the ring, then down the corridor into their cages. Doors shut, a handler made a show of feeding the lions hunks of red meat from tongs through cage bars.

The audience went wild with approval.

"Wasn't that amazing?" Gizelle clapped and turned to Trinity with a broad smile.

"Mmmm." Trinity wanted to share her enthusiasm, but she couldn't.

"And next up," the ringmaster boomed, "we bring you the most magnificent and exotic creatures on Earth! All the way from Asia! You guessed it, folks, everyone's favorite! Amazing Alphonse and his exotic elephants!"

The audience cheered, whistled, and clapped.

Trinity felt light-headed. Her stomach pinched. She couldn't watch anymore. She couldn't bear to watch beautiful, intelligent elephants go through their crowd-pleasing antics. True, she had thrilled to see them as a young girl. They'd inspired her countless imaginary adventures. But now, watching felt entirely different. She knew what was coming. The elephants, atop round balls, would prove their incredible ability to balance. The elephants, with their own high level of intelligence, would be made to bow. And at the end, for a price, they would pose for photographs with fans.

At what price to these creatures? Before she realized she'd made a decision, she stood up.

"Trinity?" Sadie asked. "Are you okay?"

"I need fresh air," she said, knowing she had no intention to return.

"Oh, but this is the grand finale," Gizelle protested. "Okay. But let's all meet up after at the White Turtle Club!"

As Trinity walked along the dirt floor and the front row, past kids and adults, she glanced back over her shoulder. Leading the elephants, a man with a long braid and purple billowing pants held a pole in the air. On its caped head, the elephant at the front of the line carried a young woman, both costumed in creations of shimmery pink and purple silks.

Then she found her way out of the canvas flap doors into the soft rays of early evening.

For a moment she felt stunned. She wrapped her arms around herself, waiting for her hearing to return, for her vision to adapt to the light as a dozen white pelicans circled above the bay.

30

WHILE THE AUDIENCE CHEERED inside the big tent, circus workers milled about outside. They smoked cigarettes. Walked dogs. Stretched muscles. Watered horses. Fried sausages. Played cards. Chatted between booths.

Trinity ducked under a tent rope and wandered past a Test Your Strength pole as two teenage boys challenged their muscles with a mallet.

She roamed, ending up at railroad tracks and the incredible length of the circus train. It was a whole city on wheels. She wondered at the folks who had chosen to live life on the rails. But had they chosen it? She supposed some had, a dream born of seeing a circus come to their own little town. But she guessed for others—the freak show performers, for instance—that working in a circus was one of the only options available. If not the circus, then a life in the shadows, hidden away from public view.

She watched her footing for manure of every sort: camel, hippo, horse, elephant, dog . . .

A flash of yellow dashed by—a blur of sparkling performance outfits—the family with five girls from the high-wire trapeze act. They talked among themselves, speaking a language she didn't recognize, and climbed into a train car.

Home, she guessed.

So much of life—for better or worse—was set from

birth. For the yellow-clad daughters, as naturally as picking apples off a tree, they attempted death-defying stunts in the air. It was what they knew. So much of her own life, too, was predetermined. But now something had shifted; she was like a paper fan, starting from its handheld base, but with any luck fanning out into countless possibilities.

The idea gave her hope.

At the train engine, its nose pointed south to forests and clear-cuts beyond, she turned back, just as the big tent emptied. The crowd poured out like ants, crisscrossing between small tents and vendors. She kept an eye out for Sadie and Gizelle.

At the dart throw tent, a boy shouted, "A bull's-eye takes the prize!"

"Try your luck at a game of chance!" called another vendor.

At a weight lifting tent, with a wooden crate of stuffed animals, a man sang out, "Show her what you got! Beat the record, if you can! You don't want your sweetheart to leave here empty-handed!"

As quickly as it had sprung up, the circus would be gone. Workers would begin striking the big tent. By nightfall, the train would pull away. And at that point, Trinity didn't want to find herself stranded with no way back to the island.

AS GIZELLE HAD SUGGESTED, Trinity headed to the White Turtle Club, a two-story clapboard building on Main Street. She entered the lobby and passed under the stuffed moose head leading into the nearly empty restaurant.

The owner greeted her from behind the soda fountain. "I think you'll find them through here, Miss Baird," he said, motioning her to join him behind the counter. As she did, he opened the half-door to the bustling blind pig. "Watch your head, now," he said.

She suddenly paused. "Do you need another waitress?" she asked, surprised at her own bluntness. But when you start seeing life filled with possibilities . . .

"You're certainly not wanting to . . . I mean, you're asking for someone else, right?"

Heat spread across her face. "No, I'm asking for me."

He squeezed her forearm gently and whispered in her ear. "Miss Baird, I think folks would feel uncomfortable with you working here, taking their orders. Everyone knows *Trinity*, the grandest boat on Rainy Lake."

"Yes, of course," she said, her fan closing to half its width.

Phonograph music filled the room, along with countless patrons, both local and from the circus. She'd been there only once before—last summer during her week back, after their day at Kettle Falls. Victor had ordered soda. Henry had put away several drinks that day but still managed to be well-spoken. She and Sadie each ordered a gimlet.

"Trinity!" Bruno bellowed from a booth. "Have a seat," he said, sitting directly across from Gizelle and Sadie. He patted the space beside him. All she could visualize was his strutting around in his bathing suit, trying to steal kisses. "Or do I scare you?"

"*Ishkabibble.* Scooch over," she told him, and when he did, she sat at the booth's edge.

Gizelle continued chatting over her shoulder with one of the trapeze artists at the adjoining booth. "No, no. I'm originally from Singapore," she said with a flirtatious smile to the man who had changed out of costume but left on his mascara and eyeliner.

Trinity didn't correct her. Gizelle had once confessed to being born to a working-class family in a tiny coal-mining town in Pennsylvania. "I reinvented myself for the stage," she'd once complained.

Well into storytelling and drinking, Bruno had managed to scoot closer. When Trinity felt his leg slide up against her own, she jerked her leg away and turned to him, pointedly. "Why, Bruno, I think you mistook my leg for Gizelle's!"

"Oh, I'm terribly sorry," he said, reaching across for Gizelle's hand as she shot him a scolding glance.

"My turn," Gizelle said, then slipped from the booth and took the small empty stage. In a smoky-sweet voice, she announced, "Wild ladies and not-so-gentle gentlemen, I give you last year's third most popular hit!" And then she began to sing out:

> Every morning,
> Every evening,
> Ain't we got fun?
> Not much money,
> Oh, but honey,
> Ain't we got fun?
> The rent's unpaid, dear,
> We haven't a bus.
> But smiles were made, dear,
> For people like us.
> In the Winter, in the Summer,
> Don't we have fun?
> Times are bum and getting bummer.
> Still we have fun.
> There's nothing surer:
> The rich get richer and the poor get children.

She belted out the last lines:

> In the meantime,
> In between time,
> Ain't we got fun!

As customers clapped and whistled, Gizelle took a bow and then returned to the booth, reclaiming her seat across from her husband.

"What a voice!" Sadie said.

Bruno beamed. "That was wonderful, my darling!" he

said, reaching across the table for Gizelle's hand. But she pulled her hand away.

"Another round!" Bruno declared.

Another kind of circus, Trinity thought. Gizelle pretended a different past, pretended their life was wonderful, pretended not to see her husband's antics and yet punished him at the same time.

"Excuse me," a waiter said, stopping abruptly at their table. He looked directly at Gizelle "Ma'am, I need to alert you—your train is leaving soon!"

Throwing her head back, Gizelle laughed.

"Oh, silly, I'm not with the circus. I'm from Hollywood!"

The waiter blushed, begged forgiveness, and backed away, as if leaving the presence of an exotic queen.

Trinity met Sadie's eyes and grinned, pretty sure they shared a similar reaction. Where does the circus end and real life start?

Sometimes it's hard to tell.

IT WAS WELL ON to two in the morning when they finally left the White Turtle. Before heading to the dock, they walked Sadie home past the community building and attached jail to the Worthingtons' home. The lights were few in the two-story home, and though Trinity had spotted Sadie's adoptive parents in the crowd earlier, she guessed they had long ago gone to bed.

"Are you sure you can captain your boat, Mr. Larsson?" Sadie asked quietly at her gate. "I'm sure Hans would be willing to pilot your boat." Hans was her grandfather and Aasta was her grandmother; caretakers for the Worthingtons, they lived in their own small house in the village.

"Oh no, no, no!" Bruno said, tottering and batting away her concern, as if it were a bothersome mosquito. "I am s'perb . . . subpurb . . . superb!"

Trinity wished he would accept the offer. He really was in no condition to pilot a boat, darkness or not.

In boisterous song, he linked arms heavily with Trinity and Gizelle, steering them away and back toward the village docks.

Clear sky had turned to clouds, without moon or star to help guide them. As they set off in the cigar-shaped speedboat, Gizelle sat in the front with Bruno, and Trinity crawled back to the bench seat and stretched out under a wool blanket.

If anyone else was driving, she would have given over to sleep. But she struggled to stay awake—the ache in her head reminding her she should have refused that last drink—and every few minutes she forced her eyes open, trying to see where they were on the channel. Despite the boat's running lights, she was cocooned in near darkness. She squinted, trying to make out the shoreline. A pine tree, a jutting point of land, but on second look she saw only blackness. How in the world was Bruno not crashing upon shore or rocks scattered below the surface that lay outside the channel's safe path?

The motor hummed her to sleep, and she woke with a jolt that sent her flying onto the boat's floor. A crunching, grinding sound followed.

"Shit! Shit! Shit!" Bruno yelled from his wheelhouse. "What the hell did we hit?"

Trinity scrambled to her feet, disoriented. The boat. Water. It was late. They'd come to a sudden stop. She made her way to the bow. "Gizelle?"

"Hmmm?" Gizelle muttered from under her blanket.

The sound of water came from every direction. She willed herself to see, and gradually her eyes adjusted. They were in the middle of a large body of water. Sand Bay, she guessed.

A spraying sound of gushing water.

"Life jackets!" she shouted. "Where are they?"

Bruno wagged his head. "Oh God! Gizelle insisted they

needed cleaning. We were in a rush to leave. Shit, shit, shit!"

"What? None?" she said.

A loon sang, its flutelike call eerily echoed by another loon, and another, their voices growing into a tremulous chorus.

31

IN THE PREDAWN GRAY LIGHT, the Larssons' speedboat listed. Its motor had stopped working. Trinity held her legs to her chest on the bench seat, avoiding the water rising on the boat's floor. The source of their middle-of-the-night collision became evident. Off the bow floated a vast expanse of logs lassoed by a boom of chained logs.

Bruno shot off a flurry of curses. "How did I know there'd be a damn log drive!"

It was a tugboat's job to usher a massive boom of logs down the lake to the mill. Trinity didn't see one anywhere. "Where's the tugboat?" she exclaimed.

As a shaft of red light dawned in the east, a strong breeze picked up from the west. It pushed logs eastward, opposite the direction the lake usually flowed.

And they were near an island. She spotted the windmill at its peak, its arms whirling in the stiff wind. *Her island,* she realized with relief, Baird Island, getting her bearings more and more in the increasing light.

She took in the situation with alarm. The strong westerly wind drove everything east, including the logs, which threatened to engulf and swallow their water-filled boat.

"We need to swim to shore!" she called. "It's not that far. You can both swim, can't you?"

Gizelle shook her head. "No! Not a lick."

Bruno added, "I'm no good over my head."

Trinity had to think. "Then stay, hang on to anything that floats. I'm going to get help."

She stepped onto the gunwale. She couldn't risk diving headfirst and hitting a submerged log, so she jumped in. As she surfaced, the enormity of the situation hit her. She had to get help or this could all end badly.

Waves rolled and crested white, higher than she'd expected, and she took in a gulp of water along with air. She choked but kept paddling, arm over arm, trying to outrun the wind. With each breath and turn of her head, she sputtered, but she found a rhythm and kept at it, stroke by stroke to the shoreline rising and falling from view.

The Larssons sounded their boat horn. *Wonk-wonk-wonk-wonk-wonk!*

Over and over again.

Bruno had tried it right after their collision with no luck. At least it was working now.

The emergency alert would surely wake up someone on Baird Island. Now, as her feet hit the sandy bottom of the strip of beach, she spotted someone on the island's leeward side, disappearing into the boathouse.

As she dragged herself ashore, she spotted George at the helm of a fishing boat as it tore out of the boathouse.

Thank God.

He'd heard the horn.

Gasping, trying to catch her breath, Trinity pressed her hands to her knees and coughed up water. When she glanced over her shoulder, only the bow of the speedboat was still above water. The couple clung to it and each other. A pocket of air, Trinity guessed, was the only thing keeping them afloat, but it could go under any second.

The fishing boat rounded the island's southern half and zoomed into view from the channel. George pulled alongside the speedboat and motioned for them to jump in his fishing boat. But the couple gripped each other, unmoving.

Shivering and wet, Trinity shouted, "Jump!" But her words were lost on the icy wind.

Seconds felt like forever as she watched.

At last the couple leapt, tumbling into the fishing boat. Without a moment's hesitation to let them upright themselves, George swung the boat's tiller and sped away from the encroaching logs and back toward the channel.

Mere seconds later, the speedboat's bow slid below the surface.

With each white-crested wave, the wind-driven logs closed over the spot and rolled closer and closer to the shore.

THE BEACH BUSTLED with activity that morning. News traveled fast around the lake, and boats showed up in all sizes, with some passengers gawking, others offering help.

A local newspaper reporter arrived by boat to interview Trinity and the Larssons about their near-fatal disaster. They gathered in the living room around a freshly set fire in the hearth. "I hear it was a close call," the reporter said, prompting them as he took out a pencil and notepad.

Grateful for a dry change of clothes, Trinity held Lou in her lap, happy for her warmth.

In true starlet fashion, Gizelle dramatically placed the back of her hand to her forehead. "Oh, my heart is still jumping. Had it not been for Trinity, who swam so bravely for shore to get help . . ." She winked at Trinity, as if acknowledging she was taking creative liberties with the story. "Without her efforts, we would surely be at the bottom of Sand Bay, along with our boat. But the Baird family's caretaker, George, arrived by boat to rescue us seconds before our own boat went under."

Bruno's eyes were bloodshot, his eyelids puffy. When asked about the loss of his boat, he said, his voice raw with emotion, "The boat's insured and I intend to order up another just as soon as possible. We're grateful to be alive. It's people you can't replace." He leaned to Gizelle and kissed her square on the lips.

"Bruno," Gizelle cooed, then she stood up. "A photo?"

Before they left, Gizelle perched herself on one of the logs recently driven ashore, her skirt skimming her crossed legs, head back.

Everyone was gathered on the beach talking when E. W. Ennis showed up in a cruiser in his usual three-piece suit. From his towering height he gazed around him, standing stately as an emperor. A shorter man joined him and followed Mr. Ennis as he marched up the dock.

"Heard about the problem," he said. "Sorry my logs escaped and landed on your shore. We need to get photos for documentation."

The Major replied, "You mean you're worried we might steal your logs and build something before you can recover each and every one of them?"

"Ah, Mr. Baird," Mr. Ennis replied. "I'd never be so bold as to insinuate such a thing. But it's done, from time to time, as you well know."

Father met his gaze, waiting him out.

"Apparently," Mr. Ennis continued, "the tugboat lost engine power late yesterday and had to be pulled to shore for repairs. But she'll be back out here anytime, along with a crew, to clear logs from your shore and get this boom heading downstream again."

With relief, Trinity watched the island clear one by one of visitors, including the Larssons, with their own brand of craziness.

Of all the retellings of what had happened, of all the questions the reporter had asked, no one had inquired or offered information—including herself—about Bruno Larsson.

Darkness and log-boom aside, he'd been drunk as a skunk.

He should never have taken out the boat.

And she'd been a fool to climb in.

It was all part of the game they played day after day in high society, called Everything's Swell.

32

FEET FIRM on the rowboat's wooden floor, Trinity sat tall, gripped the oars, and pulled, working the muscles in her back, her torso, her arms and thighs. Stroke by stroke, she rowed. It felt wonderful to leave the island—to circle it, see it from another perspective. As weeks went by, she had felt the need for more space. She set off in the rowboat every afternoon, unless the winds were too strong, and rowed around the island.

The lake went on forever, never fully knowable, and dotted with islands more numerous than could be mapped. Yet one island was hers. She knew every inch of it as if it were a living being.

A lover.

A beloved friend.

She always brought her sketchbook, pausing to drift and capture the curve of a cedar leaning over the water. Once, she rowed to the east, far enough to see the island from a distance. It was a thin strip of land rising out above the waters of an immense lake. So small and insignificant in the grand scheme of things. And yet it was the center of her universe. No matter what she envisioned for her future, it was always there. The place she hoped to always return to, as certain as an eagle returns to its nest.

One evening when Victor and Margaret joined them for

fresh walleye fried in a skillet, plus boiled potatoes, green beans, and pickled carrots, Mother set down her fork and studied Trinity from across the table.

"What?" Trinity said. "Do I have something on my face?"

"Your arms, actually," Mother said, concern between her brows.

Trinity looked at her left arm, then her right, wondering if she was erupting in a rash from poison ivy. Bare to the shoulder in the dress she'd chosen for dinner, she didn't notice anything wrong, other than her arms were more suntanned than was the fashion. But she didn't care. She had heard the same concern from Mother for years, that "ladies who enjoy the privilege of servants" must avoid too much sun, lest they look like they are of the working class.

"All this rowing," Mother said. "Your arms are showing a bit of muscle, a little too masculine."

At that, Trinity laughed out loud.

Victor cleared his throat, unsuccessfully trying to cover his chuckle.

RuthAnne tilted her head and peered closer at Trinity's arms.

Trinity decided to play along. She bent her right arm at the elbow, flexed her muscle, and pinched her bicep. "Look! You're right. It *is* a muscle, though rather puny compared to Victor's."

"He paddles all the time," Margaret said with pride. "And he's always chopping wood."

RuthAnne added with a snort, "Yes, plus he's a man."

"True," Mother said, "but I just don't think women need to try to be something they're not. What's the point?"

"Mother," Trinity said, "even if current fashion emphasizes thin arms, I see absolutely no harm in a few muscles. I'm not about to give up rowing." She smiled. "In fact, I rather like the idea of challenging Victor to an arm wrestle. If I win, I will admit to becoming too muscular. I will cease and desist my rowing trips around the island. But if he wins, then I will continue, proving that I am still a member of the weaker sex. And though I may be of the weaker, with each day that passes we grow stronger."

"Yes!" Father chimed in jovially. "Clear the table! Let's begin!"

Margaret lifted her forefinger. "Not until we taste my German chocolate cake."

Victor winked. "Ah, yes. I may need the extra strength."

Trinity enjoyed the lightness in the air. Even Mother seemed amused.

After dessert and the table was cleared, Trinity sat at one corner of the table and Victor sat kitty-corner. Sleeves rolled just above his elbows, his forearms were well-hewn and deeply tanned.

Father stood between them and held a white handkerchief above the floor.

Trinity locked hands with Victor, certain he could crush hers in his own if he was so inclined. He was stronger, and she appreciated that over the years he'd never discouraged her from activities deemed in the domain of men. It was Victor who had taught her to dive and later taken her to towering cliffs on the lake and jumped with her into the lake below. And it was Victor who had taught her how to send sparks from flint and steel to a small bit of birchbark to start a fire.

Father announced, "When I drop this, begin."

Victor met her eyes.

She grinned. "Let's see who is the stronger."

The handkerchief dropped.

Victor yielded to Trinity's strength, his arm giving way and dropping lower and lower to the table.

"Victor, stop pretending!" Mother said, no doubt worried about what it would mean if her daughter won the arm-wrestling contest.

"He's not pretending," Trinity said. "He's growing weaker by the second!"

And as his hand hovered above the table, Trinity put her full strength into her effort, relishing the momentary illusion of power, and this time he pushed back.

She gritted her teeth and did her best to throw him off.

Slowly, slowly, he lifted her hand up with his own and then over to the other side of the table. When Trinity's hand touched down, giving way to Victor, Mother cheered. "I knew he was stronger!"

"If I'm ever to be stronger," Trinity joked, with mock disappointment, "I'll need to keep rowing!"

ONE MIDAFTERNOON, as she returned to the boathouse from rowing and secured her lines around the dock cleats, George entered with his fishing boat. Oblivious to her on the opposite side, he cut his motor, tied up, and gathered a few belongings, including the gray bag they used for delivering and collecting their mail from the post office. He climbed the wooden ladder and walked out into the sunlight onto the dock.

It was strange, because since she had arrived on the island, she'd watched for any sign of mail addressed to her. She'd expected to receive an answer from the university by now. With every passing day, the chances increased of hearing . . . something. Yet neither had she received a reply from her letter to Marta nor to her three letters to Max. Every day she'd asked George if there was mail for her. Always the same answer. Nothing. It made her feel like she'd died, become a ghost, and had stopped existing in the real world. But today he returned with a mailbag that definitely carried mail.

Her heart leapt up and she hurried out of the boathouse and found him on the yacht. His back was turned as he fiddled with the lock on the large wooden toolbox, just behind the wheelhouse.

"George?" she asked.

He jumped and the mailbag tumbled off the toolbox to his feet as he spun toward her, a key in his fingers. "Trinity! You startled me."

He sat down a little too promptly on the toolbox, pulled the mailbag on his lap, almost cradling it. "Can't go scaring an old fella like that," he said, meeting her eyes. "I'm likely as not to have a heart attack!"

"Sorry," she said, her suspicion growing that something was not as it should be. Why was he acting so furtive, as if he needed to hide something? "Didn't mean to scare you, but I was wondering if there might be some mail today—for me?"

"Haven't gone through it yet. I'll let you know."

"No," she said with a firm shake of her head. She hated to order him, but she had to see for herself. "Toss it here, George," she said. "I can look."

He hesitated, working his lips, as if his life—not the mail—hung in the balance, and with a nod, said, "Of course you can."

She caught the canvas bag with both hands, stepped back from the boat, and reached in. Along with the local newspaper, she pulled out a half-dozen envelopes.

Four were addressed to Major Baird and B&B.

One was for RuthAnne from an attorney with a return address in Illinois. Something to do with the divorce, she guessed.

And the next one—she could dance!—was from Max Bern and addressed to her. "At last!" she said, waving the letter over her head, then pressing it to her chest.

George dropped his voice. "Hush. I wouldn't say anything about that just now to your parents. You know how things were when Mr. Bern left the island."

She cocked her head. "Wait. George. So you knew it was in here?"

He shrugged. "Just guessed."

She knew he was lying, which wasn't something she had

ever suspected him of before. But she didn't want to take another minute for accusations.

She strode away and crossed the beach to where Lou was busy digging. "C'mon, Lou," she called. Tail wagging, Lou pulled her snout out of a fresh hole, her black nose covered in sand, and followed.

33

A DELICIOUS WARMTH spread through Trinity as she hiked up the path and over the slope to her studio. She'd written Max several times since his banishment—perhaps more than was proper—but she'd felt such an affinity with him, she was sure he wouldn't mind. Then the long, agonizing stretch without a word—it left her feeling unsure, off balance. She locked the door behind her, ready to savor his words without interruption.

A lilting breeze fluttered the cotton curtains. Trinity ran her brass letter opener along the envelope's edge, pulled out a single page, hand-written in a neat squarish print. She smiled to see his words penned in his own hand and read slowly:

Dear Trinity,

By writing this fourth and likely final note, I risk offending you.

Fourth? Had someone made sure his earlier correspondence hadn't reached her? Her chest tightened in anger and a sense of betrayal.

By now, your parents may have convinced you that I'm nothing more than a person of scurrilous character—in short, a scoundrel. But I assure you, to

*the depths of all that is good in me, I am not. The only
offense I admit to is not being forthcoming, for until
your mother asked about my family background,
the question never came up at my employment with
B&B. No, I would not have intentionally lied. But
neither did I put all my cards on the table with you.
So many people want to categorize others by race or
religion, and as I was completely under the spell of
your presence, I didn't want to risk telling you before
you had a chance to get to know me. I did withhold
the fact that I am Jewish, an omission I now regret.
Over the past many weeks I have given this topic
much thought, especially since you have decided
along with your parents not to communicate with
me again.*

Again she stopped reading. What was he talking about?
Was he implying that her letters had never reached him?
She burned with anger and swore. George was not going to
get by with this. He'd get a piece of her mind, in no polite
terms—later.

She read on:

*We live in fraught times. Modern life moves at a
startlingly fast pace, and I think as people look for
security, they try to control not only their own
lives but the lives of others in the process. That is a
generous way of looking at things. The other way is
to see men's hearts filled with greed, fear, and hatred,
as they make up their own rules in their own little
fiefdoms and corners of the world. How else can one
explain the terrible lynchings in Duluth?*

Trinity paused, startled by his turn in subject, his harsh
tone. She pressed her hand to her mouth, remembering. The
lynchings. They'd happened two years ago, about the same
time she was going through her own emotional crisis and
being sent away. The horrendous event had been mentioned

in the newspaper, but she'd somehow deflected it, as if it were too hard to think about. As if it were none of her concern. She was struggling to stay sane. And the news made no sense. Lynchings happened in the Deep South, not in Duluth—a northern city in a northern state. There was an unreality about the news back then, as well as her state of mind.

So why had Max brought this up? Was he trying to make a connection with Father, that he was another person of money, influence, and power making up rules about society? Father would never be part of a mob; he'd never stoop to such ghastly action. But he would certainly never hire someone with dark skin. Or intentionally hire someone who was Jewish. No, he would go about his prejudice in more invisible methods, such as hiring and firing.

How could she ever abide by her parents when she hated what they stood for?

"Damn it!!" she said aloud. The island was her sanctuary, her escape. She'd thought about her privileged world when she was at the circus and then left those concerns behind when she returned to the island. But now Max had forced her to look again at the underbelly of the elite with so much wealth, so much power. She was part of that world, she could admit that much. Not that she knew what she could do about it or about the feeling she now had of a knife twisting in her stomach.

For better or worse, she was waking up—becoming more aware.

She returned to Max's words.

Kind words.

Simple words.

And then his closing:

I wish you a bright and wonderful life. Though I admit I had entertained the idea of you in my future, I see now that it was a futile and fleeting dream. I could never marry into your family. My banishment from B&B and your island caused me to look inward

and rethink my faith and my ancestry. I am proud to
be Jewish, and I aim to one day marry someone who
can journey along this path with me.
With respect and admiration, I wish you well.

Yours truly,
Max

Trinity swallowed past the rising lump in her throat and set the letter on top of her dresser. She gazed at the open beams of her ceiling. A tumult of emotion passed through her—disgust, anger, horror, disappointment, loss, grief—and she felt overwhelmed by everything his words had stirred up.

Crushed by the weight of it all.

The loss of Max in her life . . .

The three men who were killed . . . and the criminal actions of the mob . . .

The senseless hatred toward others . . .

Her parents' ignorance and narrow-mindedness and bigotry . . .

She had never thought it concerned her, that she was too removed to care, that she'd always looked away . . .

A knot of anger formed in the hollow of her stomach. Trembling, she stepped to her easel, picked up a paintbrush, and gave herself to her art, throwing lines and shapes and colors on the canvas. With each bold stroke, each feathering, she sank roots deeper into earth, into rocky crevices for soil and water, for support and sustenance. With each stroke, she stretched beyond the moment—losing a sense of time and place and self.

It was her drug, her escape. "No, it's different," she whispered, adding a wisp of midnight blue. Painting was different. Rather than numbing herself to escape how she was feeling, painting allowed her to express her emotions. That's what Dr. Stratton had tried to help her understand. *What you feel won't kill you, but keeping your true feelings secret from yourself can do great damage.* As she painted, she allowed her aching pain, her disillusionment, to wash through her and over her like a mighty wave. She painted out of raw emotion.

When she finished, she was still there, standing. The emotions hadn't killed her. She had stayed with the wave rather than running from it.

She could almost hear Dr. Stratton challenging her thinking. *You seem to believe that your family needs you to always be cheerful, the light of the party.*

It was true.

She felt she needed to be strong for her mother, steady for her sisters, charming for her father. In her family's craziness, her role was to be the one who brought balance. But her breakdown had forced her to face her own weaknesses. *Ah, but don't you see? They're not weaknesses, Trinity. You are a complex human being with all sorts of emotions. When you are willing to feel anything, then the emotions can come and go, they can pass through you as they're meant to do. How else can you find out who you are if you're always running away from yourself?*

When the dinner bell rang, Trinity set her brushes in spirits, then stood back and gazed at her newest painting. It was unfinished but promising, filled with energy and a dramatic use of line and color.

34

TRINITY HAD ENOUGH SOCIAL TRAINING and decorum not to bring up a tinderbox issue at dinner, but afterward, when they set off for a sunset cruise, she chose her moment. As George idled the engine, and the sun sent shockwaves of red and orange across the horizon, Trinity rose from her cross-legged spot on the bow with Lou and returned to the wheelhouse.

At the stern, RuthAnne and Millie were seated laughing about who knows what, and the amber rays of the setting sun set their faces glowing. Let them enjoy themselves, Trinity thought. They weren't her focus. Trinity cleared her throat. "My letters," she said, addressing the other three. "Where are they?"

George stood beside the wheel, lighting a cigarette. Mother and Father sat on the bench seat, drinks in hand.

Mother looked to Father, who raised his eyebrows.

Father looked to George, whose face was flushing crimson.

No one said a word.

Trinity counted silently to three, giving them time to come forward. Then she rushed into summarizing how she'd found a letter from Max in the mailbag. "Not until I read that this was his fourth letter did I have any real suspicions. But now, I *demand* the others."

Mother sniffed and said, "We were trying to protect you."

"Protect me! By telling me who I can care for? That's not love, Mother. It's trying to control another person's life." She felt her anger churning, threatening to close off her throat like the time she mistook vinegar for apple cider. But she didn't want to be overwhelmed by her emotions and say something she might regret—or worse still, never say what she desperately needed to say.

She would not lose this moment. She collected herself and took one deep, long breath, then another. Damn right she was angry.

"We were left shaken after reading that first letter," Mother began, worrying her folded hands.

"I don't understand. So you read all his letters?" She felt a deep stab. "My letters? How could you?!"

"No, no, no!" Father said, waving his arms. "We didn't read any that came from Max. Just that one. From your roommate's parents."

"It was addressed to the parents of Trinity Baird," Mother added. "After we read it, we struggled with what to do. I worried that you weren't ready. We honestly didn't want it to upset you—and so we held off. And then when Max's letters kept coming, we told George to hide them in his toolbox. It probably wasn't right, we know that now, but—"

"Marta? Marta's parents?" She felt only slightly better that her parents hadn't read Max's words. But only slightly. "I want to see all the letters. I am not a child."

Mother clenched her hands on her lap. "She's dead."

Moments passed.

The words moved from Trinity's ears to her throat, now burning, and dropped into her chest, which seemed to seize up with a great and heavy weight. She imagined Marta's fine cheekbones, her rose-colored cheeks, her smile . . . as well as the troubles she had faced. Trinity felt unable to breathe. "God, no. Oh no! What happened?"

"Quite sad," Father said. "The letter was short. Apparently, they said it happened one week after your friend returned home. Suicide."

Trinity pressed her palms to her face. *One week.* She was still at the asylum when Marta had taken her own life. When she'd written her letter, Marta was already dead. She hadn't known. She should have been told. She spun out of the wheelhouse and toward the stateroom at the stern. Ruth-Anne looked up as Trinity approached. "I'm guessing they finally told you."

Trinity started down the short ladder, eye level with her sister. "You knew?" she yelled. "Why didn't you tell me?"

"I didn't think it was my place," RuthAnne said matter-of-factly, as if they were discussing a misplaced shoe.

"Unbelievable," Trinity said.

Lou stood on her back legs and stretched her paws to Trinity's chest, right where it hurt the most. At the touch, and Lou's gaze, Trinity crumpled with emotion. She lifted Lou down into the stateroom and closed the hatchway door behind them.

Trinity flopped onto the starboard bed. She buried her face into the down-filled pillow as the motor rumbled to life and the yacht turned back to the island, covering up her cries. Her whole being ached: her chest, her throat, her jaw, and every inch of her skin. She hurt all over. She turned to her side and Lou licked her arm before settling into the curve of Trinity's body.

It hurt so bad knowing that Marta had killed herself. It hurt that Marta's family would not believe their own daughter's words over those of a relative who had been abusing her for years. Trinity wanted to put a revolver to the molester's heart. And Twitchy's, too, who stupidly thought there was no harm in his only touching breasts. Poor Marta. Violation on top of violation.

Trinity squeezed her eyes shut, her forehead clenched in grief, and exhaled a low groan. The abusers were the ones who should be punished, the ones who deserved death. Not Marta.

The boat slowed, the motor went silent, and the murmur of fading voices told her that everyone was heading to bed for the night. "We'll just stay here," she whispered to Lou and pulled the covers up over them.

Dark settled and Trinity lay awake, held in the boat's slow and gentle rocking. Each spring, she reminded herself, George prepared the wooden vessel before launching. From September to May, *Trinity* sat in the island's larger boathouse to the north. She'd watched once, when they had arrived early one year. She had stood beside George as he showed her cracks between boards in the hull. "I bet you can put your finger through." And she did, amazed that wood so dry and shrunken could ever stay afloat. But he showed her the trick. "She needs water. Lots and lots of water," he'd said. He showed her how he'd rigged the DC battery to a lake pump and ran perforated garden hoses through the belly of the yacht—one starboard, one port—until water poured out of the cracks. He soaked the boat like that, off and on for two weeks, until every board swelled together. Then, and only then, was she ready to launch.

She ran her fingertip alongside the whitewashed boards, perfectly joined together. In her pain, she felt enveloped by the boat, by the water and air that surrounded it, by the earth and stars and the infinite beyond.

Marta was gone.

She would never see her again.

She ached for the stupidity of it all.

What a waste of an exquisite life.

35

RAVENS CAWED from overhead boughs. Chickadees called *dee-dee-dee* and robins sang out *cheery-oh, cheery-oh, cheery-up*. Ducks swam on the other side of the hull from Trinity's pillow, quacking as if one of them had just told the funniest joke in the world. Sunlight pierced through the small stateroom windows. Trinity opened her eyes, now fully awake, still in her clothes from last evening. The news settled in again, and she wished everything about the letters had been a dream. "Oh, Marta," she said out loud.

She sat on the edge of the bed, stood, and stretched, and then opened the hatchway to discover something atop the wicker table.

A thin stack of envelopes wrapped in white ribbon.

Lou whined on the bed, and Trinity lifted her onto the deck. Her dog soon leapt from the boat to the dock and away.

Trinity retrieved the letters and returned below deck. But before she read them, she set them on the bed, then turned to the small door off the stateroom. She used the tiny toilet, washed at the ceramic sink, splashing cool water on her face to tame her puffy eyes, and dried her face with the white monogrammed hand towel.

Before hanging it back to dry, she ran her finger over the embroidered letter. It irked her. She had never asked Father to single out her name for the yacht and have her initial stitched, stamped, or engraved on nearly every item aboard.

It felt somehow very much like the gift of Lou. It came with strings, but she never quite understood exactly what kind. But the strings were all the same, tying her to her parents in ways that she felt increasingly bound—and increasingly resentful.

SITTING ON THE EDGE of the stateroom bed, she slid out a scrap of paper wedged under the ribbon. It read:

> *I'm sorry.*
> *George*

She was still angry, but she pressed the note to her chest before setting it on the bed cover. She knew she couldn't stay angry at George forever.

Her heart drummed as she undid the knot holding the envelopes together. When it came free, she turned to the top envelope, already opened. She slid out the folded sheet of paper, opened it, and read the brief account from Marta's mother. A few lines jumped off the page:

> *. . . I must inform you that only one week after Marta was released and returned home to us, we lost her to this world. We are returning your daughter's letter to you, confident that you would agree, it would not have been healthy for two troubled young women to maintain a friendship once released from the asylum. We thought all was well with our daughter until the morning we found her hanging from our garage rafters. We had hoped she'd been cured of her hysteria. She's in God's hands now.*

Trinity's chest seized up as she grabbed the towel from the bathroom and held it to her face. She imagined Marta, taking this lonely action step by step. She forced herself to be there, to understand. She tied the rope, climbed to a chair, slipped it around her neck . . . then kicked away the chair. If only, if only, if only. She imagined the weight of Marta's body on a rope, too awful and sad for words.

Time passed and Trinity was left exhausted.

Empty.

Except for one question.

What really happened?

Had Marta taken her own life, or had the uncle silenced her from further accusations and made it look like suicide?

It was possible.

She would never know.

36

A DAY AND NIGHT PASSED in a haze before Trinity returned to the stack of letters. The envelopes from Max had not been unsealed, a small comfort in her anger that she had not been allowed, until now, to read them for herself. At least their contents were still private.

Max wrote about what they had shared—their love of art, their eye for natural beauty, their ease of being together, and their "Broadway dancing skills."

She smiled.

She read each page several times, felt his longing and loss, his letting go of her with each postdated letter. He'd sent his replies back to her and had waited for her to write in return, and she would have—if her parents hadn't blocked her from doing so. If he'd heard back from her, maybe that would have changed his mind about keeping the door open to a possible future. But no matter how things might have played out differently, she would never have been able to change her family or her parents and their narrow thinking. Their meddling and utter violation of her boundaries.

She felt like the ground had been pulled from beneath her feet.

Like a fish, slit open by a fillet knife.

She hurt with each inhale.

Eventually, she drew a level breath.

Here she was, still breathing, still inhabiting her own skin. And oddly, she knew exactly what she needed.

She stepped off the yacht onto the dock. Lou was on her side, stretched out in the sun against the boathouse.

"C'mon, Lou," Trinity said.

When they stepped into the kitchen's yeasty aroma, Trinity didn't have to say a word to explain what she needed.

Agatha looked up from kneading bread, her hands dusty with flour, and her eyes filled with concern. Wearing a red apron, she opened her arms wide and Trinity stepped into them.

"There now," Agatha whispered. "There now."

37

AGATHA SAT AT THE KITCHEN TABLE across from Trinity, a deck of cards spread out between them.

"I don't understand what they were afraid of," Trinity said, setting down a pair of Jacks. "Why hold back the letter to me from Marta's family?"

"May I speak my mind freely?" Agatha asked, a softness in her eyes.

"Please," Trinity said with a nod. "I'm so tired of my family withholding the truth, I could scream."

Agatha picked up another card from the center pile. "You know that night you took ill? The night you worried us all . . . and threatened to take your life?"

Memories of that night returned, traveling up her spine in a shudder. That night was a patchwork of memories, stitched together by too much booze, a string of too many sleepless nights, and frayed emotions. Was Agatha asking her to explain her behavior that night? If so, it was a long answer, one she still didn't fully understand. But she knew it had been triggered by circumstances, her age . . . *Hysteria* was far too simplistic a word and fell short of her experience.

But Agatha didn't seem to be asking for an explanation. She simply stated, "After that night, your Mother changed."

"Meaning . . . ?" Trinity said.

"She started acting, I don't know, different."

"How?"

"After you went away, it was like she was somewhere else much of the time. With an odd, vacant look."

The opiates, Trinity thought. Now the increased changes she had perceived in Mother made more sense.

Agatha continued, "I know that here on the island no one expects 'fancy' all the time, but she . . . she stopped dressing up. Not even at their last party here."

"I don't care how she dresses, but then why does she care how I dress? You know, she ordered Sadie to take me shopping before I set foot on the island."

Agatha snapped down three eights. "I think after that night she was consumed with worry about losing you. And when you returned last summer, she fretted the whole week you were here, worrying about when you all went to Kettle Falls, worrying that you were going to have another spell. When you went home for Christmas each year, how was she then?" Agatha wouldn't know, as she and George stayed north for the winter.

Trinity shifted in the kitchen chair and crossed her arms. "Fretful. Watched me like a hawk. But what you're saying makes no sense. I mean, if she was worried about me, why for God's sake did they force me to return to St. Peter?"

Agatha folded her hands in her lap. "I think in her mind it was her way to keep you protected."

Trinity groaned. "From what? Uh, uh. I don't buy it. That's not a way to show you care."

"I think you should know: Mr. Baird strongly protested your being sent away. But then Mrs. Baird had such fits, I think she scared him into siding with her." With that, Agatha glanced at the ceiling. "Perhaps I've said too much. What do I know?"

Trinity reached for Agatha's hands, warm and comforting in her own. "You know plenty! You know how to show you care. That's *everything*." On impulse, she jumped up from her chair and planted a kiss on Agatha's round cheek. "So there."

As she returned to her chair, the scent of ham filled the air and the tea kettle hummed as it heated on the stovetop.

"Agatha, tell me more about the fits."

Just then the kitchen door swung open and Mother stepped in, her face sallow and her hair in need of washing and brushing. She gave off an odor, as if she hadn't bathed in days. "Do you realize what time it is?" she said. "Playing cards when you should be prepping dinner?"

Agatha jumped up from the table, smoothed her apron, and quickly swept the cards into a deck and set them down. "Just a quick game," she said, heading to the stove, "while the ham bone simmered." She lifted the lid on the pot and stirred with a wooden spoon.

"It was my idea," Trinity said. "And I'll give Agatha a hand."

"No, no. You don't need to," Agatha said, waving her away.

"Hmph," Mother said as she turned on her heel and left.

Trinity wanted to help and busied herself cutting rutabaga, cabbage, and carrots at one end of the counter while Agatha sliced onions and garlic at the other. She happily took instructions on which knife to use and how thin or thick to cut the slices.

While they worked, bread baked, wafting its heavenly fragrance. Lou sat on a plaid blanket in the window seat, her nose aimed at rhubarb pies cooling on the counter.

"Thanks for telling me," Trinity said, glancing at Agatha.

"Tell you what?" Agatha looked up, as if she had no idea what Trinity was talking about, but then she winked and added under her breath. "It's not my place to ever say anything, you understand."

Trinity nodded. She understood that Agatha had shared her observations in confidence. She understood that being employed by Trinity's parents was as precarious a position as she found herself in as their daughter. And she understood, too, as crisp vegetables yielded to the sharp edge of her knife, that she could have stayed holed up in her studio or on the yacht, alone in her pain. She could have shown up for dinner and pretended she was fine when she wasn't. Maybe most important of all, she understood that asking for what she needed was the first step toward not feeling so alone.

BEFORE SITTING DOWN to dinner in the dining room, Trinity dashed off to her studio to wash her face, change into a dress, and feed Lou. When she returned with the letters in her satchel, she had resolved to ask for what she needed. But what was that exactly? After how they'd tromped over her rights and privacy, what did she want? There was nothing they could do to change the nature of Max's last letter or the fact that Marta was gone.

What she hoped for was simple.

An apology.

When the large ceramic bowls and bread plates were cleared and the last fork set down after the last bite of pie, Trinity cleared her throat. "I brought the letters," she said, reaching into her satchel and setting them out on the table, one by one.

Sitting side by side, RuthAnne and Millie looked on.

"Mother," Trinity began, "you told me earlier you were worried about my reaction if you gave me this letter—" She picked one up, showing the address and return address to her mother. "The letter from Marta's parents."

Emotion climbed into the back of her throat, burning. She swallowed her feelings, determined not to let them get in her way.

"Trinity, must you?" Mother said, pushing her chair back from her end of the table.

"I must," Trinity said. "Don't walk away. I need you to hear me. Please."

Mother started scratching the side of her neck, turning it red. "I'm listening."

"It's terrible, awful news about Marta, but I want and need to know the truth. You shouldn't have kept it from me." Her lower lip wobbled. "I'm not a little girl anymore. It was wrong to keep this letter from me—and the letters from Max."

"We thought it was for your own good," Father said, sitting taller.

Mother interrupted. "When that first letter arrived, I honestly didn't know if you could handle—"

"I can handle it," Trinity said, a little more vehemently than she wished. "I'm hurting. I'm angry. But I'm here, *handling* it."

Millie leaned into RuthAnne and whispered, "Should I go?"

RuthAnne reached for Millie's hand and set their clasped hands on the table. "Stay. You have every right to be at the table. You're more family to me than my husband ever was."

Millie's eyes widened, as if she'd rather bolt than wait for what might come next.

But RuthAnne sat rigid, her demeanor unapologetic, as if she knew exactly who she was and where she belonged.

So they *were* something more, Trinity realized. But what seemed plain as day now—that RuthAnne and Millie were lovers—seemed lost on her parents. Perhaps truth was always there. But you couldn't see it until you were ready.

"Trinity, I'm sorry. We shouldn't have kept the letters from you," Father said. "Forgive us, please."

She met his eyes and, in that moment, believed he was sincere. "I can forgive you that much, but how . . . how can I ever forgive you both for sending me away?"

"Forgive!" Mother spat out the word. "You make it sound as if we did something wrong—when we were only trying to protect you! Your time in St. Peter kept you from being promiscuous and ruining your chances of a decent future. You've always been strong-headed, willful, and impulsive. It was in your best interest. And now you're back. Safe. And you're better."

"Better," Trinity said. "And how is that?"

"To begin with, you're not testing us every step of the way! At least not to the degree you used to."

"It wouldn't be in my best interests, would it, Mother?"

"No, it would not."

"You seem to be doing quite well," Father said, forcing a cheery expression. And with a full and breathy exhale, he closed the discussion and stood up. "Time for my pipe."

One by one, Trinity watched them rise from their chairs and leave.

As she cleaned the last bits of sugary rhubarb syrup from her plate with the edge of her fork, she didn't feel any closer to what she needed. What had she accomplished?

A thin apology about the letters.

An entrenched defense about sending her away.

She sat a moment longer, wishing for something more.

Something solid.

Real.

True.

Something in her life, she admitted, her family could never be.

38

IT WAS A QUIET MORNING on the lake when a speedboat appeared from the north, slowing as it entered the bay. Trinity added a few more strokes to her watery landscape, then she wiped her brush on a cotton rag and stood up from the wooden folding chair.

Lou growled, having taken full ownership of the island as well as the role of Trinity's protective guardian. No one would get to Trinity without Lou's say-so.

"Lou, it's okay. It's a friend."

Lou started barking as the Catalina eased to a stop, all polished and glistening. It was well past the middle of summer, and Henry was not much tanner than when she'd first seen him in early June at Victor's island party. Every inch of his body was covered. His fedora kept the sun off his face, and his heather brown suit, though made of lightweight wool, blocked sunlight from every centimeter of his skin. "Time for a coffee break?"

"Sure." She had been putting in long hours at her easel the past few days. "But make friends with Lou first."

He sat at his steering wheel, one hand holding the edge of the dock. Lou sniffed his hand and then wagged her whole body.

"Looks like you passed inspection," Trinity said.

Henry lifted his hat briefly above his fair skin and pale

blue eyes. "Good to know." After securing lines, he stepped toward the easel and for a few moments didn't say a word. "I like what I see. The lake has so many moods."

"Yes."

"This one makes me feel calm. Say, there's a reason I stopped," he said, turning back. "I have a few design questions, and I wanted to run them past your architect."

"Max Bern," she said. "You haven't heard?"

"No. No, I didn't hear," he said, lowering his voice. "What happened?"

"My parents sent him away."

"Was there some kind of trouble?" he whispered.

She waved away his concern. "Don't worry about whispering. Father and George are fishing and Mother and Ruth-Anne are hooking rugs on the north porch." Then she went on to explain. "They said he was doing a splendid job until they found out he's Jewish."

"What? I thought your parents were more enlightened. Or at least I would have hoped so." He walked to the end of the dock, his silhouette narrow-shouldered, his body featherweight, and gazed out.

A dozen pelicans soared in low and, with wings stretched wide, landed one by one on the water. They floated in a flotilla of white, deep yellow beaks tucked close to their chests.

For several minutes Henry didn't move. Then he turned and walked back to her, his jaw muscle tensed. "I met him in Ranier with your father. A bright, admirable fellow."

"Yes, and they fired him," Trinity said with bitterness, reminded of the loss.

"Damn. We haven't learned anything from history," Henry said. "Yet these days, there's more and more talk of that sort. Who is a true American? Who should be here? Religion. Color of skin. Bloodlines and ancestry. I thought this was a country that opened its arms to *all* people."

Trinity removed her painter's smock and hung it on the edge of her easel. "So did I. If I recall," she said, "the Statue of

Liberty says: 'Give me your tired, your poor, / Your huddled masses yearning to breathe free, / The wretched refuse of your teeming shore—'"

Henry finished and lifted his forefinger. "'Send these, the homeless, tempest-tost to me. / I lift my lamp beside the golden door!'"

Trinity turned to her paintbrushes. "I think my parents would *say* they believe the words," she said, setting her brush in a can of spirits, "but they'd add a long list of exceptions on who is actually allowed through that golden door."

She hadn't expected to have such a conversation with Henry, and she was heartened by it. And she enjoyed a peculiar freedom with Henry, who was fifteen to twenty years her senior and far too old to be a serious suitor.

"You mentioned coffee. Let's see what Agatha has in the oven to go with it."

He stepped into the kitchen after her, just as Agatha pulled round loaves of yeasty bread from the oven and set them on the counter.

"Hi, Agatha," Trinity said. "We're looking for a cup of coffee."

"Just in time—if you want a slice of sourdough bread with butter and rhubarb jam, that is."

"I wouldn't refuse," Henry said. "Smells wonderful in here."

"But only if you join us," Trinity said, motioning to the chairs at the kitchen's enamel-topped table.

"Where are they fishing?" Henry asked.

"They never tell," Agatha said, sitting down.

They visited about what kind of fish George and Father were likely to bring back for supper. "Walleye, for sure," Agatha said.

Trinity had come to expect at least one good fish fry a week, or maybe two, and loved that—whether it was northern pike, walleye, or bass—dinner came fresh from the waters that surrounded them. She enjoyed fishing now and then.

When she set a crust of bread aside, Henry must have understood it was meant for Lou. "You should look into buying that new food for dogs that comes in cans."

Agatha laughed. "Henry Densch! You're trying to fool me. There's no such thing!"

"But there is!" Henry said. "Someone figured how to take canned rations for soldiers left over after the war and turn it into something useful. Ken-L Ration, that's what they call it."

"That's plain ridiculous," Agatha said, but Trinity could see Agatha felt an easy connection with Henry, too.

From somewhere on the island shrill and frantic barking pierced the air. Whatever it was, Lou was in trouble.

"Oh dear," Trinity said. "I hope she's not hurt!" She pushed away from the table and hurried outside, following the sound. Lou's barking sent waves of adrenaline pumping through her body. She ran past RuthAnne's cabin and followed the thin and winding path, rounded the island's other towering boulder—twice the size of her elephant rock—and headed toward the massive winter boathouse, taller than a two-story building.

In the grasses outside the building's clapboard brown walls, Lou was braced on all fours, her head lowered, barking at a large rodent—some kind of animal.

"Lou, come here! Get away!"

It could have rabies.

Cautiously, Trinity drew closer, slowing her steps so as not to startle the creature into attack. Its back hairs were silvery, making her guess it was a young porcupine. But as she drew closer, she ruled out a porcupine, as well as a young beaver, as there were no quills, no long tail. A muskrat. They lived near water, and she knew George would rather shoot them than let them dig tunnels along the shoreline or raid the vegetable garden. But she'd never seen much harm in letting them coexist with humans on the island.

Standing a few yards off, she said, "Leave it, Lou." But her words seemed to have the opposite effect, and Lou suddenly lunged forward, coming within two feet—almost nose to nose—with the hissing muskrat.

With caution, Trinity moved slowly forward. She didn't want to get in the middle of a snarling fight, but she didn't want Lou or the muskrat to get hurt. As she grabbed Lou's collar and pulled her back several feet, she spotted a thin line of blood around one of the muskrat's eyes. It was wounded. An injured animal could turn mean, and a cornered animal could behave erratically, much the same as people.

Lou growled and strained at her collar.

Suddenly, Henry joined in, standing behind Trinity and looking over her shoulder. "Wh-what's going on?"

She pointed.

"What is it?"

"A muskrat."

Body smooth and round, little eyes dark and almost pleading, the muskrat slowly lifted one front foot, as if testing the dog's reaction, and then the other. But something was terribly wrong. It barely moved. And then Trinity saw the problem.

Partially hidden by the weeds, its back legs were splayed out behind it, paralyzed or broken.

"Ohhh . . ." Lou had likely clamped her jaw over its back and shook it—the way dogs do in play and to kill something. Of course, Lou had gone after it; it was in her nature to do so. But this poor animal was caring for its young or finding food or digging a den, and then this. Trinity felt sick at the sight. "What a waste!"

"What are you going to do?" Henry asked, standing a distance behind her.

"I'm not sure yet, but I'm not giving Lou a chance to hurt it worse." She picked up her dog, who wriggled and struggled to get free. "Don't let her escape, and keep her locked in the kitchen until I return," she said and handed Lou to Henry.

Henry looked relieved. "I can do that. I was hoping you weren't going to ask me to—you know."

When he was gone, Trinity stared at the muskrat.

It stared back without moving, then dragged itself forward a few inches on its forelegs. It broke her heart. There was no hope for its survival. She would have left the task up to George or Father, but they were gone. And Henry was too gentle a soul. As much as she hated the idea of ending the animal's life, it had to be done. She couldn't let it escape into the brush only to have Lou later hunt it down and shake it to death—or worse, taunt it with a slow death.

She knew how to shoot a gun. The Major made sure all his daughters could shoot in the event of self-defense, from human or animal threat. In such an emergency, a loaded rifle rested lengthwise on two wooden pegs high on one of the living room walls. But even though she was a fair shot at target practice, she hated violent noise, the kickback bruise on her shoulder. She would find another way.

Knowing that extra fishing gear and supplies were stored in a corner of the winter boathouse, Trinity stepped inside the cavernous building—large enough to store the yacht. She found a fishing net and stepped back outside with it. She hated what she had to do. How could killing something be an act of kindness?

Without allowing herself to falter, she approached the muskrat with the long-handled fishing net and swiftly drew it down over its body. The animal lunged ahead, deeper into the net. Using both hands, she brought the net under the muskrat. It hissed, and Trinity twisted the pole and net so that the more the animal struggled, the more it was tightly trapped. Then with the net extended away from her body, she lifted it and crossed the steel boat rails and walked to the short dock.

Now the verses she had memorized years ago at St. Katharine's in Davenport sprang to mind. She could almost hear the deep voice of the cantor: "A time to be born," he'd start, and the students would respond, "and a time to die." Now, almost with a will of their own, the words from Ecclesiastes rolled through her head:

> . . . a time to plant, and a time to pluck that which
>   is planted;
> a time to kill, and a time to heal;
> a time to break down, and a time to build up;
> a time to weep . . .

As she walked to the end of the dock, the muskrat squealed. Trinity felt the weight of its life suspended in the net. She swallowed hard.

> . . . and a time to laugh;
> a time to mourn, and a time to dance;
> a time to cast away stones, and a time to gather
>   stones together;
> a time to embrace, and a time to refrain from
>   embracing;
> a time to seek, and a time to lose;
> a time to keep, and a time to cast away . . .

She lowered the net as the muskrat struggled to break free.

"I'm so sorry," she said.

Then she pushed the net deep underwater, and everything went silent.

But its struggle translated through the jerking pole and up through her arms. She wanted to pull it back out, save it! But she held fast, as the bubbles slowed to a few, then one or two, until they stopped reaching the surface altogether. Still she held it underwater—she would not do this a second time—and forced herself, eyes burning and chest tight, to reach the end of the verses:

> . . . a time to rend, and a time to sew;
> a time to keep silence, and a time to speak;
> a time to love, and a time to hate;
> a time for war, and a time for peace.

A mallard and her ducklings, now half the size of their mother, drifted past.

When Trinity lifted the lifeless animal from the water, it appeared smaller somehow. She swore and hated what she'd had to do.

The island was a thin layer of soil, moss, and lichen over rock. Digging a hole would be impossible, unless it were on the sand beach, in which case it would be dug up by other predators. Or by Lou. She groaned. "I can't even bury you."

She came up with another plan and set off with the net to the island's northernmost point.

Away from the lee of the island, a strong breeze ruffled the bay. Beyond the shoreline of smooth and scalloped granite, ashen waves rolled westward.

She untangled the animal and its tiny paws from the net, sat on her haunches at the water's edge, and eased the animal's body into the flow of water.

She sat motionless, watching, until it drifted out into Sand Bay.

She felt something true, something right about what she'd done.

Something like gratitude.

Gratitude for this animal's singular life.

And for a moment—she wanted to believe—the animal was thanking her.

39

TRINITY JOINED GEORGE on his boat run the next morning. As they arrived at the Ranier dock, a white pelican lifted from a post and soared over them. Seagulls circled, hoping for a good catch of fish.

"Sorry," Trinity called to them.

When it was her turn at the post office, she stepped up and placed the empty mailbag on the counter. "Good morning. Mail for the Bairds, please."

The postmaster scurried out of view and returned with a bag brimming with letters. He traded the empty bag for the full one. "Next!"

Outside the post office, she sat on a bench and fingered through the mailbag. The thin envelope with a Paris postmark sent her heart into flight. She didn't waste a moment and opened it.

> ... happy to inform you that the admissions office
> has reserved a space for you. ... As we have students
> on a waiting list, please reply by telegram with your
> intentions as soon as possible ... as well as your
> deposit to hold your spot.

The word stopped her. How was she going to manage sending deposit money? She'd been zipping along, sails filled with wind, only to have the wind suddenly drop off.

For several minutes she stared at the letter, trying to come up with a plan. She could accomplish the first part of the request: she had enough money in her handbag to send a telegram. She would start there and let them know the deposit, in time (though she had no idea when that might be), would follow.

40

A DAMP CHILL hung in the studio as Trinity changed from her pajamas into her navy bathing suit, its white band circling her hips. Goose bumps rose on her arms and legs. She wrapped herself in her cotton robe, stepped into her sheepskin slippers, and grabbed the woven basket that contained her comb, soap, shampoo.

Lou stood on her back legs and spun once, then twice.

"Well, look at you! Aren't you the little starlet?"

Lou spun once more.

"Yes, I'll feed you." She opened a can of Ken-L Ration with a can opener, emptied its contents into the dog bowl, and while Lou gobbled down her breakfast, Trinity took the can to the shore, rinsed it, and gazed out.

Several loons gathered silently on the water. One rose from the surface, almost as if standing on the water, and stretched its wings wide, then settled to the surface. The first week of August. The loons were probably discussing plans for heading south in the weeks ahead.

Now that she'd received her letter of acceptance, she had to have a serious talk with her parents. They had to agree that she was more than ready, but she knew how it worked.

She laughed and swore at the same time.

Father would yield to avoid conflict. Her tincture-addicted mother would have the final say.

How deranged was that?

Her heart sped up in her chest.

Whatever her fate, she reminded herself of the vow she'd made on the day of her release. *She would never go back.*

She shuddered, chilled at the thought.

She'd take a sauna first.

ALONG THE PATH, she spotted a hornet's nest overhead in the arm of a dead tree and steered wide around it. Bees lifted from wildflowers as Lou dashed mindlessly after squirrels. The squat building sat next to a short dock off to the south side of the beach.

Trinity set her basket of soaps and her bath towel outside the sauna's door.

Then she grabbed birchbark and kindling from the nearby woodpile and loaded the sauna's woodstove through its cast-iron door on the outside of the building. Between two split logs, she created a small mound of bark and sticks, lit a wood match on the side of its box, and poked the small flame at the base of the birchbark. It smoked, then lit, crackling and snapping as it drew cold air in from the base of the woodstove and sent smoke and heat up the chimney pipe.

She sat on her heels and let it burn hot for another minute or two, then added a few more logs, crossing them on top of the others so they could breathe, and closed the stove door.

As she stepped from around the sauna and onto the beach, Father called, startling her, "Good morning, Trinity!" He waved and then returned his gaze to the water, arms crossed over the top of his bathing suit. "Perfect morning for a sauna!"

"I agree," Trinity said. "While it warms up, I'm going to row around the island."

"Darling," Father called to the figure bundled beside the

boathouse, "if I can't talk you into swimming laps with me, at least join us in the sauna later!"

Mother sat in a patch of sunlight on a wicker chair, a wool blanket wrapped around her shoulders, a steaming cup between her hands. "We'll see," Mother called back.

No. She needed time to think. She had wanted to take a sauna alone.

"Morning," Trinity said and walked past Mother into the boathouse.

"Mm-hm," Mother replied.

Inside the boathouse, golden light and shadows flickered in the water. A school of minnows swarmed, then darted away, followed by a northern pike. Lou appeared— never one to miss a boat ride—and jumped to the bow seat. Then Trinity rowed around the northern end of the island, glancing over her shoulder for a path between massive slabs of rock lying beneath the surface—whales on the verge of breaching—and rowed around the entire island.

WHEN SHE OPENED the sauna door, it seemed to stick.

Father yelled from inside, "Give it some muscle!"

Mother sat on the top bench, making a sour face and pulling the bottom edge of her bathing suit toward her dimpled knees. "I would prefer a long dress over this."

"Be glad we're Scots, not Finns," Father said. "At least we wear bathing suits."

"Thank God," Trinity replied. She really couldn't imagine taking a sauna with her parents in the nude. She shuddered as she closed the door quickly behind her.

Fire crackled and spat in the woodstove. The only light came from a small window near the eaves. The temperature was warm but not terribly hot. Not yet.

Trinity climbed to the top bench, where the heat was always most intense, and sat between her parents on the eight-foot-long bench. Not until they first arrived on Rainy Lake had Trinity ever experienced a sauna. They'd been invited to visit a sauna built by a Finnish family, and immediately after, Father made plans to build their own. More often than not, they took saunas in the evening, but this morning's chill was motivating.

Trinity's body tingled, adjusting to the intense warmth as it wrapped around her, penetrating every pore.

"I hope I survive it," Mother said, drawing a towel to her face, which made breathing easier in extreme heat.

"It's just starting to warm up," Trinity said.

Father added, "There's no shame in stepping out when you feel too warm."

"Trinity, dear?" Mother asked. "Would it have been too much to let us know you were starting the sauna? Too much to invite us?"

Trinity bristled at her mother's constant, caustic tone. "Consider yourself invited," she replied. "I didn't think . . ."

"No, you didn't," Mother said. "You think only about yourself."

"Ladies, stop," Father said.

But this time, Trinity had no plans of swallowing her words. She'd done that so much over the past two months. "Mother," she said, "all I feel from you is *spite*. It makes me wonder—why did you ever have me in the first place?"

"Now, now," Father said, with a tap on Trinity's shoulder. But Trinity refused to pretend everything was fine.

Mother kept the towel to her face and mumbled, "Every baby is . . . is—" But she faltered and stopped midsentence.

"A gift from God!" Father concluded.

"Would you both just please stop pretending?" Trinity blurted. "Stop pretending everything is fine. Father, you pretend not to be prejudiced, then send Max away. You pretend RuthAnne is fine, but she's drunk most of the time. You both pretend you love me, but then how do you explain sending me away?"

"You're getting worked up," Mother said from behind her towel.

"*Hysterical?* Is that what you call me for speaking my mind? Are you planning to send me back? Are you?"

"No, we're not," Father said.

"You were home for a week each Christmas," Mother said, her voice overly sweet. She removed the towel from her face and met Trinity's eyes. "And more than a week last summer."

Trinity wanted to scream in frustration. Instead, she groaned and said, "See? You're pretending again that I was fine, that those short visits home and here were enough. You don't know the truth of what it was like for me at Oak Hills. You've never asked. You've never let me tell you."

"But the postcards tell the story!" Mother mounted a quick defense and spoke rapidly, as if she'd rehearsed her lines. "It's a beautiful place. You were pampered with time to rest, heal. You had Sadie close by. She was there for you."

"No," Trinity said. "You seem to think that Oak Hills is another sanitorium for the wealthy—but it's not! It's an insane asylum! You have no idea! I didn't wear street clothes. I wore a cotton gown, same as everyone else. I slept in a room with a hundred other women. I worked, day in and day out, surrounded by many who had truly lost their minds. But good God, there were countless others, like me, who were perfectly sane and locked away by their families."

Her parents were silent. Trinity felt the armor she'd kept around herself give way. Her voice broke. "I thought I'd die there and never get out."

"Oh, no." Father's voice became contrite and he hung his head. "A few people tried to tell us, but we wanted to believe you were somewhere good. I think we were afraid to visit."

"It's getting too hot," Mother said. She stepped down to the lower bench and sat. "We did it out of love—you must believe us. We saved you from doing something you might come to regret, actions that could shame you and your family for years to come."

Trinity shook her head. "No, it wasn't love. It was a way to control me. You thought it would bring me under your thumb, but it did the opposite. So once and for all, Mother, I need the truth. It's pathetic that I must ask, but do you even love me?"

Father snapped. "You know she—"

"Let me talk," Trinity said. "Mother, have you ever loved me?"

"You insist, then I'll tell you." As if from a steam kettle, Mother's words spewed. "I never wanted you!"

"She doesn't mean that," Father said, his hand again on Trinity's shoulder, but she tossed it off.

Mother held up her forefinger. "Your father wouldn't listen. The first two pregnancies were hard on me and nearly killed me. I said no more children, but would he listen? And then I was pregnant again. Sick as a dog the whole time, and then the birth of you was a nightmare. It ripped me apart in more ways than one. You insist on the truth? Well, my dear, it was your birth. You're the reason I started on laudanum."

Trinity let the weight of the words sink in.

"That's right," Mother continued. "To help with the pain. Then to help me be a mother. To help keep my spirit from failing me. I thought it was medicine and believed it would make me stronger over time, but now every little thing drives me back to the tincture to find relief. I have become someone I barely recognize. And you have always, Trinity, from the very beginning . . . you always had a way of testing me, of bringing out the worst in me."

A quiet settled.

The fire sizzled in the barrel stove.

Sweat beaded at the roots of Trinity's hair.

Droplets gathered and ran down the back of her neck and stopped at her bathing suit. It wasn't what she wanted to hear, but at least it was honest.

"Thank you for the truth," she whispered and made her way past Mother and out the sauna door.

She paused at the end of the dock. Her chest ached, as if her whole life culminated into this moment—learning she'd never been wanted. Whatever had just happened between them was something real. She had no idea what the consequences might be, but she also had no regret for speaking her truth. As much as Mother's words hurt, at least they were genuine.

Hands over her head, she sliced into waters deep and cool.

When she surfaced, she wiped water from her eyes, then swam back to the dock and climbed the wooden ladder. She soaped up her hair and body, as much as she could, then dove, letting the water rinse her clean, leaving behind a trail of soapsuds.

Skin tingling, she dove like a dolphin and swam.

When she surfaced, she felt fresh and clean. She felt for the first time in a long time not fractured but *whole.*

An acrid smell reached her nose.

The smell of forest fires carried on the air from hundreds of miles to the north in Canada. But this scent was sharper, stronger. Closer.

When she turned toward shore, her heart jumped.

The sauna chimney glowed fiendishly red.

A black column of oily smoke chugged into the sky.

41

NO MATTER what her parents had put her through, they were still her parents. She couldn't lose them this way.

"Fire!" she yelled again and again, swimming toward the shore.

She knew the risks. Natural oils from wood, or creosote, could build up inside any chimney over time and become flammable if the fire burned too hot.

Before her feet touched bottom, the kitchen gong chimed—*ka-clang, ka-clang, ka-clang!*—a call to neighbors on the lake for help.

Trinity ran to shore, hoping to spot her parents, but the beach was empty except for Lou, digging a hole, oblivious to the terror Trinity felt hurtling through her being.

She raced to the sauna. As she reached for its wooden handle, smoke curled out along the edges of the door frame.

"Mother! Father! Get out! Get out!"

She grabbed the wooden handle, but the door resisted. If they weren't already dead, she was going to lose them any second. But then she heard coughing. She yanked again, harder this time, and the door sprung open. Smoke poured out and Trinity held her breath and stepped in, flailed with her hands to find them. She grabbed arms and pulled them, coughing and staggering, out and away from the building, now turned into a torch with an infinite source of oxygen. Flames shot up, the fire roared to life, and the scorching heat drove Trinity back to the end of the dock.

"Jump in!" she yelled, refusing to let go and tugging her parents after her into the water. When their heads bobbed up, she was grateful. They could at least touch bottom. They both seemed confused, dazed, and must have breathed in too much smoke before they knew they were in trouble. She guided them through the water like children, farther away from blowing embers and closer to the opposite end of the beach and the boathouse dock.

"Sit here," she said.

Father began hacking and stood back up. "I can help."

"No, you can't," she said, forcing him down at his shoulders, just as George emerged from the boathouse with a hose. He dragged it across the beach to the sauna and sprayed water at the billowing flames.

"George has the water pump going. You can watch."

Then she rushed to George's side. "Let me help."

He opened his mouth in protest but then said, "We need buckets!" He handed off the hose and dashed to the boathouse.

Trinity aimed the hose at the building, trying to wet it down, trying to keep the flames from leaping to the pine branches above. The hose bucked as it drew water from the lake. Trinity gripped hard and held fast with both hands as she sent water up and down the sides of the building.

The bell continued to clang—bless Agatha!—and George set bucket after bucket on the dock, along with an ax. "Help will come, you'll see!" he shouted as boats zoomed toward their island.

Black smoke and orange flames mixed with white steam. Trinity fought the flames, getting as close as she could, but her face burned and she choked on smoke.

People showed up, boat after boat—running with buckets to the lake and then toward the fire. Neighbors filled buckets with water, passed them along a human chain that ended by emptying buckets onto the flames.

But it wasn't enough.

Fire shot up through the roof, then jumped higher, like a giant hand grabbing at nearby pine and cedar branches. If one tree caught fire, it could turn into a flash fire, treetop to treetop across the whole island.

Trinity aimed higher and shot water up overhead and into the treetops, bringing ashes down around her. To her relief, the flames drew back from the overhanging branches, abandoning the trees.

"Here, let me help!" It was Henry. He reached to her hands and began taking the hose away from her.

She refused to let go. "Let me do this!"

But the moment those words slipped out, she started to cough from deep in her chest, and her coughing increased until she was forced to let go. "Take it!" she shouted, giving way.

Her lungs felt clogged as she stumbled backward, away from the billowing clouds of steam and smoke. Her arms had turned to rubber.

She was relieved to see her parents staying on the end of the dock, but the wind had shifted and was blowing directly at them. She rushed to them, their faces both looking more exhausted than she'd ever seen them. She had to take charge. "You need to get away. You've breathed in more than enough smoke already."

Mother's entire body trembled and Trinity held out her hand. "Come, this way," she said and guided her along the path with Father following. Trinity stopped a safe distance away. In that moment she caught a glimpse of the years ahead and the changing nature of their roles.

"You . . . ," Mother said, squeezing Trinity's hand. "You probably saved us."

"Well . . . ," Father said but then began coughing. When he stopped, he tried again. "Well done."

"Please. Go," Trinity said. "Change into dry clothes. Rest if you need to. We've got things under control."

To her surprise, they didn't fight her and walked away, each supporting the other.

Trinity sped back. When she reached the half-log bench behind the boathouse, she felt her chest tighten. She doubled over, coughing, spitting out ash and phlegm.

Her eyes stung.

Her lungs hurt.

She ran her hand over her singed eyebrows.

But she was okay, she assured herself. Her parents had survived.

RuthAnne suddenly appeared at her side, staring at the rescue efforts beyond. "What the hell? We just woke up. Must have slept through everything." She tugged Trinity to sit down beside her on the bench. "We can watch from here."

"It happened fast," Trinity said, not taking her eyes off the scene as Henry aimed at the base of the fire and others tossed buckets of water. Most flames were replaced by smoke and steam. A sludge of ash and water poured from the sauna's smoldering base.

"What happened?"

"I started a sauna," Trinity said. "Mother and Father joined me."

RuthAnne huffed. "Yeah?" Her tone was caustic.

Trinity spun to face her. "What are you insinuating?"

"To get attention," RuthAnne said. "Maybe to get back at Mother and Father—for not throwing money at your feet."

"How can you say that—or even think that? What could I possibly gain by doing that? I'm not trying to give them reasons to send me away. RuthAnne, they nearly *died* in there. I had to help them out."

Trinity remembered Mother's painfully honest confession, and turned back to her sister. "Since I can remember," she began, "you've always held something against me. What have I ever done to you?"

RuthAnne clenched her jaw, forming a visible knot. "Okay, you asked. I was seven when you came along, and Mother was deathly ill and spent days on end in her room. When she seemed better, she still stayed away. For a few years, Liz and I thought our governess was our mother. And then as you grew up, you turned into a bright-eyed little darling who stole all the attention. I tried to make peace with it. But then Father named the damn yacht after you. People always ask, 'Why did he name it after Trinity?'" She threw her arms upward and let them drop. A flush of red climbed from her neck and spread across her face. "What the hell do I say to that? 'She's his hands-down favorite'?"

Trinity steeled herself against her sister's jealousy and bitterness. "If I'm such a favorite, then tell me why they sent me away."

RuthAnne looked off toward the boathouse. "Because you scared them."

"What?"

"They couldn't control you. They said you were overcome with hysteria that night and threatened to take your life. They needed to send you away for your own good and so you didn't bring shame down upon the family name."

She'd heard the same words from her parents before they sent her away. She would never know if they sent her away out of the need to protect her or their social standing. "And you agree with their thinking?" Trinity asked.

"Absolutely not," she said. "That's why I didn't return here asking for anyone's permission to get a divorce. I knew I had to tell them how it was going to be, like it or not."

At that, a cough struck again. Trinity bent forward, doing her best to clear her lungs of gray matter. When she stopped, she sat up straight. She sensed a fragile bridge forming between them, and she started cautiously, one foot in front of the other, across it. "How did you find the strength to end your marriage?"

To Trinity's surprise, RuthAnne's eyes brimmed with

emotion. "I'm finding strength every day. Don't get me wrong. I don't miss that bastard, but I miss that we were this thing—a couple—and together we somehow fit neatly into society with all its expectations. Outwardly, it made life easier. But being together, I died a little day by day, pretending to be something I wasn't. I never loved him and never will. Now the truth is out." Her chest rose and fell with a deep exhale. "It's better this way."

For several moments, they didn't speak.

Trinity gazed at the sauna building, now reduced to a billowing cloud of white and gray. The rescue effort had relaxed. People slowed, rested, gathered in small groups, and talked.

Then RuthAnne said, "I guess I can be a real ass sometimes."

Trinity was stunned. "Sometimes."

"I'm sorry," RuthAnne added.

Trinity pulled her head back, as if seeing her sister from a new angle. She'd never in her whole life had any sort of apology from her sister. She'd always felt at arm's length without understanding why.

It was a huge step.

"So you don't really believe I burned down the sauna."

"Nah," RuthAnne said with a shrug. Then she leaned in and planted a kiss on Trinity's cheek. "And about all that other stuff in the past, I don't give a flying rat's ass anymore. I have someone in my life who cares about me—and honestly, I've never been happier."

BY EARLY AFTERNOON, after a thank-you lunch of sandwiches, pickles, and Agatha's buttermilk cake, the crew of volunteers left by water.

Except Henry, who leaned against the water well's rock foundation as Trinity surveyed the sauna's remains.

Nothing was left but a smoldering pile of charred wood. The blackened barrel stove tilted at an angle, its chimney pipe gone. The lowest branches of the nearest white pine were crispy brown and bare of needles, but the fire had been contained.

"If you don't mind," Henry said, "I want to stick around and keep an eye on it. Make sure it doesn't flare up again." Ash smudges covered his face. The tip of his nose was black with soot as he gazed at the rubble where a few thin wisps slivered upward.

"Thanks," she said. A sour, chalky taste remained in her mouth and nostrils. Her throat felt raw each time she swallowed, but she breathed easier knowing that the whole island hadn't burned to the ground. It would have without the help of neighbors. She had passed small islands burned by lightning strikes; not much remained but ash-covered granite and a scraggly skeleton tree or two. If their island were to ever burn to the ground, it would be stripped of its charm and would require years and years to recover.

She started coughing again, forced to spit off to the side. "Excuse me," she said, wiping her nose. "Not very ladylike, sorry." She spit again and her chest felt a little lighter. "Henry, thank you for your help."

"You may not know this about me," Henry said, taking off his hat. He untied the bandanna from around his neck and mopped his forehead of perspiration and grime. "But I love to help others—especially my friends."

She had wondered how Victor could support his trip to Europe. Hadn't he mentioned a benefactor? "And you're helping Victor," she said. There was nothing subtle about her statement.

"Did he let the cat out of the bag? He was to keep the support confidential."

"No," Trinity said. "He did nothing wrong. He told me he had a benefactor, and when you mentioned helping people, I guessed, that's all."

"And did he tell you the latest?" Henry asked, walking toward the burned sauna with a long stick. He stirred here and there in the muddy ashes, finding occasional pockets that sent up steam, smoke, and flames. "I've been helping him develop his photos of moose using some new techniques. I'm quite close, I believe, to finding a means to create photos in color."

"Oh?" she said, surprised to learn of his creative abilities.

"And," he said with a grin, "he has invited me to join him to travel around England."

"That's great," she said, feeling both happy for him and a pang of self-pity.

"Truth is," Henry said, stirring again, "I'm a little worried, to be honest. He wants us to travel around by bicycles."

"Bicycles?" She laughed. "When everyone is dreaming of cars and aeroplanes, I would expect nothing less from Victor. Though he may want to try getting there by canoe!"

"Ha! I wouldn't put it past him. I'm just worried I won't be able to keep up with the old man."

She smiled. Though Victor was the younger of the two, they both seemed younger than their years. She found it difficult to think of either of them as old. "Henry," she assured him, "you'll do just fine. And maybe you'll set a reasonable pace and keep Victor from killing himself. I admit, it's pretty hard to believe he has a weakened heart."

Satisfied that he'd apparently churned through enough of the ruins, Henry stepped back and set his stick against the stone well, facing her. "I've never met anyone more fit, more filled with vitality in my life, have you?"

Trinity agreed. "I think he's charmed as a leprechaun."

"Or woodland elf," Henry said.

"Pixie," Trinity countered.

"Puck," Henry said with a grin.

"When will you two set off?" she asked.

"Seven days."

"Oh," she said, caught by surprise. "That soon?" They

hadn't left and she already felt abandoned. "I'm sure you'll have a wonderful time."

"Say," Henry asked, "have your parents come to their senses about funding your studies abroad?"

The question hit her hard. "Ha. No, I think they're farther from their senses than ever. But yesterday, I read that the librarian in International Falls applied for another job. She's leaving the end of this month and her position is opening up."

"No, I hadn't heard." He motioned her to the beach and sat in the sand. "Come, sit down a bit. Tell me."

She sat beside him in the warm, dry sand, facing the waters stretching west.

Henry stretched out the legs of his wool trousers. The right knee of his pants was scorched with a hole the size of an orange. He'd probably never looked so untidy in his entire life.

"Did you get burned?"

He probed his kneecap with his forefinger. "No. Lucky, I guess."

Trinity continued. "I plan to apply. I have to. I'll find a place to rent. I can work and save up until I have enough funds to return to school."

Henry drew his knees up to his chest and clasped his arms around them. "You could, and I can't tell you how much I admire your determination."

She cocked her head sideways and flashed a grin of appreciation. "Why, thank you, Henry."

"You could work and save and put off your studies for a few more years, or . . . or you could let me help you."

It was tempting to put her hand out for financial help, but she jumped to her feet, hands on her hips. "No, Henry," she said. "Thank you for your offer, but I need to stand on my own two legs. I've promised myself to never give power to someone else over my life again."

"Okay," he said, drawing a circle in the sand with a small

twig. "You're in a rough patch with your family, I know. But you have talent and you need options." He acted as if it were a simple numerical problem to be solved.

Trinity's hands dropped to her sides. "Henry, even though you're a friend, how could I not feel diminished if I accept your money? Or that I owe you something in return? I'm *not* poor. Someday I'll inherit . . . It's just that . . . right now, I'm . . . I'm . . ." She exhaled with finality. Several moments passed, and she watched him, her back warmed by the sun.

He ran the twig slowly around the circular groove he'd created in the sand, over and over.

As a seagull flew overhead, squawking, Trinity breathed in the mingling smells of smoke, pine boughs, and lake water.

In the distance, a fishing boat hummed.

Finally, Henry stopped drawing circles, looked up, and met her eyes. "I didn't ask for it, but I have been entrusted with managing my family's estate and finances. I try to be responsible. I invest in businesses. I look for reasonable opportunities to grow. And I am *always* looking for ways to do some good with my family's insane amount of wealth."

She began to protest, but he held up his twig, as if it were a scepter. "Be empowered," he said, "and let me help you." He extended his hand up toward hers.

She hesitated, grappling with his offer, with her identity, with her choices. Her chest rose and fell, rose and fell, rose . . .

His eyes were calm, not demanding.

He was offering a gift that was hers to take or leave.

He waited.

Sometimes she was astonished she'd survived. Since her meltdown, she'd gone over a waterfall, stuck in the force of its dizzying current; but now, at last, she was free from its power. Now, in spite of it all—in spite of the loss of her sense of self-worth, the wrenching loss of Louise and Marta—she'd never felt more solid, more sure of herself.

She knew herself, treasured her deepened self-aware-ness, and because of it she could face whatever might be around life's next bend.

She didn't have to accept his gift.

She wasn't backed into a corner.

She could choose.

She could take the job at the library and patiently gain financial independence.

Or she could accept the help he freely offered. With an exhale of relief and a simple nod, she reached her hand toward his.

42

FROM THE GALLEY OF THE YACHT, Agatha served a pork roast dinner, complete with carrots, potatoes, and fresh applesauce.

Water sloshed alongside the boat's beams as they drifted, dining above deck in the stern.

"It almost feels as if we're celebrating something special!" Mother said, and for the first time in forever, a smile—a genuine smile—passed across her face as she looked around the table, her eyes landing on Trinity.

Was it possible that such a change in her demeanor, Trinity wondered, could be a consequence of their each speaking the truth? If so, then it was as if everything that Mother had built around her to keep Trinity out was crumbling, a grain of mortar at a time. It was too soon to know if such a change could be lasting, but Trinity realized she didn't need to know the future. It was a start.

"We are," Trinity said, "and I'll let you know after dessert."

At which point Agatha cleared the table and returned with servings of her famous whipped cream lemon cake. "Agatha," Trinity said. She didn't want to make this announcement without them. "Would you and George please join us?"

Because there were not enough chairs at the stern, Agatha and George sat on either side of the stateroom's low roof. With the whipped cream frosting threatening to melt, everyone lifted their forks and devoured the cake. When the last fork was set down, Trinity pulled her letter from the pocket of her sundress.

"It is a *very* special day," she announced. "Yesterday I received my readmittance letter! I'll leave in a week to study in Paris."

"But you have no money," Mother reminded her. "You could scarcely pay your own passage, let alone tuition and living expenses. Don't you think you first want to discuss this with us?"

But Trinity sat tall. "Thank you, Mother, but I have my own means."

A frown of disappointment settled across Father's face. "You actually think that taking that position at the library will somehow finance your studies? Ah, you'd do well to cover your living expenses in International Falls. And if you managed to have a little bit left over, it would be years before you could actually save enough to return to Paris."

Trinity let him finish before she said, "Yes, I thought about that. But no. I have another means. I have a benefactor."

RuthAnne wagged her head. "This is interesting. *Do tell.*"

"It's Henry Densch," Trinity said. She looked around the table, trying to gauge the response. She expected they would drum up some reason to protest.

"Oh, my," Mother cooed like a mourning dove. "Well! That's a different matter entirely." Her eyes lit up. "And might I assume this comes with a promise of marriage?"

Trinity laughed. That's what Mother would think. "It's not like that at all."

"Then what?" Father asked, his tone skeptical.

"Henry believes in me. He wants to support my art. Simple as that."

A dozen questions followed, and Trinity was happy to answer them, one by one. Yes, she planned to leave in six days by train with Henry and Victor to New York City. From there, they would all take passage on an ocean steamer to

South Hampton. Henry and Victor would go on to tour England while Victor gave lectures about his Hudson Bay expedition. Trinity would proceed to Paris.

"Well, we can't let him pay all your expenses," Father said. "What kind of parents would that make us?"

"I prefer it this way," Trinity said. "No strings attached."

"Well, we'll see," Father said, a light in his eyes.

As she sat in her wicker chair with Lou in her lap, feet planted solidly on the polished deck, she felt a shift—an unstoppable forward motion—as if she were already under-way on her transatlantic crossing.

"But what about Lou?" Mother asked. "You seem fond of her. Are you going to just abandon her to our care?"

Trinity stroked the top of Lou's head. "I adore her," she said, meeting her parents' eyes. "I can't thank you enough. I needed her more than I realized. I thought I might leave her with Agatha through the school year. But I can't leave her behind. She's coming with me. Besides, everyone seems to have a little dog in Paris. We'll do just fine together."

"Which leads me to my question," RuthAnne blurted. She lifted her whiskey-filled tumbler to her lips, took a drink, then set it back beside her empty dessert plate. "I understand why you gave Trinity the dog. You wanted to cheer her up when she returned to the island."

Millie pressed her head closer to RuthAnne's and whis-pered. "Are you sure you want to—"

RuthAnne patted Millie's arm and continued. "But, Father, why in the hell did you name this boat after her? Why not Mother? Why not me? Why not Elizabeth? It has always pained me, Father, that you so blatantly picked your favor-ite in the family and made such a public display of it!" She exhaled and took another gulp of her drink.

Father tilted so far back in his chair that Trinity thought he might go butt-over-heels backward. Somehow, he bal-anced himself. He chewed on his lips, as if preparing for how to answer. Then, as if he'd found resolve, he pulled himself forward in his chair, stood up, and placed his hands on the table. "It was never about favorites. I never dreamed . . . and I'm quite sorry for any misunderstanding."

RuthAnne opened her mouth in protest, but he stopped her, holding up a finger. "Let me finish."

Turning her gaze skyward, RuthAnne acted as if she didn't care.

"I named her after Trinity because she's the one who is most deeply and profoundly connected here. She loves these waters, this wilderness, as I do. She loves this boat, as I do. And even though it looks as though she'll be leaving for a time, she's the one who will return here, who will be here long into the future." He stretched both arms wide. "She's the one who will keep this legacy going."

Trinity tried to take in his words.

Why had he never shared this with her or anyone in the family? Never expressed his prediction or hope that she would carry on their island tradition? And though no one could ever fully know the future, she had to admit—his words felt true.

"But Father . . . ," RuthAnne protested. "You know I love it. Mother loves it."

"Yes, I know, I know," Father said. "You love it for a season, and then you go back to Chicago, or Davenport, to your worlds of social duties and delicacies. And that's true for Elizabeth, too, out in New York. And there's nothing wrong with that. Nothing at all. It's who you are. But this—"

He expanded his arms wide as if to encompass the lake, the sky, and the setting sun. "I believe *this* is who Trinity is."

For years, she'd misjudged Father's motivation and decision to put her name across the transom. But now she pictured him every morning at the water's edge, no matter the temperature. His swimming routine. It wasn't merely for exercise; it was his religion—his way of connecting with the lake. As was the yacht. They had this in common. There was a reason she carried the island within her, even in her darkest moments. He was right. Rainy Lake—in all its wildness—was forever in her blood.

A soft clapping sounded. Trinity couldn't tell where it was coming from until she looked across the table. Hands half-hidden in her lap, Mother was clapping.

"At last," she said, narrowing her gaze at Father, "you're out with it. I must say, I've wondered, too."

"I was sure I'd told you all," he said, looking perplexed.

"Dear, thinking it," Mother said, "is not the same as saying it."

RuthAnne laughed out loud and lifted her cocktail. "To putting all our cards on the table!"

Trinity hesitated.

A dozen white pelicans soared past, then dropped low, skimming the water. Beyond the silhouetted flock, the sun sat on the horizon, a fiery globe framed by hazy layers of apricot-orange, lilac, and cobalt blue.

One moment couldn't erase the past or promise sweeping changes for the future.

But she raised her glass and joined in the toast.

It was a beginning.

43

WHEN SHE AWOKE, Trinity opened her windows to let the lake sounds float in. A painted turtle plopped from a nearby rock into water. Waves lapped against rocks and boulders on the shore. Loons called softly around the islands and bay. A beaver slapped its tail on water. A fishing boat droned along the channel.

She breathed in pine and cedar, lake water and wood smoke, overlaid with a hint of fall. She loved every moment on the island, but it was time to go.

She finished packing her toilette, nightgown, robe, and slippers in her traveling trunk. Then she closed its top, trimmed ornately in silver and oak, and stood back, examining each panel now painted with tiny images: a fern, a chickadee, a birch, a blue flag iris . . . images to remind her of the island while she was away.

She smiled, pleased with her late-night efforts.

There was only one thing left to do.

She'd been putting it off, not sure what she wanted to say. Needed to say.

She sat down at her writing desk, pulled from her satchel her pen and a sheet of stationery, and began:

Dear Max,

I am terribly sorry your letters never reached me. My family hid them from me until just recently.

*Can you believe it? Let me tell you, I was fuming
with anger, and who wouldn't be? They had their
reasons, though I don't agree with their thinking.
And you had your reasons for writing your last letter
to me.*

*I refuse to let this door between us slam shut. I
may never fully understand your choice to stay
within your tradition and faith. If that is your final
decision, I will do my best to respect it. But perhaps
we could bridge our differences by writing to each
other. As you said, we share an artist's eye. And
maybe more than that. Whatever it was, I value time
shared with you, no matter how brief. You held up a
mirror and helped remind me of who I am—at a
time when I sorely needed it. For that, I'm forever
grateful.*

I was broken, but no longer.

She inhaled, filling her lungs to full capacity, then
exhaled.

She went on to explain her funding to Paris, her excitement at returning to school, and included her future
address. Then she paused, trying to find the right words in
closing:

*My sincere hope is that we remain friends. When
you were here, I never shared my dream with you.
I was afraid you might think I was painting a future
with you. And we were only getting to know each
other. But here is the dream I have imagined. One
day, I will return to Rainy Lake to build my own
island home. A chateau, perhaps, built among
towering trees. I will need to find an architect who
understands how to blend such a structure so that it
does not try to dominate Nature but, rather, to rise
out of it naturally. If that day ever comes, I know
exactly who I will ask to help bring my vision to
reality.*

In the meantime, I wish you every goodness and every bit of happiness.

> *Your loving friend,*
> *Trinity*

She tucked the letter in an envelope and put it in her leather satchel, planning to mail it before her train departed. She took one last appreciative glance around.

There was a quiet knock on her screen door.

"Are you ready?" George called. "Don't want to rush you, but I'm here to gather your luggage."

When she stepped outside, George waited with an empty wheelbarrow. Lou danced around his ankles, her entire body wagging.

"Suddenly, I hate to leave," Trinity admitted. "All summer I've waited for this day, but now I want just a little more time."

"That's okay," George said. "Skip that train. You and Lou can stay on with us. Just have to move into town during the winter. You'd be more than welcome. We have a little sofa you can sleep on."

He chuckled, and she knew he was kidding.

It felt good to laugh.

Then he rested his hand on her shoulder. "Seriously. If you need to leave Lou, it's okay with me. It's the least I could do after what I did. Agreeing to hiding those letters from you. I'm so darn sorry, but I just haven't found a time to say it until now." He met her eyes, and she could see that he carried an unfair burden of responsibility. He was employed by her parents, after all.

"Trinity, can you ever forgive me?"

She wrapped her arms around his neck. "George, of course I can."

The moment she let go, Lou placed her paws on the hem of Trinity's dress and gazed up, her dark eyes keen with pleading.

"Don't worry, Lou." Trinity reached down and kissed Lou on the top of her head. "I'm not leaving you!"

Within moments, George had secured Trinity's traveling trunk, satchel, and portfolio in the wheelbarrow, all expertly balanced. As he lifted the wooden handles, he motioned with his head for her to go first.

She took a few steps. His voice came from behind. "You know, while you were away, well . . . Agatha and I, we sorta moped around here like two lost sheep."

She stopped and turned to face him. His words touched her, and she placed her hand to her heart.

"So we sure hope," he added, "that you'll be back next summer."

"Oh, George," she said. "I wouldn't have it any other way."

AUTHOR'S NOTE

When I wrote *Frozen,* set in 1920 on Rainy Lake, I never envisioned writing a companion novel, *Ice-Out,* and now, *Waterfall.* Sometimes I feel that I am doing the bidding of my creative master, Muse, whatever one might call it. What I know is that characters present and pester me to explore their stories. And I do, but it is by no means "channeling," as that would be too easy. No, the stories haunt me until I begin writing and then torment me while I figure out *what* I'm writing about. The *why* often comes later . . . sometimes years later.

What I didn't know at the beginning was that each of these books would reflect a unique voice in the early 1920s from different social and economic strata. In *Frozen,* Sadie Rose (whose mother was a prostitute, inspired by a woman I read about who was found in the snow in Koochiching County) represents a layer of society that is often hidden—or not considered at all. With Prohibition as the backdrop, Owen Jensen's ambitions in *Ice-Out* go dangerously beyond those of his working-class father, the local creamery operator. *Waterfall* follows Trinity Baird, inspired by the wealthy Roberts family who summered for decades on Rainy Lake, the daughter whose name graced the family yacht.

As a reader of historical fiction, I always want to know what's true, what's inspired, and what's imaginative. But as a writer of historical fiction, I know that those lines cross and crisscross and often blur in service to the story. In every character and detail, I have tried to reflect individuals and events of history on Rainy Lake in this era. With the exception of author Sinclair Lewis and the Princess DeBourbon of Spain, names of actual persons are changed. Names of islands have been changed too, but I have retained the more familiar set pieces of this unique setting: Rainy Lake, Rainy River, Ranier, Kettle Falls, International Falls. My hope is that these actual names will give readers who live outside this region a stronger sense of geography and interest in this wilderness area on the Minnesota–Canada border and Rainy Lake, now protected as Voyageurs National Park. En route by boat from Ranier to the national park, visitors may pass through a channel with a small log cabin perched at the water's edge on the left—the art studio of Virginia Roberts. (In fact, her studio is featured on the cover of Doug Ohman and Bill Holm's book *Cabins of Minnesota*.)

Virginia (Roberts) French at Rainy Lake in the 1920s. Photograph courtesy of Ernest Oberholtzer Foundation.

Decades ago, while on a writers' retreat on nearby Mallard Island, I was in the former study of Ernest Oberholtzer and stumbled on a black and white photograph of a young woman in a wool swimsuit, standing at the end of a long plank, or improvised diving board, somewhere on Rainy Lake. I wondered about this young woman, who appears fit and tan in an era when women had just shed corsets and hid their fair skin under parasols. She possesses a quiet confidence and appears completely at home in the wilderness. I learned her name was Virginia Roberts, a lifelong friend of "Ober," a budding environmentalist.

Years later, while I was starting to work on *Frozen*, I serendipitously met the owner of another island—Roberts' Island, more often known as Atsokan Island. Its owner, Jim Hanson, keeper of the island and curator of its stories, was eager to share his knowledge of Atsokan and the Roberts family, including Virginia Roberts. Family friend Oberholtzer had purchased the island on behalf of Major Horace Roberts. Oberholtzer was often called *atisokan*, or storyteller, by his Ojibwe friends; the name Atsokan is now commonly used for the island, though maps will say Roberts Island.

Atsokan Island is a treasure. For much of the past decade I have been gathering there annually for a week-long writers' retreat. On my retreats with other authors, we share our works-in-progress each evening in the lodge's living room or north porch. When it's chilly we build a fire in the hearth under the glass-eyed gaze of a stuffed moose head and are surrounded by oil paintings created by Virginia Roberts. Above the dining room table, regularly set with dozens of white candles, hangs her self-portrait. A dark and brooding work, it always strikes me as at odds with photographs of Virginia as a young woman. Instead of vibrant and smiling, the self-portrait is dark and brooding, ever watchful, and haunting.

Virginia Roberts, an artist who studied at the Sorbonne in Paris, began summering on her family's island on Rainy

On Atsokan in the early 1920s: from left to right, Harry French, Virginia Roberts, Major Roberts, Virginia's sister Rosara, her mother Dorothy, Ernest Oberholtzer, Virginia's oldest sister Dorothy, and Ober's mother Rosa. Photograph courtesy of Jim Hanson.

Lake around the age of twelve. Later, Major Roberts purchased a fifty-foot Elco yacht in the 1920s and named it after Virginia—a puzzling fact since he had a wife (from a wealthy shipping family in Canada) as well as two other daughters. The Baird family in *Waterfall* closely, but imperfectly, mirrors the wealthy Roberts family from Davenport, Iowa, and without my planning it, Virginia Roberts inspired Trinity, who stepped unbidden as a character into *Frozen* and eventually demanded her own novel.

Though Virginia Roberts as a young woman was never committed to an asylum, I imagined such a unique individual might have been at a time when women were expected to hold to conventional behavior and standards. She was an artist, a nonconformer, and I found it an easy leap to believe that an impetuous, artistic, outspoken young woman of that era would have caused alarm in her family with the subsequent decision to send her away—at least for a time. It was a plausible leap, especially since the Roberts, like so many families, dealt with its share of mental health issues. Rosara, another daughter in the Roberts family, was institutionalized several times.

In the early 1920s, mental health issues were handled far differently from how they are treated today. These days it's very difficult for a family to commit a family member to treatment, unless that individual poses an imminent threat to self or others. But back then, family had the power to commit another family member, often for life. As a way of dealing with the loss of a family member to an institution, families often ran obituaries in their local newspapers, perhaps a means of lessening their sense of family shame rather than admit to supposed defective genetics in the family.

One common diagnosis that was used to lock up teenage girls and women was *hysteria*, an umbrella diagnosis that covered everything from being promiscuous (i.e., sexually active and unmarried) to depressed (including postpartum blues), to anxiety and disobedience. As part of my research, I visited the museum for St. Peter State Hospital for the Insane in southern Minnesota with hopes of accurately

St. Peter State Hospital for the Insane, St. Peter, Minnesota, 1920s.

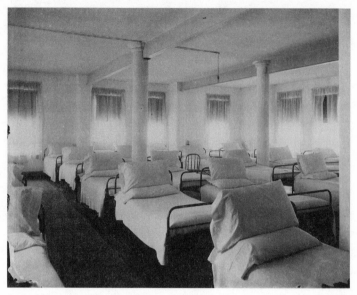

Women's dormitory at St. Peter State Hospital.

reflecting treatment of patients in the early 1920s. I don't include shock therapy in my novel because that form of treatment was not yet used in 1922.

Other characters in *Waterfall* have connections with historical figures from northern Minnesota. Henry Densch is inspired by Harry French, a wealthy Harvard graduate and close friend of Oberholtzer, whose family also summered on Rainy Lake.

I had great fun creating Gizelle and Bruno Larsson, patterned after Bror Dahlberg and his second wife, Gilda, who played several Hollywood roles. It was actually Bror's first wife, Mary, who had a tepee built and furnished on Red Crest Island for visiting author Sinclair Lewis, who wrote part of *Elmer Gantry* during his stay.

The character of E. W. Ennis is fashioned after E. W. Backus, paper company owner and powerful industrialist who aimed to harness the region's vast watershed for hydro-power. His perpetual thorn was Oberholtzer, who took

Sinclair Lewis visits Rainy Lake with Mary Dahlberg *(left)* and Princess DeBourbon of Spain.

the fight to protect wilderness all the way to Washington, D.C. In time, Oberholtzer, with the help of others, thwarted plans for at least a dozen hydropower dams, which would have turned the watershed of the BWCA (Boundary Waters Canoe Area) Wilderness and Quetico Superior Wilderness into giant reservoirs instead of keeping them natural, accessible, and wild as we know and appreciate them today.

IN THANKS

This book would not exist without the unflagging support and encouragement of many. To those of you who kept me going when I felt overwhelmed, thank you. I am humbled by your generosity and deeply grateful.

First and foremost, thank you to Jim (James Conrad) Hanson, dear friend and owner of Atsokan Island, for sharing its lore and history and helping to illuminate the early years of the Roberts family on Rainy Lake. Thank you for every visit to the island and every ride on the lovingly restored yacht *Virginia*. Each time is a step back into history and a celebration of wilderness preserved.

Thank you to Beth Zabel, curator of the St. Peter State Hospital Museum in St. Peter, Minnesota, and to staff members Ilene Holt and Jane Haala. Thank you for the personal tour and for sharing your insights into the early practices of mental health at this facility. Walking through the doors of the asylum was a visceral experience as I imagined being committed as a patient with doors closing behind me. As life would have it, shortly after and during the writing of this story, I needed to make an emergency visit to see a dear young relative who was unexpectedly sent to a psychiatric ward.

I'm grateful to the Koochiching County Historical Museum and its curator, Ashley LaVigne, and to Beth Waterhouse and the Ernest Oberholtzer Foundation for your invaluable help.

IN THANKS

I'm sure I'll forget someone, and please forgive me, but a huge thank you to my editor, Erik Anderson, at the University of Minnesota Press, who helped bring out the heart of this novel; my agent, Fiona Kenshole, for championing my work; to those who have heard or read parts of this story and offered insight, including my writers' groups: Margi Preus, Polly Carlson Voiles, Sheryl Peterson, Marsha Chall, Catherine Friend, Kelly Dupre, Anne Ylvisaker, and Lauren Stringer. Also, a huge thank you to Priscilla and Al Jones, Julien Appignani, Lynn Naeckel, Kate Miller, Jim Hanson, Gail Nord, Karen Franchot, Chris Koza and Kate Casanova, HaeWon Yang and Eric Casanova, and my wonderful husband, Charlie Casanova.

Mary Casanova is author of thirty-nine books, ranging from the picture books *Wake Up, Island* and *Hush, Hush Forest* (Minnesota, 2016 and 2018) to historical novels, including her young adult titles *Frozen* (Minnesota, 2012) and *Ice-Out* (Minnesota, 2016). This is her first novel for adults. Her books have earned the American Library Association Notable Award, Aesop Accolades from the American Folklore Society, Parents' Choice Gold Award, *Booklist* Editors' Choice, Midwest Booksellers' Award, and two Minnesota Book Awards. She lives with her husband in a cabin on sixty acres in northern Minnesota near the Canadian border.